Miriam Coles Harris

Phoebe

A Novel

Miriam Coles Harris

Phoebe
A Novel

ISBN/EAN: 9783337001155

Printed in Europe, USA, Canada, Australia, Japan

Cover: Foto ©Andreas Hilbeck / pixelio.de

More available books at **www.hansebooks.com**

PHOEBE

A Novel by the Author of "Rutledge"

BOSTON
HOUGHTON, MIFFLIN AND COMPANY
New York: 11 East Seventeenth Street
The Riverside Press, Cambridge
1884

CONTENTS.

CHAPTER		PAGE
I.	OVER THE LEFT SHOULDER	1
II.	A PRETTY PIECE OF NEWS	14
III.	WIDOW HOLDEN	27
IV.	JUST A WOMAN'S NOTION	45
V.	WEARY-FOOT COMMON	54
VI.	HUMBLE PIE	61
VII.	THE NEW DAUGHTER	70
VIII.	TARTAR	87
IX.	MARROWFAT	125
X.	HONOR'S WOUNDS	142
XI.	A DAY IN TOWN	149
XII.	LUCY HEARS THE STORY	156
XIII.	LEFT BEHIND	162
XIV.	ISOLATION	177
XV.	A DIDO OF TO-DAY	183
XVI.	PEYTON EDWARDS	197
XVII.	BARRY'S RETURN	212
XVIII.	A BUTTON OFF	234
XIX.	HAGAR	242
XX.	THE COOK ASSISTS	249
XXI.	RACING AND CHASING O'ER CANOBIE LEE	266
XXII.	GRAY SHINGLES ON A WET DAY	270
XXIII.	OUTSIDE THE KITCHEN DOOR	284
XXIV.	AFTER ALL!	296
XXV.	IN MY LADY'S CHAMBER	321

PHŒBE.

CHAPTER I.

OVER THE LEFT SHOULDER.

A CLEAR but brief November day had ended. Though not yet six o'clock, the sky was almost without color, and a slender silver crescent just above the trees, almost as one looked, grew sharp and filled with light. A young girl, who was sitting at a window, with her fair, round cheek close against the pane, looking idly out at the falling leaves and the darkening landscape, lifted her head suddenly, and saw the new moon and started.

"Oh, mamma, it's over my left shoulder!" she exclaimed, petulantly. "What horrid ill-luck are we going to have? It never fails. I hate to see it over my left shoulder."

The words she said chimed in uncomfortably with the thoughts of the lady whom she addressed. There was a third person in the room, — another young girl, seated at a piano, playing softly in the twilight, so absorbed that her younger sister's ex-

1

clamation did not draw her attention. The lady
by the fire did not turn her head, but shivered a
little, and said, reproachfully, after a moment, —

"Then you must have seen it over the other
shoulder uninterruptedly for the last sixteen years.
I don't know anybody who's had better luck than
you, Honor; or, for the matter of that, than all of
us."

"It depends upon what you call good luck,"
said Honor. But she did not continue the subject, having very little to say on her side of the
question; and, besides, it was not an hour to talk.
So she leaned against the pane, and gazed out at
the silver thread in the clear sky, and at the vine
clinging to the wall, from which the leaves were
dropping at every breath of the now sinking wind,
and thought her own young thoughts. The room
was at the front of the house, and the window at
which Honor sat looked out upon the entrance.
Up to this she expected every moment to see the
carriage drive, bringing her father from his day's
toil in the city. This room was a library, with
warm, dark walls and a good many pictures; there
was no lamp in it, but a fire blazed on the wide
hearth. Beyond was a dark room, and beyond
that, again, was the dining-room, lighted with
shaded lamps. A glimmer of silver and glass
and a quietly moving maid told of the coming
dinner-hour. The mother, sunk in her deep chair
before the fire, had been looking around the walls

of the room, all encrusted as they were with the ornament of sentiment, that had grown on them with time as lichen grows on stones. She followed the fire-light as it fell on her fair-haired daughter, whose fingers touched the keys, and on the slender young creature who leaned against the window; on the dog at her feet, who lay gazing at the blaze. She loved the smell of the wood as the sap oozed from it, of the flowers that stood on the table across the room, even the scent of cigar smoke in the book that lay upon her lap. They were the smells of home, the sights of home, and they were dear to her. She remembered twilights long ago in this very room, when the girl at the piano had scarcely reached the keys standing on the points of her tiny toes; when Honor, in her nurse's arms, had drummed on the pane waiting for papa at that very window. For years the sap had smelled like that, and the flowers had lived and died for generations of flower life in those very vases; the cigars that had been smoked by this very fireside, with long talks and midnight confidences, as she sat beside her once young husband, — who could count or recall them? Yes, she had had a peaceful home, a sheltered life, prosperous to the world's eye, more prosperous, even, to the soul's sense. Her children! — she always looked at them with such a gaze of love and satisfaction that it must have been like sunshine and ripened them, one would think. There had been

but one break in the family life, while the only
son of the house had been away in the usual exile
of school and college days. But that was nearly
over now; in a few months he would be at home
again, and they would be complete.

Complete! That was the word she had been
saying over to herself with a sort of fear just before Honor caught sight of the moon in that unlucky attitude. What life could be more complete than hers? Who had ever had a fuller one?
Everything about her, from the lovely contour of
Lucy's head, to the soft depths of the chair that
yielded to her faintest movement, gave her a sense
of satisfaction, of security, of comfort. Just at
that moment, when her senses were so satisfied,
her heart so contented, there came a vague note of
alarm, like a knock at the outer gate. She put it
aside, but the faint, muffled sound had shocked
her nerves; she could not get it out of her ears.

And then Honor had spoken. Her silly little
superstition irritated her mother, as it joined itself
to the train of thought that she was trying to ban-
ish. She was glad when the sound of the wheels
outside came, and Honor sprang from the window
and ran into the hall to meet her father, and Lucy
left the piano and followed her. A great rush of
cold air came in before the outside door was closed.
The girls' sweet, merry voices were all she heard
for a moment, as she moved forward to the library
door. She detected, before he had passed the

threshold, a harsh tone in the father's brief answer to their pleasantry. When she kissed him, he scarcely returned the caress, and did not look at her. When the firelight shone on his face she saw that it was pale. She had too much tact to say, You are not well. His was too reserved a nature to be reached by direct routes or rapid moves. She must wait to know what troubled him till they are alone, and till he chose to speak. But speculation was not idle. She sat down again in her chair, and a hundred alarms passed through her brain. Lucy always went with her father to his dressing-room, and saw that it was lighted and that he had all he needed. How she wished she could to-night take Lucy's place, and shorten her suspense! Presently Lucy came down, and ordered dinner put upon the table, and went and sat on the other side of the fire, while Honor was tearing open some letters by the dining-room light.

"Papa seems tired," said Lucy.

"He is very busy this week," said her mother. "I suppose he has been in court all day."

And then they were silent. When he came down he did not stop at the library fire, but saying that he supposed dinner was ready walked directly in to the table, and they followed him. At dinner he was unwontedly critical of the food, eating little, and not attempting to talk, answering his daughters' questions shortly and absently. He never made any disguise of his feelings when any-

thing troubled him; an effort at gayety or interest in passing matters he never thought of. His
wife watched carefully, and tried to judge whether
some serious professional disappointment had occurred, or some matter of more personal concern.
Honor attempted once or twice to draw his attention by a half impertinence, which, as the youngest
in the family, was in a way her privilege. Lucy
looked troubled, and tried to talk on matters that
would engage them all safely. At last Honor said
abruptly, —

"Any news from Barry to-day?"

"Yes," said her father, shortly, not absently,
nor as if his thoughts had been called from somewhere else.

"Oh, why did you not tell us before! Show me
the letter, papa. Or is it in your overcoat pocket?
May I run and get it?" And she half rose from
the table.

"I have no letter from him," he answered.
"Sit down."

"Oh!" she said, a little confused by his unusual
manner. "I — thought you meant you had had
a letter from him."

"Barry is not ill?" said the mother, startled
out of her resolution to be silent.

"I have not heard of it, if he is," returned her
husband, not looking at her, as he poured out a
glass of wine.

Then she knew that the trouble was about

Barry, and that it was not illness. She was so materially and inbornly a mother that the first feeling was one of relief. If that dear flesh that she had nourished and cherished was safe and well, she could bear all the rest. Barry had done something to displease his father. That was hard to know; but it would come right. Whereas if he had typhoid fever, or had broken his collar bone, it would be much less certain to do so. She thought his father was severe in his judgment of Barry, always; not from lack of love, but from excess of it, and from an ambition that was not measured by probabilities. Two male human beings could not be more dissimilar than they were. The father was sternly intellectual, with an intellectual man's temptations and provocations. The son seemed to have considerable mental force, but withal put in such an overpowering mortal mould that the balance was always wavering between the two. He was so fine an athlete that even his masters forgave him for not being a student. You began by admiring his mind, and you ended by admiring his body. You condemned his indolence, and you found your eyes following him with perfect satisfaction. How could you blame a youth for not trying for the first prize in Greek, when without trying he could get the first prize in everything else outside? But his father blamed him, and could see no excuse for his lack of ambition. He himself had never known the temptation of pleasure-seeking. It simply offered no attraction for him. Work and rest were the two poles of his battery. An early and satisfying marriage had closed the door of the world to him, which, however, no loneliness would ever have driven him to open. It never would have occurred to him that recreation or solace could be found in society; he would as soon have thought of burrowing in the earth for it. With a generous confidence in the allotments of fate, he took it for granted that his only son was the exact pattern of himself, and looked forward to his career as his own amplified and made perfect by the removal of obstacles. In all his professional life, he had one guiding purpose, —Barry's future. And when this superb young animal, with undoubted abilities, but undoubted distaste for using them, was launched on his college career, and made himself adored of everybody, but ahead of nobody (in Greek), he grew hard towards him, and bitter. The mother had need of all her tact and patience to mediate between the two. But her efforts had not been fruitless. Just in his last year he had roused himself, more from affectionate desire to please them than from any other motive, perhaps, and had done so well as to surprise and pacify his father. Now he was away, studying at a law school in a remote country town, it being a fancy of his father's that there, at least, he would be free from the distractions of society,

It must not be supposed that Barry had shown himself a wild and reckless fellow. On the contrary, he seemed a son to be proud of, if one would take him as the gift of heaven, and not as a manufacture of one's own. He did not fill his father's bill, certainly, but that was scarcely his fault, as it would have been necessary for him to make himself over *da capo*, to accomplish that, and at twenty one does not take to reconstruction kindly. Barry loved his father, and wanted to please him ; but as he could only do so by giving up every impulse of his nature, and acting upon impulses which he did not feel, and only faintly wished he could feel, it was disheartening work, and he naturally had no enthusiasm for it.

Just now, however, things were working better. They had good reports of him from the remote country law school, and his father's hopes were reviving. That some disappointing account of his want of application to his studies had come was the worst his mother feared. It was very bad, very discouraging, certainly, but it would come out all right. Since he was n't ill, bless him, she could bear it, whatever it might be.

After dinner, she played a duet with Lucy; she had a long consultation with Honor about the crewels for her screen ; she read, or tried to read, the evening paper. By half-past nine o'clock she acknowledged to herself that she cared more than she thought, and that the suspense was fretting her unbearably. Lucy saw it, and managed to draw Honor up-stairs a half hour earlier than usual, and husband and wife were left alone together.

Mr. Crittenden had been sitting at a small table beside the fire, looking over some papers. His wife knew very well he was only making a pretense of occupation. It was no real work. He pushed the papers into a drawer, at last, and leaned back in his chair. He looked across at her where she sat, and their eyes met. She had not pledged herself to anything but silence; she let her eyes fasten on his with an anxious appeal.

"I have some pretty news for you," he said, after a few moments, in a hard, grating tone.

"You won't make it any prettier by keeping it from me, will you?" she said, in a suppressed voice.

"I have n't kept it any longer than was necessary. It is n't exactly the kind of news one would lay before young girls."

And then he paused again. From being the defender and advocate of Barry for so long, Mr. Crittenden had come to have the tone of regarding his wife as a partner in his son's misdemeanors. She had made light of his faults so often, that her husband naturally felt they did not pain her, and it was with a feeling that he was the only one wounded, and not with any wish to spare her, but rather as one injured, that he always made his complaints.

"I ought to have been prepared for this, but I confess I was n't. I might have known there was but one natural result of a life without purpose."

Mrs. Crittenden got up and walked once or twice across the room, then sat down resolutely and folded her hands, and looked into the fire with sealed lips.

"You and I have never agreed about this matter," he went on. "I have never been able to make you understand the dangers of your method with the boy. I can't expect your sympathy with my disappointments."

"I have not been disappointed," she said, stoutly. "I see no reason to despair of Barry. He is n't what we meant him to be, but he 's a fine fellow for all that, and one whom any father might be proud of."

There was a bitter sneer in the father's tone as he said, "A particularly fine fellow; the pride of any household. Read that."

And he laid upon the table a letter. His wife got up and went to the light and took it up. It was in an unfamiliar hand, a man's, and bore the postmark of the town where the law school was. She opened it and read it, standing by the lamp. As she read, her breath came quicker. She put out one hand and steadied herself by a chair that stood beside her. When her eyes had flashed through the letter once, she let go the chair for an instant to turn back the page and re-read it. She was generally self-controlled, and she counted upon her strength, but for once she had overrated it. She reeled a little when she lost the support, dropped the letter, and sank into the chair. Then she sat quite still, her eyes on the floor, the color surging up into her face and going back again. Her husband, full of his own trouble, was not looking at her. She had never allowed him to pity her before in the matter of Barry; he did not think of beginning now.

"I have n't answered the letter yet," he said, "but something must be done." He got up and went to the fire, and replaced a stick that had rolled down. "Something must be done at once," he said, standing and looking into the fire. "We'll have to send him away from there. We might as well face it. We'll have our hands full keeping him out of trouble. This is but the beginning."

As she did not answer him, he added, after a moment, a little impatiently, "I suppose it does n't surprise you?"

"I feel ill," she said, speaking in a faint voice. "One of those attacks is coming on. Give me a glass of water, will you?"

He went across to the dining-room to get the water, thinking as he went that it was an unfortunate time for her to have one of her attacks just when it was necessary for him to talk this matter

over with her.　He did n't associate the attack
with his pretty news in any other way.　She had
always been so brave about Barry, it was not altogether to be wondered at.　When he came back
and gave the water to her, she drank it, and seemed
better.　He hoped the attack was n't coming on,
after all.

"Do you feel better?" he asked.

She said, "Yes."

"Keep quiet a few minutes, then, and perhaps
it will pass over.　I want you to be able to settle
with me what's to be done about this matter.
You would not be satisfied to leave it to me."

"Oh, Edward, don't be cruel to me!" she exclaimed, burying her face in her hands.　He went
quickly to her, and bent over her.　She caught
his hand, shivering and crying.

"This blow will kill me," she moaned.　"Help
me! help me!"　He put his arms around her, and
she clung to him.　The "dull, hard stone" within
him melted as he felt her tears, and his own eyes
filled with the slow, unaccustomed moisture.

One feels as if children must have some fatal
penalty to pay for calling forth the awful tears of
disappointed parental love.

CHAPTER II.

A PRETTY PIECE OF NEWS.

THE letter was from one of the professors of the law school, who had been a classmate of Mr. Crittenden's, and to whom he had written when Barry went there to pursue his unbeloved studies. There was no intimacy between the two men. There had been a strong rivalry in youth, but the city lawyer had so distanced the country professor that all that had died out. The unsuccessful man was none the less convinced of his own merits; the successful man always felt that perhaps luck had been unduly on his side. The latter had felt a faint hesitation in asking the professor to look a little after Barry, when he sent him to the law school. The people who have been important to us in our youth always retain a certain prominence in our minds. Few men of Mr. Crittenden's acquaintance were of less worldly importance than Professor Smythe, but from few of them would it have been as painful to him to receive the following letter : —

MY DEAR CRITTENDEN, — When your son introduced himself to me, and presented your letter commending him in a measure to my care, I felt as if it would not be much that would be required of me, besides enjoying the sight of and occasional intercourse with such a fine young fellow. I have not written before in answer to it, because, in fact, the letter did not seem to require an answer, and because the young man seemed to be doing so well as to make it superfluous to send you any report of him. Within a few days, however, such a painful rumor has reached my ears that I cannot feel myself justified in letting you remain in ignorance of it. When I speak of rumor, I must add that it is not of mere report I speak; but before writing I have taken pains to verify the story, and not to distress you unnecessarily.

You will remember that last summer your son and a companion went off on a walking expedition during the vacation. Their journey did not extend very far. I am told that they, or at least he, did not go farther than Malden, a small farming village about twelve miles from here, and there spent the entire three weeks. He has, I believe, been there at various times during the autumn. Latterly, I have noticed in him an unusual application to study, and a gravity, I might almost say anxiety. I know very little of the lives of the young men, and am not thrown at all with them except in the lecture-room, and I knew nothing of this matter till it had become town talk, and of such importance as to reach my ears. It appears that the ruin of a young girl living somewhere near Malden is laid to his charge, and that the people of the neighborhood are much excited by the fact. She is the daughter of a widow, and has no brother or near male relative, or I suppose there would have been some scene of violence. According to the popular idea, however, this only makes the worse case against him. I must add, I understand the young woman to have borne a good character hitherto, and to belong to an entirely respectable family, though in very humble circumstances.

I need not say, my dear Crittenden, how painful it has been to me to write of this to you, but I have felt it my duty to let you know the facts. You will understand enough of life in a small town to know that it is not wise for him to remain longer here, and I fancy, by withdrawing him at once and quietly, the scandal of an expulsion can be avoided. You know you may command my friendship in the matter to the utmost.

I am yours faithfully,

ERASTUS B. SMYTHE.

It was late at night when Mrs. Crittenden re-read this letter alone in her dressing-room. The agitating talk had worn her husband out, and had left her worse than sleepless. While he slept, exhausted, she paced the floor in ever-increasing distress of mind. The night wore on, and found her still up, still unable to accustom herself to the thought of what had befallen them, still unreconciled to the Power that had not restrained her child from sin in answer to her prayers. This room, above all others in the house, was associated with those prayers. She turned with a bitter heart from the sight of the prayer-desk where she always knelt. His picture lay under the cross, and had lain hidden there ever since he left her first. There was a feeling in her heart that Heaven would understand it as a mute prayer for him every hour and moment of the day that she could not pray for him with words. There came back to her some words of yesterday's Psalter. They had been sounding in her ears all day, in an unmeaning, unappropriated way, just as words. " No man may deliver his brother, nor make agreement unto God for him. For it cost more to redeem their souls, so that he must let that alone forever."

She had tried to make agreement; she had failed. Had her faith been a childish one? It had lasted so many years; she had been so confident, so patient. It was late to begin to know what and who to believe in. It was hard to have spent a life-time in a service, and to find out in a minute there had been neither master, nor wages, nor rules, except in credulous fancy.

She thought of other women whom she knew, commonplace, easy women of the world, whose sons had turned out good and honorable men; who had never had this horror, this shame of heart, this burden of inward degradation, to bear. Oh, those prayers, — what had they availed? Those petitionings of Heaven day and night, — what answer had they got?

She was a woman whose serene dignity gave no idea of the depths of her emotional nature. People said she was just to her children rather than enthusiastic about them. No one, perhaps, not even her husband, suspected the absorbing nature of her love; the romance, the poem, that each young life was to her. Her pride and reserve made it more possible for her to conceal it from herself than to reveal it to others. And she had so concealed it. She only saw when the knowledge of her son's fall came to her how high had been the place she had given him, what an impossible perfection she had required of him.

She pulled from her dress a miniature that she had worn ever since he was a baby; she did not look at it, but shut it up in a drawer and locked it in. No one knew that she had worn it. She wished she could forget that she had. She turned from his picture on the wall. If he had been dead it would have been easier to look at it. To do her justice, it was in no wise the scandal that abased her. She had not come to regard that yet. But it was the sin, the deception, the grossness of the fall. She was so much a woman that she felt she could have yearned over and longed for him if he had been in prison for some dishonorable sin for lucre. But she did not yearn over him now. She did not long for him. She felt estranged, turned cold and unnatural.

> " As if, fond leaning where her infant slept,
> A mother's arm a serpent should embrace."

She had made so many excuses for him. She had had such full faith in his goodness of nature, such patience with his light-heartedness and love of pleasure. She had felt herself so much wiser than her husband. She had never wavered, not for a moment, in her belief in him. He would come out all right. If one understood him, there was nothing to make one doubt. He was conscientious and affectionate, and so much under her influence. Her influence, — ah! She shuddered. Only two months ago he had been at home with her, and she had not seen any difference in him. What wisdom, what intuitions! How fit she was to guide and influence him! Oh, poor mother! not only had her idol fallen in the dust, but she herself had fallen with it. In all our abasements that is generally the worst part.

The fire in the grate had burned out; the room was cold. The house was still, with the early-dawn stillness, when it is also the coldest. She could not remember a vigil that had not been because of illness. She thought of the nights —

not many of them — when she had watched anxiously by the beds of her children, and had seen
the dawn break. Ah! there are different trials
in life, "afflictions of all sizes." She wondered
if there were anything yet reserved for her that
would make this night's anguish pale, as this had
made those earlier ones. She could believe anything of suffering, as she was living through this.
She paced up and down the room, and then went
out into the hall, now dark and still. Her heart
swelled as she thought of the little feet and merry
voices that she would never hear in it again.
She felt as if their family life were dead. She
could not imagine merriment ever again among
them. (She was a woman, and exaggerated.)
She went softly to the room where her two young
daughters slept, and, shading the candle she held
with one hand, gazed down at the fair, sleeping
faces. Honor had deserted her own pretty nest,
and crept into her sister's.

"Thank God!" she murmured, "*they* are mine
still. I cannot lose *them*."

And the dry sirocco of the night's anguish was
relieved by a rush of tears. But at that moment
there came a sharp, pricking thought into her
mind. She started away from the bed where the
young girls slept, and went back to her own room.
Her tears were sent back to their source; there
was a tight feeling about her chest, a nervous energy about her movements. "Never!" she said,

between her teeth, as she pulled aside the curtain and looked out at the dark sky where there were still faint, cold stars. "Never!"

She was not thinking of the stars, nor watching for the dawn. She mechanically dropped the curtain, and walked again up and down the room. Then shutting the door, and throwing a wrap about her shoulders, she sat down by the dead fire, and tried restlessly to rekindle it, as if some opposition had taken the place of her abandoned misery, and must find practical expression. She entered into the details of the fire-making as if there had not been anything else to think of; and when her determination was rewarded by a faint blaze and rustle, she leaned back in her low chair, and gazed at the flicker, and repeated, "Never!" with her hands firm set together.

Never what? The thought that had turned her pain into such a changed channel, as she gazed at the innocent loveliness of her children, was this: —

"There is a mother who to-night cannot look with such solace on her daughter's face. I am not the only one who suffers. Which is the worse load to bear, — hers or mine? *Can I help her?*"

Up to that moment she had not thought of the mother. She had thought of the ruined, degraded girl with repulsion, with angry, furious resentment. She could not change that feeling now, but thinking of the mother gave her a feverish

anguish. She could not hide it from herself that *she* was an object of just compassion. However low her station, it was certain that she suffered. In all stations of life, the sight of a daughter's shame is counted the sharpest ignominy possible. And these people were not low enough to be accustomed to immorality. They were undoubtedly far less sensitive, and missed much of the finer pain of finer culture; but there were certain instincts of nature which were not wanting in them. This woman was suffering; then, innocently suffering, perhaps, from her son's ill-doing. Could any human power help her? Yes. There was but one way; and there was but one person, perhaps, who had the power, and she was that person. She knew that if she set her face to have the reparation made, in all probability it would be made. It was then, with her heart as flint, that she said, —
"Never!"

She was not a person ignorant of, or indifferent to, the world's judgment. There was a Judgment she set far above it, and to which she looked with an unusual fixedness; but she was human, and she had not lived forty-two years among selfish men and women without a little seeing with their eyes and hearing with their ears. She knew that what her son had done would be only a temporary injury to his worldly prospects; she knew that in her husband's eyes the worst feature of it was the portent of his future recklessness. That might be tempered by the discipline of circumstances, and sobered by maturer years. He might yet be "as other men are." A little money would bridge over the scandal. Outwardly everything might yet be well. It did not pacify her heart at all. He was "strange to her," this son she had borne. But she had another side than the midnight, heart-revealing one which we have been looking upon. She had strong common sense, and a nice appreciation of what was acceptable and profitable in life. She had been successful in her small way. She had found it so easy to succeed that she had not valued her success very much. The strong religious feeling which I have described had never been brought into serious conflict with this easy, smooth popularity - possibility in her nature. She had had such a sweet, good, happy home she had been satisfied, and had thought little about it. Duty and pleasure had gone hand in hand. She had not been obliged to define herself ambitious, because she had had poured into her lap all she wanted, and had never known what it was to be hungry. Now, in her secret heart, she found she was ambitious, — not for herself, but for her children. But she found it out only when the pleasant fruits lying in her lap were being snatched away.

She had imagination enough to know what a galling, degrading yoke an ill-assorted marriage is. To what depths would she sink her already fallen boy, if she insisted on his making this reparation? Why should she set her judgment against the judgment of the world; of all the intelligent men and women who believed otherwise; of her husband, whose strong dissent she felt sure of? Her judgment!—she had not much reason to respect it at this crisis. No, she would not listen to the faint but unceasing voice within her. "*Never!*"

The fire was not much of a success. It flickered and burned blue; it curled around the bars of the grate, and spit out little gusts of smoke that made a nasty odor in the room. She grew chill and weary. She would go to bed. She got up and began to undress herself. As she stood before her dressing-glass, a sudden faintness came over her,—not so much, if one could make the distinction, a physical swoon as a mental one. She walked quite steadily to the chair and sat down, and lay leaning back in it, with her eyes closed. It seemed to her the bed for which she was making ready was her death-bed; that she was laying aside for the last time the adornments and the habiliments of earth. She should need nothing henceforth of the things of time; she was leaving all behind that could not be carried with her when she lay down in the "wormy bed." She knew the parting with her children had come; all her labor and planning for them was done; all work was at an end; no more now was permitted her to do, but what she had done would be living on after her. With keen,

awful sight she saw what had been well done, and
what amiss and with a low aim ; for those few
strange moments everything stood out in the clear,
high, cold light of eternity.   Little details of long-
past times, a decision about discouraging this companion and encouraging that, the selection of this
school in preference to that, the giving up to certain prejudices of others, — all came before her
with startling familiarity and yet more startling
newness.   The gloss faded off some pleasures, a
new lustre grew on others.   All seemed new, yet
old; awful, yet real.   The worth of to-day's short
success against to-morrow's long retrospect, — the
balance, in fact, of time and eternity; the praise
of men, or the praise of God. .

A half hour passed.   A little more light came in
at the window.   The steps of a servant going down-
stairs shufflingly broke the stillness of the house.
Day was come, and the household was rousing
itself afresh.   "The sleep and the forgetting"
were over for this night.   The weary watcher shivered, and lifted her head.   Life had begun again
for her.   The momentary faintness was a trick of
the nerves.   Whatever you might call it, it had
done its work, and was gone.   She knew very well
she was not going to die, but going to live, and to
suffer, and be tempted, as of old.   Everything
seemed inexpressively commonplace and cheerless,
— the cold room, the dead fire, the gray light
creeping through the curtains, the yawning ser-

vants making their sleepy way down-stairs. She had come back to life, but she had been to its very brink; and a responsibility lay upon her not to let slip from her memory what she had seen when she stood there.

CHAPTER III.

WIDOW HOLDEN.

YOU are not apt to feel very fresh and vivacious after being awake all night, even if there has been nothing to wear upon your nerves but the loss of sleep. Most people are familiar with the uncompromising character of such depression. It is not only that your spirits are low, but your nerves are strained; not only that to-day is a bore, but the recollection of yesterday is hateful, and the anticipation of to-morrow without attraction. If, in addition to your vigil, you have had any mental conflict to pass through, all that has changed color with the daylight. Your tragedy has become melodrama, your tears taste of brine, your heart's blood looks very thin and poor; you feel not only ashamed of your emotion, but out of temper about it.

Mrs. Crittenden found it very hard to meet the requirements of this every-day day, which was yet so unlike every day. It was raining dully. If it had not been, she would have gone to the city, or somehow got away from this insufferable yoke of family life for a few hours. She had done all

the thinking, feeling, resolving, of which she was
capable, and she had a sense of impatience at
the stagnation at which she had arrived, even
while there was a feeling of relief that there was
no more that she could do.   No, there was nothing more that she could do.   She had made her
resolution in cold blood, and there was nothing
but to carry it out.   The conflict with herself
had been the real, scorching trial; now there was
only the hard, practical business of keeping herself to what she had promised.

She shut herself up in her dressing-room, and
sat down by the window, against which a slow,
persistent, chill rain was pattering.   If the wind
had roared, if the trees had bent, if the sky had
been black with storm!   But it was a commonplace, raw November rain, chilling one like a
peevish, exacting, low-spirited woman in a house.
The few leaves were not swirled off in a gust, but
fell dispiritedly into the pools and rivulets that
had formed in the carriage-way before the door.
The vines hung despondently against the house:
they did not moan or sway; they only creaked
exasperatingly in the little peevish wind that occasionally moved them slightly.   The ground had
a soaked look, as if it had had enough of it; the
sky was even, monotonous, mediocre, grim.   The
thermometer was not very low, but the dampness
was unspeakable.   The stems of the trees looked
water-logged and unwholesome; from the twigs

hung drops that the weak wind did not shake off.
There was little life or motion within sight from
the window. The house was too far from the road
to distinguish passers easily, and into the grounds
no one, at this hour and on such a day, would be
likely to come. The grocer and the butcher had
paid their morning visit. Mrs. Crittenden had
already gone through that penance. There was
nothing, there was nobody to come. She sat at
the window with the feeling of a person who
knows there is nothing to see, but who must gaze
on with the bitter idleness of grief. She could not
occupy her hands or her thoughts; her eyes roamed
over the dreary scene without, and were less pained
than when they rested on the ordinary and familiar things within. Her door was fastened. There
was no danger of intrusion : the household orders
were given; Lucy and Honor would respect her
haggard looks. She leaned wearily against the
window and gazed out. The only feeling that
was not distinctly painful was that she would be
let alone, that nothing would be required of her,
that in a certain dead way she could rest. Suddenly she saw an approaching vehicle turn in at
the gate. It was one of a shabby class of hacks
that waited about the depot, and sometimes
brought chance visitors from the train. Who
could be coming? She rose from her seat.

Before the cab was near enough for her to see
any one in it, she had made up her mind whom

it contained. From the window she could see it drive up to the door, and could see who alighted.

The visitor was a middle-aged woman, rather slight, dressed in black, a little shabby. She wore a close, old-womany bonnet, from which a limp black veil hung, tied under the chin, in the fashion of twenty years before. She got out, and in a tremulous, wavering manner looked at the door and then at the driver. At last she decided (if that might be called a decision which seemed the result of inability to see anything else to do) to ring the bell, which was promptly answered. Then she went back to the cabman, and took out her purse to pay him. Her hands trembled very much; she had difficulty in making the change, or in understanding what his charge was. Her gloves were rather loose, and a good deal creased about the fingers. They were of foxy black, and had probably been her best gloves for a number of years. Because of their clumsy size, or perhaps because she was not accustomed to wearing them, she could not manage the small change; some of it rolled upon the ground. The trim maid came forward, and, smiling superciliously, picked it up for her; the cabman smiled a little, too, and looked at her curiously. At last it was all settled, and the visitor followed the maid into the house. In a moment more came a knock upon her door. "A person, madam, asking for you."

Yes, she knew it. She was getting ready for

the person; that is, all the evil in her was dressing itself to appear, and she seemed to be turning
to ice and granite to go down to meet her. As she
went down the stairs she saw that the visitor had
been left in the hall, sitting on a chair near the
library door. The woman looked up, and rose
agitatedly.

Though the house was not a grand one, by any
means, it had a good staircase and a wide hall.
" Mamma looks like a lady in a story-book when
she comes down the stairs with a long dress on,"
Honor used to say.

" Will you not come in by the fire? " asked
Mrs. Crittenden, as she passed by her visitor, and,
entering the library, shut the door after them, and
gave her a chair.

" You won't be likely to know who I am," began
the stranger, in a voice which she could scarcely
control.

" I can imagine," said the other, looking at her
coldly.

" How? You know, then? You have heard? "

" I know you are probably from Malden. I have
not heard your name."

" It is Holden. *He* was of the Holdens of Greene
County, related to the Waterburys on the mother's side. His folks are looked up to all about
our place."

And a faint flicker of pride was indicated in
her manner, washed out in the next instant by a
rush of recollection.

"He?"

"My husband, I mean. He has been dead these twenty years. I thought you knew about it, may be. My girl never saw her father. She was born six months after I buried him."

"I did not know anything about the — circumstances of your life."

"I don't know what you know!" cried the poor woman, unable to endure the slow torture of this manner. "I have seen a great deal of trouble in my life, — death and sickness, and hard enough work to get along; and my own people are poor, — I don't deny it, — and things ain't with us as they used to be. But there's one thing I can say: this sort of trouble, *this*, *this*, is new among us. It's the first time that one of us could n't hold our heads up among decent people. I thought I 'd had trouble before, but — but" —

And the poor woman struggled with a handkerchief that lay deep down in a low and very full pocket, and when she got it out put it before her eyes. This action brought out in high relief the baggy gloves. I am sorry to say, none of these details were lost on her hostess, who sat watching her rigidly. The face that was revealed, when at last the stranger took the handkerchief and the gloves out of prominence, and essayed to speak, was a sensitive, not unrefined one. It was quite possible to fancy she had once been a pretty woman, though hard work and the unjust burden of

American lower-class life had aged her prematurely. She was probably not very much older than the more favored woman who was passing judgment on her, but a careless observer would have said there was at least a difference of fifteen years in their ages. Her skin was dried and brown, a thousand fine wrinkles networked it; her eyes looked tired and old, and as if they had shed endless tears; her mouth was sensitive and weak. She was timid, distrustful of herself. One could not help seeing what a fierce convulsion must have been needed to drive her out of her homely seclusion to face cold and unfriendly strangers. But Mrs. Crittenden did not feel sorry for her. She hated her. I am sorry to have to say this of the woman who kept her boy's picture under the cross on her prayer-desk; and who for forty-two amiable years had been the admiration of her neighbors for her charity and tenderness; and who, better than all, had made up her mind to do right in this cruel matter. Perhaps the last bit of evil was coming out of her in this struggle; perhaps, if she had done this blamelessly, she would have been too perfect to be required to walk further among the thorns and flints of this bewildering world. Perhaps — but there is no use in speculation. She had turned hard and cold, and, so far from pitying her adversary, felt a sort of satisfaction in knowing that she suffered.

"I 've — I 've come to see you about this, but

3

she does n't know it. She would n't have let me do it if she 'd known."

" She ? " interrogated Mrs. Crittenden, who refused to recognize pronouns.

" Phœbe, my daughter."

The lady shuddered. Phœbe, — that was a name to bring into the family annals! Her only associations with the name were, that it had belonged to a greyhound of her brother's, and also to an old mulatto cook, very stout and of much good-humor, who used to give her doughnuts when she was a child. Phœbe! Well, that was a very small matter. She waited for her visitor to go on.

" She would have said it would n't do any good. She would have kept me back."

" I think, if you 'll excuse my saying so, she would have been quite right about it."

The color flushed into the dried, brown cheeks. " I did n't know you would be so hard to talk to," she said. " I thought, being a woman, and having daughters of your own " —

" Oh, *my* daughters, — we will not talk of them, if you please."

The thrust was not lost upon the stranger, and the agitated color spread again over her face.

" You feel very safe about them " — she began.

" I said, we would not talk about them, if you please."

" No, I did n't come to talk about them. I don't know how you 've brought up your children, or whether it's your fault that other people suffer by them. Girls are not so different from boys. Sin is sin. And in our part of the country we don't think our girls too fine to mention, and in the same breath let our boys go free, when they've broke the laws of God and man."

" I 'm afraid, in Malden, you are *not* very careful in the education of your girls."

A passionate answer rose to the woman's lips, but again the tide of recollection swept over her, and made her silent.

"I am afraid," went on her tormentor, "that you give them too much liberty, and do not teach them to respect themselves. A woman's position is very different from a man's."

" We teach them out of the same Bible!" cried the poor mother, trembling with the vehemence of her feeling. " What's sin for 'one is sin for the other. There ain't twenty commandments, one set for one and one for the other, but only the ten that 's stood all these ages, and served for men and women both. That's the way we read Scripture in Malden."

"Malden is a small place," said her hostess, coldly.

" If it is, it's a God-fearing place."

"Ah? Among the men, you mean?"

" Yes, among men and women both, though you do jeer at me for my girl's misfortune," groaned the stranger, turning away her head, and beating nervously with her gloved hands upon her lap.

" Your girl's misfortune, and my boy's sin, — is that the way they put it in Malden? With us — in the world, I mean — it goes just the other way. It's a misfortune, unlucky, you know. It's rather a disadvantage to a young man, but nothing permanent. It doesn't injure him in the eyes of the world. He gets over it, he marries, he goes on as if nothing had happened."

" He shan't!" cried the poor creature, rising in her feebleness, and putting her hand out in her impotent wrath. " He shall feel it. It shall hurt him. My girl shan't be the only one to suffer."

" How will you manage it? You can hurt him to the extent of a few dollars " —

" We don't want your dollars. You can keep your dollars, — wicked, hard people that you are. But we will have our revenge, — we will have our revenge."

" How? Pray tell me how. Calm yourself. We might as well talk this over quietly. It is very bitter to both of us, no doubt. Such things are trying to the temper and to the feelings. Sit down again, if you please. There is nothing gained by this sort of excitement, as you must see."

She sat down, involuntarily obedient to her superior.

" When I tell you there is nothing that you can

do beyond applying for some pecuniary salve, I tell you the truth. The very pillars of society rest on woman's purity. If there were any looseness permitted about that, what would become of family honor? It is hard that it should be so, but this law is as old as society itself. We have to make up our minds to take things as they are. Men are permitted license that women cannot take. Society has to protect itself, and that's the way it goes to work to do it. Its laws are hard upon women who sin, — very hard, I must admit."

"I don't care about the laws of society," moaned the poor mother. "I care about what the Scripture says. *You* know what the Scripture says about — about " —

And she hung her head. It was new to think of her girl as of one at whom the stones of the Jewish mob might have been cast. She was just getting acquainted with her grief, which was always presenting fresh and unexpected phases.

"The world, you know, does n't concern itself about the rules of Scripture. This thing always has been and always will be so. The world casts out and degrades the woman who sins, and takes back into favor her partner, and does the best for him she can. I'm not saying it's right, but it's so."

"God will punish him!" cried the woman. "God won't let him go off free."

"Ah! very likely not. There you may be right.

And that's what you'll have to rest upon. For
you can't do anything about his punishment, believe me."

"I'd better not have come. I thought — you
would be different. I didn't know you'd brought
him up that way. I don't wonder now, — I don't
wonder in the least."

"Oh, as to that, our children do not always
illustrate our teachings. I suppose your daughter, now, was brought up according to the theories
you've mentioned?"

"She was brought up after a godly sort. Her
grandfather was a minister. Her father's folks
were all great hands for meeting. My people
weren't that kind, but I brought her up as I
knew he'd have wanted her to be brought up.
I did my best. I never let her stay home from
Sunday-school, rain or shine. She got a prize for
reading the Bible through three times in one year,
when she was only twelve years old. She knew
all the kings of Israel by heart, and there wasn't
a river or a mountain on any of the Scripture
maps that she couldn't put her finger on in half a
minute; and there wasn't a beetle or a bug of the
Holy Land that she couldn't tell you all about,
before she was turned of ten."

"Ah! And yet you see, hard as you tried,
her education has not been a practical success."

"Her education!" cried the poor woman. "Nobody can say I didn't do everything I could for

her. I 've put up with being alone from Monday morning to Friday night for the last four years, while she 's been away at Brixton at the high school. I never let her do a stroke of work. I 've sewed for her, and washed for her, and mended for her, and starved myself to pay her board and schooling. And she did me credit, — yes, she did me credit. She was the head of her class, and she never lost a day all the four years at Brixton. Her teacher in algebra said he 'd never had such a hand for the higher mathematics. And the day of the exhibition she did a proposition on the blackboard before them all. And everybody was talking about her. No, no, there can't be anything thrown up against me about her education, music and all. Heaven be thanked for that ! "

If there had been anything needed to harden Mrs. Crittenden's heart, it was this picture: a pert, vulgar, higher-mathematical, over-educated, under-bred country girl. The geography of Palestine and the propositions on the blackboard obliterated the last touch of pity.

" I think you would have done better," she said, serenely, " to keep her at home with you, teaching her to do housework, and be a modest, well-conducted girl."

" I don't say but I should. I never felt that it was right that I should be left to bring her up alone, with nobody to look to. I was not the kind to be left alone, to be at the head about

things. Perhaps God knows what He took him
away for when we 'd only been married inside of
a year; I could never see."

And she rocked herself backward and forward
for a few moments, while a bitter look came over
her recently tearful, pleading face.

" But you," she said at last, — "you had your
husband to help you. You had a plenty, and all
ways of bringing him up to choose from. Why
did n't *you* do better with your boy? You twit
me. But I 'd like to know which has the most to
be ashamed of, you' or me. I 'd like to know how
we 'd stand before the judgment of God. I don't
care about men. I don't care about their judgment now. But I tell you, I 'd rather be the
mother of my Phœbe, with all Malden pointing
their finger at her, than the mother of your bad,
black-hearted, fair-spoken son, that 'll go scot-free,
and never be the worse for it, you say."

She panted; this flood of words was as unnatural to her as the agony that brought it forth was
new.

" I don't see that there is much to choose, in the
matter of pride," said Mrs. Crittenden. "But that
is neither here nor there. I suppose we must bake
as we have brewed, and it seems we have neither
of us brewed very well. It does n't help me that
you have an unworthy daughter, nor does it help
you that I have an unworthy son. I do not see
what can be gained by talking of it further."

" There is nothing gained!" cried the woman, starting to her feet. " I ought n't to have come. I — I — might have known — I 'm a poor hand to talk. Lawyer Brent would have come, but I would n't let him. I was 'most wild. I thought I could make you see what was right; but it seems he 'll have to come, after all."

She pulled her shawl about her throat, folded her trembling hands over it, and went towards the door.

" I would advise you, for your own sake, not to send the lawyer," said the lady, steadily.

" I shall do what they tell me," she cried, opening the door that led into the hall, " if I ever get home to tell them about this. I did n't believe anybody could be like you. I ought to have listened to 'em. I — I — never will trouble you again."

" Stay," said Mrs. Crittenden, following her. " I have something to say to you. Come back."

But the woman pushed on to the front door and opened it, and would not look back, much less come back, but with hurried, uncertain steps and swaying figure crossed the shelter of the porch, and passed out into the rain and mud. Mrs. Crittenden called her, eagerly, loudly. The widow shook her head, and did not look around, but went wildly splashing through the pools that stood in the road, as if she did not see them, and not pulling her veil down to protect her face, as if she did not feel the rain that fell upon it.

" Come back ! "

It was easy to say Come back, but how to get her to do it? If she ran across the lawn in her slippers and morning dress, the household would be roused, there would be a scene, everything which she had planned would be destroyed. If she sent a servant after her, she would perhaps refuse to come, and certainly would say something that would set the servants talking. No, there was nothing for it but to let her go, uncomforted by what in the end she had meant to tell her.

Mrs. Crittenden doubted the woman's ability to get away alone ; she saw that, even as she reached the road, she looked wildly up and down ; it seemed but a happy chance that she turned in the direction of the depot. It would take twenty minutes to order and get out the carriage, and even then there was little hope of overtaking her. If, however, Mrs. Crittenden did overtake her there would be that said that the coachman ought not to hear before she would consent to return. If they met at the depot, all Marrowfat would know the story before night. The woman's natural shyness might keep her silent about her sorrow, if no one spoke to her or questioned her. But in her present over-wrought state, the sight of her hard-hearted hostess would, without doubt, open the flood gates again.

No, there was nothing to do but to shut the door and go and warm herself, chilled to the mar-

row by the raw wind, and to trust that the unwelcome guest would get safely away by the twelve
o'clock train, locking the secret in her breast.
She knew she had been cruel and cold; she felt
sharp compunction; but she had meant to be just,
and to convince her that whatever might be done
would be done of free grace and no compulsion
from outside. She certainly never meant to let her
go away without this tangible relief. She knew
that she scorned and hated her and her child, but
the knowledge that she meant to do right by
them as far as in her lay, even to the gross dam-
age of her own best beloved, took away the self-
condemnation that would have followed the hatred
in any other case. It all seemed a piece of her hideous trial, — hideous, hideous, like a nightmare;
revolting, unlightened. She went up to her room,
and sat down in the window, and looked out again,
watching. May be the woman's strength would
fail her, and she would fall down, and they would
find from whence she had come, and would bring
her back. May be even now she was pouring her
incoherent tale into the ears of some crowd
gathered around her prostrate body. May be the
limp veil was even now being dried before the
fire of the first gossip of the town whose house
she had to pass on her way to the depot. It was
an unusual sight in Marrowfat, — a respectable
woman out in such a drenching, all-day rain, without any protection but a limp veil and a thin black

shawl. When, however, no news came, and the
distant whistle sounded at twelve o'clock, there
seemed a reasonable hope that the train bore away
with it the importunate widow and her ugly story.

"Mamma," cried Honor, "was that shabby
body a candidate for your Widow's Society? You
might have lent her an umbrella, if you did n't put
her on your list."

CHAPTER IV.

JUST A WOMAN'S NOTION.

"THAT'S a woman's notion, — just a woman's notion," said Mr. Crittenden, impatiently, pushing back his chair and rising. This was the last, the very last word of many spoken in the midnight silence of a country house, when even the ticking of the lowest-voiced clock was audible. The fire had died down, having been replenished. many times while they talked. She was satisfied to have it die down, for she knew her husband's gesture was final, and that there was no more to say to-night. And she was not ill satisfied with the result of this, the last of many long conferences. Though he had not seemed to acquiesce in what she had urged upon him any more at the end than at the beginning, she felt that his objections were softening, that he was harboring the plan, that he had given it place, at least, in his consideration. She knew very well that in this affair his convictions had never been unalterable, while hers had been. And indeed, our conquests are generally regulated by the strength of our convictions. From missionary work up, it is a matter of conviction, whether we succeed or not. The world belongs to the brave, to the stout in his purpose, to the clear in his seeing, to the undoubting of his path.

Mrs. Crittenden was not very self-willed in domestic interests. She did not have her own way invariably. The laundry tubs were a standing grievance to her. The new kitchen floor was put in entirely in opposition to her judgment. In many points about the education of the children, she had silently surrendered her opinion to a husband who was not tyrannical, but who had a man's preference for the emanations of his own brain. She was just enough to recognize his right to do as he wanted to — sometimes. She bided her time, and this was the time she had been biding, evidently. For it needed all the memory of her many concessions, as well as all the strength of her strong convictions, to make him yield in this most vital matter. He was a very fair modern Christian, always on the side of right in public and social matters. But when it came to such a step as this, it appeared that his religion had been considerably weakened by the current of worldly life that had flowed so near it _for so long a time. The banks must have got washed down a good deal in some places, in the course of fifty years of such dangerous juxtaposition.

A woman's notion! What was just a woman's notion, in this case? Briefly this: that this son of theirs, who had sinned, should pay the penalty of his sin, and make reparation for it in the only way possible to him ; that he should save his unborn innocent child from shame, and the woman, who was at least no more guilty than he, from lifelong degradation.

"A pretty mess," he said, "society would be in, if all were of your thinking. What sort of blood would you get into our veins? What sort of mixtures would you make in families?"

"That is not any concern of ours. Right is right, if the heavens fall."

"You are putting a knife to the throat of the boy ; let me tell you that. You might as well kill him as make him do this thing."

"I have considered all that."

"In a few years, if you don't force him into this, he may steady down, marry well, and be a credit to us."

"With that sin on his soul, and that child an outcast? I don't want such credit."

"I have told you I will provide for the child."

"You cannot provide it a name and a place in the world."

"That is fine talking. Its place in the world would not have been very grand, with that lowbred woman for a mother. I tell you I have the poorest opinion of those people. You don't know what you are about. You have let a sentimental fancy run away with you."

"On the contrary, I have looked our duty in the

face from the first, and it is bitter as gall to me.
I know every detail. I have counted what it will
cost us to the fraction of a penny, to the fraction
of a pang. I know that I am giving up the boy's
future as far as this world goes. I know that I
am injuring our daughters' prospects. I know
that I am damaging very seriously our material
prosperity ; that I am putting a yoke upon us as a
family ; that I am pulling all those dearest to me
down to a lower level in the eyes of the world.
But — I ask it, all the same. Edward, it must be
done. God knows I am not fanatic, I am not enthusiastic. The happy and approved life we have
been leading has been as sweet to me as it has
been to you. I only knew how sweet when I saw
it being broken up. I like a high position. I like
the favor of the world. I have found out only now
how boundless my ambition has been for Barry,
where I have always put him in my thoughts. I
know if he makes this marriage he steps out of
notice, — he becomes the obscurest and most ordinary person. I know that the girls will suffer
in a thousand ways from the loss of his popularity, and from the difficulty that will be made in
receiving his wife. I know that our income will
be barely sufficient ; that we shall be heavily bur-
dened for many years, perhaps, in the support of
his young family. I tell you frankly, I see no
bright side to it. It fills me with dismay. I wish
I could see any other way out of it, but, Edward,

there is none. He must marry her ; he must do what is right. We must trust Heaven for the rest. Suffering is better than sin. *This* is a heavy burden ; but what would be the burden of a wrong unrighted, a debt uncanceled, all through our lives, tainting everything ? I don't want any such prosperity. I don't want any child's cry, any woman's moan, to haunt my sleep. Let us do right, and bear what comes of it. Let us be brave about it. Life is short. Why should we care so much? If the thing is *right*, we 've got to do it."

And so on through hours of midnight fireside talk. Sometimes, I am afraid, her husband said, Stuff and nonsense ; sometimes, I am afraid, he walked about the room with his hands driven deep down in his pockets, and his forehead wrinkled with the angriest opposition. But it was not in the nature of things that such conviction should fail to convict. " Only believe." The result was certain, nor was the process very slow. Within a week the following conditions were settled upon : —

Mrs. Crittenden was not to write to her son, nor in any way influence him or communicate with him. The father was to write him, more or less sternly (more, probably), about the disgrace and dishonor he had been to them, but putting before him the choice between two courses. He could, if he chose, marry the girl at once, remain where he was for the winter, and in the spring come home with her, in which case his father

4

would take him into his office, allow him a salary
of two thousand dollars, and expect hard work of
him.   He would give him as a home a small cottage on the place, that had been hitherto occupied by the gardener.   He could promise him no
further assistance, and warned him that his life
would be of the hardest and humblest nature.

As an alternative, he could go at once, within a
week of receiving this letter, to China, to take an
inferior position in a large mercantile house with
which his father had influence, where he must at
least spend the rest of his youth, depending wholly
upon his own exertions, and having no allowance
from his father beyond his passage money and his
necessary outfit.   The situation was secured, if he
chose to take it.   The steamer sailed on the 20th;
a stateroom was at his disposal.   The letter was
short and business-like, and was not calculated to
leave any doubt in the young man's mind that his
misconduct had ruined his prospects for life, and
that his father was not very much averse to seeing him well out of the way.

Three days passed, — three days of very considerable anxiety to the parents who waited for his
answer.   China or Phœbe?   The father thought
China; the mother believed Phœbe.   The great
fear the mother had was lest he should be driven
by his pride to do something against his conscience, and go away, stung by his father's curt
dismissal of him forever from the family life and

by her silence. But she had promised not to write, and could do nothing but keep her promise. The father trusted that he would choose his freedom; at all events, if he had a repugnance to the woman, he had that door to escape by. A pretty narrow door, to be sure, and none too inviting, but he had it, and he could not complain.

At last an answer came, curter than the father's, and as business-like. He elected Phœbe and the two thousand dollars and the gardener's cottage and humble pie generally. It was evident to Mrs. Crittenden that they would never know from him whether he turned his back upon freedom and adventure because of his conscience or his pride, his love of Phœbe, or his hatred of hard work. To feed himself had not been Barry's idea of happiness hitherto. He had been so lovingly fed, he had never objected to the process. It now remained to be seen whether his pride would interfere with his digestion, or whether his laziness would uproot his pride. His letter gave no evidence of a penitent spirit. He desired an early remittance for present expenses; he did not speak of his mother, and sent no message to his sisters. He took the attitude of an equal with his father; treated the allowance as his right, and made the whole arrangement strictly a business one.

It was part of the compact between the parents that in writing to him henceforth his mother should not allude to the matter otherwise than in its commonplace aspect; that she should bind no burdens on his conscience, and let him know nothing of the conflict that he had occasioned them. This was in deference to the father's judgment that she had always enervated him by her sympathy. It was easy to agree to that, when she was gaining so much more important things; but it was not so easy to keep to it, when time passed on, and each letter grew colder and shorter, and the distance between them lengthened.

But she must bide her time. Spring would come, and when they were once more face to face the ice would melt.

When the letter came announcing his marriage, the fact had to be communicated to his sisters. The young girls held their elder brother in a sort of idolatry. He was their hero; they had both associated him very intimately, in their secret hearts, with their own future. Lucy was prepared to sacrifice herself to him, if he would accept her, and to live unmarried to serve him and to further in any way the great career which lay before him. Honor, more worldly, dreamed of marrying him to some one of great wealth and beauty. She felt sure the lovely being would have a brother who would be her own fate: they would wander together, an ideal quartette, through lands of song and picture, they would build houses side by side, they would roll in wealth, they would exult in all gifts of nature and of fortune. Poor Honor!

it was a considerable downfall to have to hear
that her brother was already married to a young
woman living in a country village, whose name
was Phœbe, and who probably "did up" her own
collars and cuffs, if not the more bulky portion of
the family " wash." Honor was scarlet with shame
and disappointment, Lucy white with hurt feeling.
There were sore hearts in the house for many
days, but "young flesh heals quick." They had
been spared, wisely or unwisely, all but the fact
that he had married without telling his sisters
anything about it. They were at liberty to suppose that everything but that was as it should be.
Lucy healed her heart's wound by reflecting that
such absorbed love as would permit him to forget
their existence must be heroic. She dedicated
herself henceforth to the care of his children, and
to the building up of the fortune which he had
forgotten, in his haste; to which practical end,
she discontinued two reviews and countermanded
an order for some books which she had felt very
necessary to her before this new necessity arose.
This gave her a sense of having risen to the occasion, and then things resumed their ordinary
course. Honor soon became interested in her
preparations for Christmas, and her enthusiasm for
her brother being cured, she reconstructed her
day-dreams, leaving him out, and was, all things
considered, as happy as before. It is always easy
to supply vacancies in day-dreams.

CHAPTER V.

WEARY-FOOT COMMON.

But while the young girls thus happily accommodated themselves to the change in the family, their elders had more difficulty in reconciling themselves to all that it involved. Mr. Crittenden was not a rich man, in any solid sense. His professional income was large, but so were his expenses. He had felt that he had many years of good work in him yet, and up to this time he had not taken very heavily the anticipation of the future for his family if those years should be denied him. Now, however, anxiety took hold upon him : he acknowledged that the easy years past had been unwise. The provision for one family was inadequate, and here was another laid upon him. He refused to believe that Barry would ever do anything for himself. Expenses that before had seemed necessary and justifiable now fretted and galled him. He grew nervous and irritable. The setting off two thousand dollars for Barry's use, and giving up the cottage to him were really inconsiderable sacrifices ; if he had been in his ordinary health and spirits he would not have esteemed them heavy. But ap-

prehension for the future took possession of him.
It was not unfounded apprehension ; he should
have had it long before. They had spent too
much money. The proper provision had not been
made for the future ; but that was not Barry's
fault, and should not have been laid at his door.
The fact was, it had appeared probable to both
father and mother that Barry would step into a
large fortune that was waiting for him in the hand
of a pretty young cousin, who had, with all the
rest of the world, seemed entirely devoted to him.
They had not talked about it even to each other,
nor schemed about it. They were not the sort of
people to do that. But in the secret heart of each
had been the conviction that after a few years of
liberty Barry would settle down to that, and be
among the rich men of his day without over-ex-
ertion of brain or muscle. It changed things so
entirely to think of his needing as much or more
provision than his sisters. The burden grew intolerable. Men are much more irrational than
women when they get off their balance. They
seem unable to distinguish between necessary and
unnecessary expenses. Economy with Mr. Crittenden became a hair-cloth shirt without grace. The
details of the family expenses stuck into him with
so many sharp points. Every bill presented
opened a chasm of ruin before them. His wife
was clear-sighted enough to know that the situation was not very seriously changed except in their

imaginations; she felt that the only good in it was
that they had come to see, before it was quite too
late, that they were living with unwise liberality.
It was hard that it should have happened just
when the girls were growing up. But what will
you? One is never ready for discipline. Like a
wise woman she fitted her neck to the yoke and
went on steadily, retrenching, soothing, smoothing,
enduring, but not enjoying the process more than
another.

It had been their intention to spend this winter in the city, to give Honor the advantage of better masters, and to let Lucy have her first glimpse
of the gay world. It had been talked of for
months, and all the arrangements made. Every
ten minutes one or the other of the young girls
said something about it in some way. Honor was
wearing her old walking-dress, and saving the new
one for the city. Lucy was assorting her music,
and deciding what books she wanted to take with
her; she was paying her last visits to her poor
people, and making out a list of what they would
need before she came back to them. It was one
of the steps on her new path of discipline that the
mother least enjoyed telling these happy young
planners that they would have to stay at home
and unmake their plans at their leisure. She
scarcely knew how to tell them; she put it off
from day to day, and fretted in secret over it.

"Mamma," said Honor, tapping at her door on

the afternoon of a day on which she had pledged herself to tell them the bad news before night, — "mamma, may I come in? My new habit has just come by express. I put it on for you to see if I don't look — very nice — in it."

And, pushing open the door, she stood on the threshold, looking very pretty and very certain of admiration, in a new riding-dress, the sight of which smote the mother with dismay. In the pressure of recent events, she had forgotten all about this extravagance. A month or so ago, she had taken Honor to be fitted for an expensive habit. The bill; the uselessness of the dress now, since there could be no saddle-horse bought, and no riding-lessons taken; the child's disappointment; the pride they had always felt in her graceful riding; the unlikelihood of her now ever having that indulgence again during her girlhood, — all mixed themselves up bitterly in her thoughts, and she turned sharply away from the sight of the slender girl, who stood with one hand lifting up her skirt, the other holding back the door. She looked so confident of her mother's fond approval. Her habit was perfect. She was high-bred looking, with a slight figure, soft, blonde hair, *nez retroussé*, delicate coloring. It was the sort of figure and face that belong to high civilization, that demand wealth and costly surroundings, that seem out of keeping with middle-class life. The riding habit had cost enormously, — Mrs. Crittenden remembered, sharply, the very sum; but it seemed, even now, as if it belonged to her of right, as if no one would ever dream of ordering anything but the best for that young aristocrat. Thrift, economy, self-denial, — none of these fitted Honor. She would be nothing if she had not her right setting, everything if she had. She was a worldly little girl and a self-willed little girl, but infinitely piquant and winning. The mother knew of sincere depths below the glittering surface, and had meant to wait till this all melted in the sun of love. Now she felt it would be crashed and broken by the thwarting of circumstances, and she could not answer for the consequences. She had meant Honor to have a happy girlhood. It was easier to think of Lucy suffering. Her face contracted with the pain the thought gave her. She had a momentary feeling of rebellion and anger. Honor started and flushed as her mother turned sharply away.

"You don't care to see it?" she said, straightening herself up, and retreating a step.

"No, I am busy. I cannot attend to you now."

She did not look up; the door closed. She knew that for the first time in her life one of her children had come to her for sympathy and had not got it. She had shut out poor little Honor, and sent her away wounded and angry. She did not know herself. A great many such surprises await us on our road, at a great many turns of which we do not know ourselves. They prevent monotony for one thing, and promote humility for another. It abases pride considerably to find that one's cherished perfections are the result of circumstances, of an absence of provocation to be imperfect. What one thought an elevation of principle was merely an elevation of income, forbearance and charity, an unimpaired digestion, indifference to the world, an abundance of its benefits.

The winter could not fail to be a trying one. Though the young girls took their disappointment, in the one case with sweet submission, in the other with stormy but short-lived anger, and though the family life moved on without much perceptible change, all felt, in one way or another, the darkening of that light that had always shone from the mother's eyes, the break in the serenity that had always made them serene. Indeed, to her the strain at times seemed greater than she could bear. The alienation from her son, the changed future for her daughters, the effect of the disappointment on her husband, were the great things. The little, who can enumerate? Gloomy weather; overstrained nerves reacting on digestion; petty economies, that tried pride as well as love of ease; curiosity of friends; annoyance at her husband's depression, almost contempt for it; continual vexation at the change in herself, — all these things together made her days dark and painful. There was nothing that she could do to appease her restlessness. She could not pour out her love

and solicitude in long letters to Barry, of whom
she could not help thinking night and day. She
could not even, with her hands, fit up and make
less miserable the poor little home for him, for till
spring it was in possession of the then-to-be-done-
without gardener. Her household ways were so
well ordered and of so long standing, she could not
employ herself much on their adjustment. She
was too restless to read with profit, too sad to visit,
too sore to bear any companionship. On what was
nearest her heart she could not speak to Lucy, for
she had kept her in ignorance of it; nor to her
husband, for they were not of one mind about it.
It certainly was none the better for her that she
had to keep it locked up in her own breast. She
began by longing for the spring "as they that watch
for the morning," and then to dread it, and to fail
in her convictions, and to doubt all things, beginning with herself.

CHAPTER VI.

HUMBLE PIE.

IT was a perfect afternoon in the latter part of May. The garden and grounds had not yet begun to show the absence of the deposed gardener, for they had all been put in order by "days' work," and were yet trim from the process. The house had been painted the year before, and was darkly olive-green and deeply red where the vines did not hide it. There was certainly no look of pinching poverty about it. It was a charming home, built upon the site of somebody else's perhaps less charming home, and so, rich with old trees and wealthy in vines and shrubs and hedges. The grounds were three or four acres in extent. Other well-appointed homes were near it, but you could not quite look into their windows, and you could not by any means talk from one piazza to another. At the back, the ground sloped down into a sort of ravine. On this slope lay the garden and the stables, and an orchard that had been white and pink with blossoms but a few days ago. Across this ravine you looked over tree-tops to blue hills that rose beyond. It was an old place and a new house, a very comfortable combination. The house had been built some twenty years, but the site was the old homestead of a well-known family, which in his early married life Mr. Crittenden had bought.

The old house itself had been torn down, but the farmhouse, a very small and inconvenient one, being of rather more recent date, was left standing, and had served as a house for the gardener. It stood at one side, quite up against the hedge half-way between the road and the house, and had been rather an eye-sore to Mrs. Crittenden. It was not near enough to the road to be a gate-house, and was, besides, too far from the stables, and too much under the nose of visitors and passers-by. The gardeners' wives were apt to be careless about potato-parings and tin pans; their children were sometimes untidy and noisy. It was a standing offense to Barry, who had always wanted it pulled down. But there it had stood, and there it was to-day, the home to which he was bringing his wife. Honor called it "Humble Pie," in a whisper to her sister, which their mother heard with a bitter smile. They did not know half how humble.

The transforming of Humble Pie from a very shabby Irish shanty into a picturesque cottage had been the occupation of the spring. Very little money was permitted, and very much labor was required. It was a poor little place. The small

front door opened into a room which was to serve
for dining-room and parlor. It had three windows, all of different sizes and in undesirable
places. A small kitchen adjoined it at one side.
A narrow staircase opposite the front door led up
from the parlor to the two sleeping-rooms above.
These rooms were under the roof, and the ceilings
slanted very much, and the windows were small,
and the closets could never be anything but musty.
There was a loft over the kitchen, which was to be
the dormitory of the one servant, though it had up
to this time been the dormitory of the rats and the
receptacle of old garden tools and obsolete pots
and pans. One of the two bedrooms was fitted up
for Barry's dressing-room. Dressing-room! The
window was so low, there was not a spot where he
could get light enough to shave without going on
his knees, or sitting on the floor. There was no
place where the press for his clothes could stand
save directly behind the door, which consequently
would open only a few inches, and which would
make it necessary to squeeze in with great com-
pression of the person. One can squeeze in through
a door once, but for a "constancy," as they say
in the country! It was hard to fancy Barry keeping his temper through this daily ordeal, — Barry,
the most exacting member of a dainty, luxurious,
smoothly running household. The architect of
this ancient building had not been an advanced
ventilationist. There was no accredited way in

which the air could get into the sleeping-room,
or, having got in, get out. The window was not
opposite the door, but modestly behind it; and it
could be raised only a matter of five inches, and a
dense growth of evergreens shut it up from without. The little lobby had no perceptible mode of
ventilation save from below, and as the stair-door
opened into the parlor, and was not ornamental
when open, it was safe to say it would generally
be shut. " They will both have typhus fever and
die," said the mother. The father refused even to
go into the house and look at it.

˙ " He has made his bed, and he will have to lie
in it," he said. " If he wants a better house, let
him bestir himself and go to work and get it."

But pretty paper and muslin curtains and a
little fresh paint made it quite a delight to the
young sisters, who did not care much about ventilation as a principle. The vines outside, and a
very inexpensive new porch, and some hoods over
the " unthinking " windows, and a coat of paint
certainly rendered it not unattractive. Lucy and
Honor, with step-ladders and tacks and hammers
and spoils from their own rooms had flitted in and
out, as happy as nest-building birds. The mother,
with anxious eyes, had superintended the " pointing up " of chimneys, the putting in of kitchen
shelves, the clearing out of drains. The garrets
at home had been ransacked, the upper shelves of
china closets overhauled : scarcely anything new

was bought,' and yet Humble Pie was comfortably furnished and a not unpleasant-looking little place.

What could be unpleasant looking, in this warm, sweet, late May weather? Fresh shoots from the vines hung about the porch and windows; the thick screen of evergreens had renewed itself, and was bright to match the season. Not a weed had presumed to obtrude itself on the freshly made path, and the new sod that had been laid to obliterate the gardener's children's foot-prints had become naturalized, and was green and bright.

It was afternoon when they arrived, Barry and his wife alone (for the little baby, for whose good name so much had been sacrificed, had died before it saw the light, and had had no need of a name, good or bad, in this or perhaps any other world). His mother had sent away the two young girls, when she heard the whistle of the train sound. The journey had been long, and they would be tired. The meeting would be agitating. It was well the travelers should rest, and see their home by themselves, and come over at seven o'clock to dinner. The mother alone would stay to meet them and give them a word of welcome, and then leave them to the lunch already prepared, and to the inspection of the house, that could not fail to have as much interest to them as to those who had with so much affection made it ready for them. The new servant in the kitchen was ner-

5

vously moving about and glancing out' of the window.

Yes, in five minutes they would be here; in five minutes would come the minute of which the mother had been thinking for, let us say, a hundred thousand minutes, since that November new moon shone through the library window over the left shoulder of pretty, pettish little Honor. She should in five minutes see again her alienated boy, — see the face she had never left off seeing day or night since then, and see the dreaded, despised, and all unknown woman who had taken him away from her. Her breath came short and quick : it makes great draughts upon one's strength to rehearse so often the moment which is so slow in coming. How would it be? Would she be strong enough to conceal any repulsion that she might feel towards her? Would she be self-controlled enough to show just the right tenderness to him, not overwhelming him with that for which perhaps he had ceased to care, and not chilling him by a change from the welcome to which he had been accustomed? One needs to be saint, statesman, one needs to be filled with wisdom, human and divine, to be a parent.

She looked again about the little room. It was all in order : flowers in the pretty vases, dainty china for their first meal on the small square table, pictures and books and ornaments disguising the plainness and poverty of the place. The

sunshine came in through the fluttering green
shadows of the vines outside; the soft muslin curtains moved faintly with the summer breeze;
there was verbena among the roses and mignon-
ette on the table, and the odor was delicious.
Honor had brought down one of her canaries,
among her other welcoming gifts, and it hung in
the porch and sang its best to the admiring robins
and bluebirds in the trees overhead. But ah,
what a home to which to welcome her boy! It
was a cruel travesty of all her ambitions for him.
The first-born of the house, the admired young
Adonis, the planned-for, speculated-about, carefully
educated, exceptionally gifted son, coming home
with his bride to the gardener's tumble-down
shanty, on the outskirts of his father's not too am-
ple grounds! It all seemed a miserable burlesque.
Had they been thinking themselves of too much
consequence for the past twenty years, and was
this the waking up? Was this the fit beginning
for the son they had reared, or was it fit only for
him because he had failed to profit by their rear-
ing? There are times in our lives when confusion
of the elements makes it impossible to take our
reckoning, and this was one of those times. The
only thing she could hold by was the certainty
that when she had made the decision she had
done what she thought right, and by that inward
compass she must steer and wait the chances, or
the providences, or whatever they were.

She felt too overstrained to meet the new-
comers now; she wished she might put it off.
She walked about the room, her cheeks flushed,
her lips firm-set. She was a small woman; in youth
she had been very slight, but the after-forty fullness was now rounding her figure, and making
her less girlish, but not ungraceful. Her hair was
light and waving; her eyes were gray and fine
and expressive and rather far apart; her nose
retroussé; her mouth not small, firm and yet
sweet. Her motions were quick, but her manner composed. She gave you the idea of being
younger than she was. Her voice was very sweet,
and she had a manner of attention and sympathy
which made her much beloved. Withal she seemed
to be judging, weighing, even in little things, and
yet she was not cold; she was even impulsive,
when she approved her impulses. People thought
she probably had n't any impulses which were not
to be approved. She was very much looked up to,
and for years had known that her opinion was of
weight with the persons among whom she moved.
Now all this seemed part of the huge mistake in
which her life was engulfed.

There they were; she heard wheels at the gate,
— the wheels of one of the shabby hacks. For
their carriage was put down, and Honor's pony
sold, and the shabby hacks at the depot were all
their reliance now. How would Barry relish bringing his bride home in one of them, — home to the
gardener's humble shanty?

As the hack drew up before the little door she went back a moment more to collect herself. She caught sight of Barry as he stepped out of the vehicle; she saw him glance quickly and curiously up at the front of the little house, with a contraction of the brow. How tall he looked, how broad-shouldered and handsome. It was more incongruous than ever to think of him under this low shelter. Then she came forward and stepped upon the porch to meet him : his companion was standing behind him. Barry approached her, and stooped down and kissed her. She did not even meet his eye, in her agitation. She saw that his cheek was a little flushed, and that his hand trembled slightly, that was all that she could be definite about, when, in her own room, she thought the meeting over. She had carried away no impression of the young wife, save that of a tall, well-formed woman, wearing a dark traveling dress and having a veil tied over her face. Nothing had been said, save the acceptance of her explanations and arrangements. She had left them almost the moment after their arrival, and now there was nothing to do but await the hour of dinner, and the beginning of the new life that must be so full of consequences to them all.

CHAPTER VII.

THE NEW DAUGHTER.

THE evening was warm, even though it was still May, and at seven o'clock it was much more attractive out of doors than in. The sky was full of lovely tints, scarcely yet to be called sunset ones, and the air sweet with the thousand odors of late springtime. There was a honeysuckle on the piazza that had put out its first faint blossom; and it was a faith of Lucy's that the green leaves of all the vines gave out a perfume during the first few weeks of their innocent lives. The piazza was hung with twenty years' growth of vines: Marrowfat was a warm place, and all summer the family lived as much outside as inside the house. There were one or two tables and plenty of bamboo chairs and lounges on the wide piazza, and brackets and shelves, and generally an afghan or two and some footstools, and a leather screen. When a shower came, there was a rush for the piazza to secure the properties; but the thick vines made it a tolerably safe place even in a shower. This evening all the windows were wide open, back and front; the sunset was at the rear, and shone through, and made house and piazza light and warm-colored. Lucy sat with a book on her lap, but it need not be said she did not read. Honor wandered about restlessly ; now going into the parlor to glance at her pretty little person in the mirror, now coming out on the piazza and peering through the vines, to see if they were coming.

" If papa had only got back in the early train," she said for not the first time. " It would have been so much nicer for him to have been here to receive them. But he acts exactly as if he did n't care a straw about their coming. I almost think he had forgotten it."

Certainly it would have been nicer. It was one of the small contrarieties that darkened his wife's life nowadays that he had not come in his usual train. She only hoped it was not with a purpose. - She was a woman who made her little plans and rehearsed her little scenes with a strength of imagination that made their disarrangement a very vital matter. She had hoped they would all be together at the steps to welcome Barry when he first came up them with his new wife. She had thought the father's coldness would be covered by the general movement and distraction. Now the meeting was to be done all by itself, and no one would fail to see just how unwelcome both son and daughter were to him.

" Here they come," whispered Honor, flitting

out from behind the vines. Lucy closed her book
with a throb of the heart, and rose. The mother,
quite pale, but with a sweet welcoming smile came
forward to meet them. They were crossing the
lawn, Barry a little in advance, as if he were
not thinking of his companion, but were nerving
himself for something, which he proposed to get
through with as quickly as might be. He was
well, even elegantly dressed ; with maternal omnis-
cience the mother knew that his clothes must be of
last year, for he had had no money to get new ones
since. There was something about him so above
this sort of mean fact. He was commandingly well
made ; he carried himself with an innocent pomp,
an absence of disdain combined with a conviction
of supremacy. He was so strikingly handsome
that people turned and looked at him, both men
and women. It had always been, "your handsome son," " that splendid boy of yours," ever
since he wore petticoats. Who could look at him
without pride, that had any part in him? His
skin was not dark, rather clear, and with a redness
that came and went, but was not in the least ef-
feminate, any more than the smile which was continually glimmering across his face, and which seldom went entirely out. (It was out now, though,
out utterly.) His hair, which had a *soupçon* of
a wave, was of a bright, lively chestnut, as was
his mustache. It was abundant, rich, thickly
growing hair, which asserted itself, though kept

shortly cropped. Indeed, there was no suggestion of want of abundance about him : the pity was all the greater that it should exist in his pocket. His eyes were gray, large, and expressive, and with a sort of flame about their glance that one does not look for in gray eyes. They had very dark and long lashes, a part of the amplitude of his tonsorial endowment. The ready-coming color and the long lashes would have risked the manly appearance of another, perhaps, but Barry was too tall and too self-asserting and his manliness too pronounced to be endangered by such trifles.

At this moment he was pale rather than flushed, however, and the seriousness, almost constraint, of his face struck his young sisters as unnatural. The gravity of the occasion began to oppress Honor uncomfortably; she scarcely dared to look at her new sister. Did people always feel like this when they had been getting married? Barry stooped and kissed his mother, who came half-way down the steps to meet him.

"And Phœbe?" she said, with a tender smile, going down another step and putting her hands out to the young woman, who was still standing on the ground at the foot of them. This position brought her a little above the level of the head of the new-comer, who was as unusually tall as she was unusually short. She kissed her almost on an equality, and then, keeping her hand, led her up the steps towards the two girls who, having hur-

riedly greeted their brother, stood shyly awaiting
her. Phœbe tripped slightly on the middle step.

"Oh why did you trip!" cried Honor, involuntarily. "It's bad luck."

"I'm sure I hope not," murmured Phœbe, almost inaudibly.

"These are your new sisters," said Mrs. Crittenden. "And this one, I need n't say, is the su-
perstitious one. You must try and cure her."

Phœbe did not look as if she had a mission to
cure any one of anything : she looked as if she had
all she could do to get through the ordeal and
cure herself of the desire to run away, though she
did not impress her young sisters with anything
but an appearance of stiffness and reserve. They
kissed her and led her to a seat on the piazza, and
sat down beside her, and covertly looked at her
while they talked to her.

Phœbe was a person you could not well help
looking at any more than at Barry, for, like him,
she was notably handsome, though without the
finish of good dressing and easy bearing. Not that
her bearing would not have been easy on her native hills, or among her own people ; but it takes
a pretty stout easiness of bearing to stand up
against the first meeting with your husband's relations, particularly when they look at you covertly
when they talk to you, and have reason to.

She was, as has been said, very tall, and rather
fuller and finer than it is the fashion to be nowa-

days. But she was quite capable of making a fashion for herself. She was a beauty. Her shoulders were well shaped, her head well set upon them. Though she wore an abominable shiny black silk dress, which fitted with home-made smoothness and total want of style, you could see there was no fault to be found with her figure. You had . faith in the perfection of the arms you did not see, thanks to the odious, ill-made sleeves, and to the purity and roundness of the throat that had a stiff linen collar close about it, fastened with a big brooch, which had a good many quirls and turns of chased, cheap-looking gold. She was large, if that is any objection, but large correctly, in proportions that satisfied you. You knew that she would move well, with a certain full grace, when she was at ease, and not being looked at by her husband's relations. Her skin was clear, and her cheeks and lips had a warm color. Her rich brown hair grew low on her forehead and waved without assistance. It was as badly arranged as might be, for the *ingénue* style had not reached Malden, and the maidens and matrons of that neighborhood still wore fortresses of hair on the tops of their heads. It was easy to see, however, that Phœbe had so much that she could, when enlightened, dress it in any style demanded. Her nose was straight, and her mouth, while not fuller than everything else about her, was certainly not indicative of undue sternness of

purpose or a lack of physical life. But it was
sweet and well formed; the indentation of the
upper lip was deep, and her slow, infrequent smile
brought out a look of innocence. Her eyes were
large, and brown, and soft. They were appealing
and affectionate, like the eyes of a setter dog.
She was evidently rather a silent person, whether
from shyness, or from a natural disinclination or
inability to communicate with her fellow beings, it
was not easy at once to see. While Barry was
standing by his mother near the steps, and the
others were sitting down a short way from them,
a hack drove in at the gate.

"It is your father," said Mrs. Crittenden, a little
nervously, looking at her watch. Barry, perhaps
from nervousness as well, moved away from the
steps and joined his sisters.

"Papa is late," remarked Lucy.

"Why does he come in that old thing?" asked
Barry.

"Oh, don't you know," cried Honor, "that
we've given up the carriage?"

"What for? In consequence of your getting
to be a young lady?"

"Why, no; more in consequence of your getting to be a married man! Don't you know
economy is the order of the day?"

"A very disagreeable order," muttered her
brother, the color coming into his face. It had
not receded, nor his brow smoothed, before the

hack stopped at the steps and was battered open by Mr. Crittenden from within, who emerged, tired and rather pale. He did not look at once up to the piazza, but turned and gave the man some directions, and then opened the dilapidated carriage door again, and searched about for something he had left. If Mrs. Crittenden had not engaged with herself at an early age not to pull the wires of her male puppets, she would have said, " Barry, go down and meet your father and take his bag."

She trembled with the eagerness that she felt to say it; but she was a wise woman, and forbore. Barry did not go; very likely would not have gone if he had been asked. He stood with a contracted brow, looking across the lawn till his father came up the steps.

" How do you do?" asked the latter, after speaking to his wife, reaching out his hand to him in a matter-of-fact way.

" Phœbe," Barry said, stepping back, after he had dropped the perfunctory hand, " this is my father."

" Ah," said Mr. Crittenden, looking towards the group, from which Phœbe made an uncertain slow step forward. " This is your wife? How do you do?"

And he put out his hand. It seems probable that during a critical instant he debated with himself whether to kiss her or not. If that were so,

he decided in the negative, and let go the hand
he held without any further advance or welcome.
The girl became slowly very white, and drew
back to her place behind the two young daughters,
who in their turn were greeted without effusion by
their. father, and kissed him lightly. . Lucy ran
forward and took his bag, and, as usual, went up
with him to the door of his dressing-room.

Dinner was a little stiff; it could not have been
otherwise. But Honor's vivacity was unfailing.
She liked events, and this was an event of mag-
nitude. She was too young to read between the
lines of her elders' forced talk, and not imagina-
tive in the way that Lucy was, who was making
a volume of romance out of every change of color
in the young stranger's face. She simply found it
delightful to have had a marriage in the family,
and it was a treat to see a bride, even if one of
six months' standing, and such a very odd one. It
was a break in the monotony of the home life.
For the winter had been dull, and the spring had
been worse, and summer was not yet on its feet.
At sixteen one likes things to happen. Honor
was watching always for something to happen.
This taste of hers was quite a boon to the family
on that evening, as one person in very sincere
good spirits must be to a tableful of doubtful or
depressed ones. Before the meal was over, life
looked a little more possible to one or two of the
party, and a little more promising. to one or two

others. Honor's lively chatter brought again before Barry's eyes the old life, and recalled his interest in trifles long forgotten. A good dinner warmed his blood; it was something to bask again in the sunshine of civilization. Lucy always consented to be happy if others would be so. The mother felt the long strain on her heart relax a little. The father, unconsciously to himself, was relieved that the first step was taken, and promised himself that the succeeding ones should not affect him equally. The tie of blood was imperceptibly asserting its magic force. The young alien felt them drawing together, and knew herself an alien. When they were leaving the dinner table, —

"After all," said Honor, "it's very generous in me to be glad to have Phœbe here, for she's not becoming to me. Don't you see? She makes me look little, and thin, and poor. Lucy does better beside her, — she's taller than I am, and isn't put out completely: she makes rather a nice contrast, with her light hair. But I, — I'm blown out; there isn't a flicker left. Phœbe looks like a great Jacqueminot rose, and I like a piece of white clover, a little browned at the edges."

"I should n't have called you a field flower, exactly," remarked her brother, touching the scarf of her delicately embroidered French cashmere. "This looks more like Solomon in all his glory."

"Don't you think it's nice?" asked Honor, drawing back a step and looking over her shoulder with a complacent vanity. "It's a French dress mamma ordered for me last fall; and it did n't get here till Christmas. It was to have been my nice dress all winter, but as we did n't go to town it will do for my nice dress all the spring and fall. Don't you see? I 'm getting very thrifty. I have n't worn it once. I would n't waste it on Marrowfat in the winter. But this was such a great occasion."

"We feel it," said Barry, briefly. He could have wished she would n't talk about the family economies so much. They went back to the piazza for a while, as the evening was so warm. The sky was still bright with the sunset tints. Lucy went down the steps and picked some flowers, which she gave to Phœbe, who held them as if she did n't know what to do with them.

"She does n't like flowers, I 'm afraid," thought Lucy, with a sinking of the heart. What did she like? Evidently not clear soup and lobster pâtés and salads and meringues, for she had left them successively almost untasted on her plate, and would n't have taken them at all except for a look from Barry. She did not appear to like pretty rooms and wide piazzas, for she did not look at them with any interest. And it was to be doubted whether she liked her new relations very much, for she was very irresponsive to all their graceful advances.

And how did they like her? The mother

looked at her affectionate, dumb-pleading eyes, and forgave her, and almost loved her. The father took in at a glance her unusual beauty, and his heart hardened towards her, and softened towards the son who had been led away by it. Certainly there was excuse for Barry. We don't love the splendid horse that has thrown and killed some one dear to us, nor the fine dog who mangled our pet, nor the keen blade that made such a quick end of our friend. Their individual perfections do not render the sight of them any less painful to us; rather, more.

Lucy watched covertly the constrained, undemonstrative manners of the new-comer, her passive grasp of the nosegay that she gave her, her unsuggestive answers, the little interchange of glance and word between her and Barry; and Lucy was perplexed and somewhat downcast, — poor Lucy, with her dreams and her small experience.

And Honor looked at the ill-made black silk and the flamboyant breast-pin, and wondered, — wondered till she almost forgot to talk.

Mr. Crittenden had wandered away to look at the garden, after dinner; his wife had hoped Barry would go with him, but he showed no such intention. So they all sat on the piazza watching the fading sky, and drank their coffee when it was brought out to them. There were many things to tell Barry. He would not ask questions, but it

6

was plain he was interested in this and that, and
Honor had a sprightly way of imparting gossip
that her brother had always rather approved.

"And Tartar's coming to-morrow. Did you
know that?"

"My cousin Tartar! You don't tell me so!"
cried Barry, getting up and walking across the
piazza with his hands in his pockets, evidently
much interested. "It's — a great many months
since I've heard a word of Tartar. How is she
getting on? Is she engaged or anything?"

"Ah, no, Barry," said his mother, with a soft
sigh. "Tartar isn't engaged. You know you
did n't expect to hear that."

"Upon my word, I don't know why not. I did
n't 'expect' anything about it, if I must tell the
truth."

"Tartar is a dear girl," she said, in the same
tone. "I shall be glad to see her again."

"I 'm sure you won't be gladder than I."

Barry stood leaning against a pillar of the
piazza before them in an easy, graceful attitude,
his face quite lighted up with interest in these
things, all new to Phœbe. Though she had never
heard Tartar's name before, she knew the whole
story in a moment, the mother's soft sigh, his sudden awakening. She had vaguely known that
there was some one who had been intended for
him. It was this cousin, then, that they had meant
him to marry, — this cousin who was coming to-
morrow.

" You know she 's been ill. We have n't seen her since before the holidays," said Honor. "She went South early in January. Everybody was frightened about her. She had pneumonia, and it left her with such an ugly cough."

" I had n't heard of it," said Barry, dryly. It seemed his interest did not abate, though he did not ask Honor to go on.

" We went to town to see her just before she sailed. She was so thin, her hand seemed like nothing, only it was so hot. And she talked, talked, every minute we were there. Lucy and I simply did n't say a word."

" Tartar never was what you 'd call reticent," Barry said, with a little laugh, bending over his cigar, in which he was cutting with a very sharp knife a very small incision.

" Why do you laugh, Barry ? " asked Lucy, with a hurt expression.

" Would you have me cry ? I take it she 's better, since she 's come back from the South and is expected here to-morrow."

" She is better, but she was very ill. You ought to be ashamed for making light of it, when you and she were such friends," said Honor.

" I 'm showing my feeling by being glad that she 's well, not by being sorry that she was n't."

" Ah, much feeling you show ! " cried Honor. He certainly did not look much moved. Phœbe knew it was passing through his mind that in De-

cember the news of his marriage had been made
public. She tried to think whether it would please
her to hear that any man had been made ill by the
news that she was married (always provided of
course that he had got well again before she heard
he had been ill). It hardly seemed to her it would
have given her much pleasure ; but she could not
tell, — it might. And then one must make allowance for a man : men are so different from women
about such things.

"Her Aunt David went with her, as usual,
though she had to be carried on the steamer, stiff
with rheumatism. But she was so frightened
about Tartar's cough she would n't let her go
without her, and now she won't let her out of her
sight. She 's coming up with her to-morrow. I 'm
afraid Tartar 'll never have her liberty again."

"There might be · worse things than having
Aunt David as a permanent attachment. And
have they got an apartment ? Where are they
living ? "

"At a hotel. They feel that Tartar won't be
able to spend her winters at the North any more,
and so they have given up their apartment, and
are floating population." ·

"Talk about liberty ! There 's liberty for a
young woman : the world before her, and nobody
in it belonging to her but one old woman, who
does just as she tells her to ; and more money than
she knows what to do with. If she can't be happy,
who can ? "

"You forget," said Lucy, "that liberty is n't all women want."

"They generally think it's that they want as soon as they have got husbands."

"And Peyton Edwards is coming up, too, to-morrow. I thought you 'd be glad to see him," added Mrs. Crittenden. " It's so long since he's been here, I feared he had forgotten us; but last week I got a note from him, from which I inferred he would be glad to come. So I wrote him that you would be home, and he must come to-mor-row."

" He waited till the mud was dried up," cried Honor, with fine scorn. " Barry, nobody's been here all winter, — literally nobody. I shall know now who are to be counted on."

" That's unreasonable, Honor," said Lucy, ear-nestly. " There was nothing going on ; we did n't ask anybody. You could n't expect to have young men coming here in winter, when Barry was n't home, without being asked."

" You'll see ; they won't wait to be asked now it's pleasant weather ; they 'll remind us of their existence, as Peyton did."

" Poor old Peyton," exclaimed Barry, with a laugh ; " he's the last person you 'd accuse of be-ing a fair-weather friend."

" Or of angling for an invitation," said his mother, with a smile.

" Poor old Peyton, indeed! He's about two

years older than you are, Barry. He may be poor, but he won't be long, the way he works and the way he does n't waste his money! He 's the kind that everybody calls reliable, steady-going, and that sort of thing; but for all that, I say he is n't any better friend than any of the others. You know yourself, mamma, you 've wondered that he has n't come all winter."

" Oh, well, that will be explained some time, my child. Trust your friends."

" If you 've got any to trust! Barry, did you write to him and tell him about — about your getting married ? " asked Honor.

" No," said her brother, shortly.

" Perhaps it 's that. You ought to have written to him, the most intimate friend you 've got."

It became more and more apparent that a young and enthusiastic person, who has not been told all the truth, is a very uncomfortable member of a divided family circle.

CHAPTER VIII.

TARTAR.

THAT night, when Phœbe went up to her room, she walked thoughtfully to her glass and looked in it.

"Why did n't he tell me they did n't wear pins?" she said to herself, pulling out the great gold brooch and thrusting it out of sight in an open drawer. There was something in the gesture that showed vehemence of feeling, — vehemence, but not haste, as if the fire had been kindled some time ago, and had just now ripened into a steady blaze. Now that her new relations were not looking at her, Phœbe moved without constraint, and with a sort of concentrated purpose. She took off the black silk, which she had learned to hate, and put on a white wrapper, and sat down on her trunk, with the waist of the dress in her hand, and pondered deeply. Not a detail of the costume of her slender young sisters-in-law had escaped her. She exaggerated the defects of her own, and thought of herself as an unwieldy monster, and of the black silk as a disfiguring abomination. Presently she took a pair of scissors and rapidly ripped up the sleeves; then she tore off the tight little band around the neck, and cut half an inch or so of the shoulder seams. She gave a sigh as she thought of the anxious care with which those stitches had been put in, not many weeks ago, she and her mother and Amanda Whittemore giving their nights and days to them. How much more she knew now, now that she had been three hours in company with French dresses! If she were only back there at home, with the clatter of Amanda's machine, and the simmer of the tea-kettle on the stove, and her mother's tired voice in her ear! She smothered the homesick throb, — there was no time now to be homesick; she must bend her whole mind to reconstructing the black silk before to-morrow night. It must be tied back, she said, shaking out the skirt, tied back in two places, and some of the fullness taken out of the back. What had Amanda been thinking of! She had made her a "figure of fun." Then she had a happy thought. She went into the depths of her trunk and drew out some lace, soft and pretty, and quite presentable in these imitation days. She had bought it of a dreadful woman who went about the country with a big basket covered with oilskin, and perjured herself many times a day for twenty cents a yard, at every farmhouse. Phœbe unwound it and shook it out. She turned up the sleeves of her dress to the elbow, basted the silk ruffles around them, and then put a double row of

lace below. She looked with satisfaction on her
naked arm and wrist. She turned back the front
of the dress, with its vile satin buttons out of sight,
and pulled the lace around her neck, in the form
of a fichu that Lucy had worn. Yes, that was it, —
she had it; and she gave a sigh of relief. She put
all the things away in the trunk, lest Barry should
come up and see them ; and then she shook down
her beautiful hair and brushed it out, standing before the glass and knitting her brows as she
thought of the difference between her forehead
and Lucy's.

"I can't look like Lucy," she reflected, "but I
can wear my hair down in my neck."

She certainly could wear her hair low in her
neck. It went into that formula with soft docility.
It was the most "biddable" hair, like a fine poetic
nature with no resistance in it. It fell down in a
coil around Phœbe's arm as she took out the comb,
and with an instinct of caress she raised her arm
and laid it against her cheek. It was the sort of
hair you wanted to touch, and smooth, and lay
against your cheek.

Yes, she certainly could wear her hair twisted
in the back of her neck, like Lucy's. That was
demonstrated, and still deep in thought she began
to get ready for bed. Deep in thought, indeed; it
seemed as if she were being swallowed up in a
flood of new thoughts, impressions, fears. She had
the intuitive courage of youth, and her want of ex-

perience was in her favor, as experience of failure
is not inspiriting. She was so alone, she was at
such a disadvantage ; she dared not guess with
what eyes these people looked upon her. And her
ignorance ! — from the forms at their table and the
fashions of their dress to the sentiments of their
hearts and the religion of their souls, she was in
an ignorance the most profound. She dared not
ask Barry; she did not want him to know she did
not know. She could only gaze, guess, apprehend
with every sense, study with her whole being, put
every faculty into the silent work. She was perceptive, she was young; she had the keen surface
intelligence of our countrywomen, and the habits
of mind fostered by the common-school system.
She had conquered the beetles and bugs of the
Holy Land. She would conquer the spoons and
forks of this higher civilization. She was self-reliant because her nature was deep, and because in
it lay purposes and an experience that weighted it
beyond the wont of natures of her age. Her loneliness was only comparative now. She had never
been used to confidences with her mother, and she
had outgrown her few school friends and been separated from them since she left the illustrious seat
of learning where she had perfected herself in the
higher mathematics, and attained distinction in
chemistry and mental philosophy. As they said,
she had not been " a great hand " for intimacies,
and her little home had been rather smaller than

any of theirs, and much remoter; and after her
distinguished success in graduating at the head of
her class, she had rather sunk out of sight of her
companions, and been only a tradition in the high
school town, for the year that had succeeded. It
was not new to her to feel alone, and not unnatural. All the same, in this strange land, she
longed, with a tight feeling in her throat, for the
sight of her mother's anxious face; for the sound
of Amanda Whittemore's shrill chirrup, for the
thump of the dog's tail on the bare kitchen floor;
something that was not new; something that had
grown familiar in long, easy years; something,
just some one thing, that would not shock and
make her think; something that she could look at
or listen to, not speak to. It was not a necessity
to her to speak, happily.

The next evening, at seven, when the two
crossed the lawn on their way to the parental dinner, Phœbe was a little in advance of her companion.

" What have you done to your dress ? " he said.
" Has Honor been teaching you how to get yourself up ? "

Honor, indeed! thought Phœbe; but she only
said No; she had n't seen Honor since the night
before.

" Well, then, you 've done it very well by yourself."

She certainly had. The soft lace subdued the

shiny black silk, and her white throat and beautiful arms made one forget the offensiveness of it.
At her belt, just where she had seen Lucy put her
bouquet, she wore a bunch of splendid red roses.
The change in the arrangement of her hair made a
marked improvement in her appearance.

Barry repeated in a tone of complacency, " By
Jove, you've hit it exactly."

When a lover admires, it is adulation, homage,
he offers; when a husband approves, it is a mere
expression of complacency. The approvable qualities belong to him; he feels that a demonstra-
tion of satisfaction is but one remove from ego-
tism. It is all right, of course, but it is not quite
so pleasant. Phœbe gave a little inaudible sigh to
the memory of a happy past, and then accepted
meekly her husband's approbation. It was better
than his disapprobation, at least. At first she
had felt, rebelliously, that it was worse; but she
was not an unreasonable woman, and she was
making use of all her powers to fit herself into
her place and to be reconciled to it. Mental philosophy and the higher mathematics had helped
her: she had cause to be thankful that all that
stimulates the imagination had been left out of
the arid curriculum of the Brixton High School.

She certainly had reason to be glad that she had
passed muster, as they walked across the lawn into
the very jaws of criticism, seated in solid ante-
dinner phalanx on the piazza. Barry's commen-

dation, though it had chilled at first, like a cold bath, invigorated her courage and sent a warm glow through her as a secondary effect. The eyes of her rival should not daunt her, since Barry had said she had "hit it exactly."

The rival, the rival's aunt, Mr. Peyton Edwards, and her father-in-law had all arrived in an earlier train than the one in which the latter had come the evening before, and had been driven up in a superior carriage that had doubtless been ordered from a livery stable to do honor to the guests. As they had passed the cottage, there had been an eager looking out. Barry had taken a holiday, as he was not to go into business life at the office till the next day. He had been loafing about all day, unpacking his pipes and his books, rather enjoying his discoveries about the little domain, planning improvements and talking over ways and means. The dread of the meeting was over, everything had proved so much better than he had anticipated, the getting home had been so pleasant in many ways, that he had had a very contented feeling. The day had been fine, even warmer than yesterday, and it was bliss to be alive, and he was young besides. When that superior carriage passed, he was sitting in the little porch, in a very loaferly attitude, smoking. He had forgotten it was time for them to arrive. He had forgotten that visitors must come sometimes, and come awkwardly near his poor little door, and look in-

quisitively in at his poor little windows. He had
thought about it often enough, all winter long,
but he had spent a whole day, the world forgetting, in a sunshiny, simple content, in which the
instincts of new home-making were entwined with
the memories of old home-loving. The rumble of
those wheels broke the charm. He started up and
returned the greeting of the new-comers very
gayly, but Phœbe from the window saw the dark
flush and contraction of the brow that succeeded.
He came hurriedly into the house and said it was
time to dress for dinner. During the hour that
followed, he found everything wrong: the dressing-room door, the low window, the unutterable
stupidity of Mary Ann. How well Phœbe, though
the high school had not stimulated her imagination, knew why the house had that moment grown
too small, the lot to which he had bound himself
too oppressively obscure! His cousin Tartar, with
her golden coins all jingling, had passed by. Dis-
content had fluttered noiselessly in at the open
windows on little stinging wings, and when would
there again be peace at Humble Pie?

But when they were dressed and both of them
out in the calm summer afternoon, Barry re-
covered himself a little. It always mended his
mood to be well washed and well dressed. He
felt his empire when he was *point device*. Nothing ruffled him like being shabby and dusty. And
it was especially soothing to him that Phœbe

looked so handsome. Handsome was a poor word;
it was not the word that fitted at all; it was stiff,
and wooden, and red-cheeked, and middle class.
You could not call her regal, with eyes so affectionate and appealing; nor splendid, in her thin
black silk and imitation lace; nor magnificent,
with her silent, half-frightened manners; nor spiritual, with all that wealth of flesh-and-blood perfection (as flesh-and-blood perfection is considered to be incompatible with spiritual perfection).
Beautiful is a word that like manna has a flavor to
each man of what he likes best. Perhaps each of
those who watched her come across the lawn and
approach the piazza thought, each in his or her
own way, How beautiful she is, after all! Aunt
David put up her glass to her elderly eyes, and
made the comment sharply *sotto voce*, nodding
her head as she did it. Mr. Crittenden, his head
a little bent down, looked out at her from under
his dark brows, and in his mind emphasized the
adjective which he had overheard. Peyton Edwards moved aside as she came up the steps, and
his eyes followed her with something like wonder.
Honor had been telling Tartar about the black
silk, and Lucy had been looking deep reproach
at her for her disloyalty. Tartar almost caught
her breath, — with surprise, shall we say? — as
this singularly beautiful young woman entered
upon the scene.

She went through the introductions tolerably

well; that is, she did not color, or stammer, or put
out her hand in the wrong place. She grew
rather pale, and did not do much but drop her
eyes and move her lips quite inaudibly as she was
presented to each person. It certainly would have
been better if she had bent her head a little, but
she seemed to have forgotten about that, or did
not know. Aunt David insisted on shaking hands
with her, so she had to look up for an instant during that ceremony.

She saw a thin old woman, with a great many
wrinkles and a very bright eye.

"I've alwayth felt ath if Barry were my own
thon," she said, holding Phœbe's irresponsive
hand for a moment. "I hope you'll let me feel
that I have thom thiare in you."

Phœbe looked again furtively. She did not
make up her mind on the instant whether she was
prepared to say Aunt David was welcome to a
share in her or not. Aunt David was very in-
teresting. She was distinguished-looking; you
could see people always wanted to listen to her,
though she spoke with such a funny lisp, and liked
to look at her, though she was twisted with rheumatism and wrinkled with age and yellow with
years of conflict with an ungrateful liver. The in-
definable flavor of beauty hung round its ruins; no
lack of physical completeness could take from her
the power to attract and please. She had been a
clever young woman, and she was a clever old

woman, with a fire and force of will that made itself still felt.

The meeting between her and Barry was very
warm. She took both his hands, and they had so
much to say to each other that he seemed almost to
have forgotten Tartar, who had spoken to Phœbe,
and was waiting to speak to him. At last he
turned to her; probably he had not forgotten her,
after all. She was evidently a little embarrassed,
but she did not fail to cloak it with a sharp little
flow of sarcasms, for which her sobriquet would
have prepared a stranger. Her name was Sarah,
but she had been called Tartar from her childhood, which had been a very tempestuous and
spoiled one, under the guardianship of her Aunt
David, who had as sharp a tongue as she. Aunt
David publicly said she was the worst child in
the United States; but as she seemed to love
her better than any other child in the world, it
was rather offering a premium on badness. Aunt
David was strong-willed, but Tartar was stronger-
willed. With great frankness, they quarreled in
public as much as in private. Tartar openly be-
moaned her bad temper, but set it down to inheritance, as if it had been rheumatism. Aunt David
was very worldly, and acknowledged it. Probably
they were both better than they chose to admit.
Tartar's temper was not unpleasant, and Aunt
David had a good deal of heart, notwithstanding
her worldliness.

7

Tartar was rather taller than Lucy; not of course so tall as Phœbe. She was dark, with blue-black hair and flashing black eyes, a low forehead, a thin, tolerably well-formed nose, deep dimples, a fine mouth, a little too large, and teeth so white that, in conjunction with the dimples and the eyes, a smile had the effect of a sudden display of fireworks, it was so sudden and dazzling. She was decidedly thin, eminently well dressed.

Phœbe watched her furtively as Barry, after a moment's welcome of Peyton Edwards, turned back to her and began a low talk with her. She stood by a pillar of the piazza, with the vines at her back, slender, supple, aristocratic-looking, her thin, small brown hands opening and shutting, but not sharply, a fan that hung from her waist, her very tiny and well-shod feet visible below her short dress, one crossed before the other. There was such a well-trained look about her, you could not imagine her not having done everything before.

Phœbe could not hear what Barry was saying to her. (One hopes, of course, that she did not want to hear.) He had an excellent manner with women; it must have been native, for no one remembered when he did not have it. There was something between a caress and a supplication in his tones. While he did not show any lack of self-confidence,—on the contrary, his acts were all based upon it, — that quality was not at all brought to the front; it was used as a base, nothing more. Mistaken men, who allow it to appear above ground! He possibly had a chivalrous regard for women (also native), and he acted out its dictates with a tentative sort of amusement. He was never tired of the success of his experiments; they were a continual source of innocent enjoyment to him. It was delightful to him to awaken Aunt David's enthusiasm; it was equally charming to him to know that the two young ladies whose tickets he had picked up in the cars yesterday would thrill at the thought of the adventure for a week. What could be more harmless, more amiable? It was surely adding to the sum of human happiness. One ought to use one's gifts. If a person has a knack at fascination, it must be the right thing to fascinate,— within bounds.

Phœbe was not quite prepared for the development of this talent in her husband. She had naturally been gratified at his popularity with her mother and Amanda Whittemore. He had not been thrown into any other female society in Malden. As he was equally a hero in the eyes of Joe, the "hired man," she had simply concluded that he was perfect, and that every one of both sexes must know it, sooner or later Experiences were multiplying upon her, and she did not know distinctly what she was to think about anything. Probably she had a look upon her face that in-

dicated this frame of mind, for Lucy and her
mother both came towards her, with the object of
making her feel more at home and happy.

Now Phœbe was fatally quick in some of her
intuitions, and she instantly divined their purpose.
She was not obstinately bent on feeling unhappy
and not at home, but she did not find the condition removed by the consciousness that they
were making this amiable effort to remove it.
Lucy did not dare to try the flowers again, having
found that her new sister did not respond the
night before. She also had a misgiving that they
would not have read the same books, that in lit-
erature they had not any common ground. The
little search in her mind for something to talk
about made itself apparent in a want of ease and
sympathy of manner. Whatever it was she talked
about, it had, so far, led to nothing but " I don't
know," and " I had n't ever thought about it."
Lucy looked so discouraged that her mother, who
had taken a seat on the other side of Phœbe,
and who was disguising her intent and anxious
listening by great attention to a piece of embroidery in her hand, came to the rescue by asking
some question about the little *ménage.* Did
Phœbe think that she could get along with Mary
Ann, by having some one in to wash?

Now to Phœbe Mary Ann herself was an unprecedented luxury. What could she need of a
woman in to wash? What radical difference was

there between the keeping of a little house in Malden and the keeping of a little house in Marrowfat? What did these people expect her to do? She answered in much confusion that she did n't want a woman in to wash, she thought.

"Perhaps you may need her just at first," said the mother, "before Mary Ann gets quite accustomed to her work. I am afraid she is very inexperienced. But you and Barry will always come over here for your dinner, and that will make it lighter for her."

"Oh, I'm sure we shan't have to do that, ma'am."

The prospect of an endless chain of dinners like to-day and yesterday took away her breath and startled her quite out of her confusion and embarrassment. She spoke with a sincere deprecation there was no mistaking. The mother smothered a sigh as she saw the chagrin and apprehension on her face. She could fancy Barry would not prize the tête-à-tête dinners cooked by Mary Ann as much as she would. She had hoped they as a family would not be so terrible to her; but she had no one to thank for it but herself. She thought of the poor bewildered, despairing mother in her limp crape veil and shabby black dress, making her way across the lawn in that November rain. No wonder her daughter felt she was in an enemy's country.

The way did not look very clear to Mrs. Crit-

tenden as she bent her head over her embroidery.
All around her there was the sound of voices,
easy, merry, such as she had been used to hearing
in the happy times that were past. The piazza
looked like the old life. One could have imagined
it last summer, but for the silent daughter-in-law
at her elbow, whom Lucy was taxing her ingenuity
to entertain. Barry bending toward his gypsy-
dark cousin with his manner of devotion looked
like last summer: the picture of the two figures
had always given her keen satisfaction before,
and now it was with such a pang she looked at
them. Whichever way she turned, whatever she
saw, there came one thought. It was like a long
song with one termination to each verse. Have I
done right?

Peyton and Honor were talking to each other.
Mr. Crittenden was listening to Aunt David with
a half-absent smile, occasionally his eyes wandering to the pair standing by the vine-clad pillar.
The declining sunshine shone across the piazza
from the west; the soft air was full of the faint
twitter of birds and the faint perfume of flowers
and leaves not yet matured. The shadows on the
lawn were making the rich, pure green of the new
grass beautiful where the sunshine struck it. The
external peacefulness and beauty of her home had
never seemed greater to her than at that moment.
But for the presence of the girl beside her, the internal peacefulness and beauty might have been

as great, it seemed to her. Had she done right? Ah well, nothing could put them back to where they were last June. It was useless to recall the past. If Phœbe were not here in bodily presence, there would be an intangible sin that would interfere as much, perhaps, with the internal calm. But it is difficult, in all moods, to credit the intangible with its full power.

This Phœbe was a nightmare. Why was she here? If she were not, all their contented pleasant dreams would have seemed in the way of fulfillment. Had they done right? She never could divest herself of the feeling that she was accountable for the marriage, and she alone. Without his father's aid and permission Barry simply could not have married, and she had no clew to the part his wishes and his conscience had had in the matter. Since she had seen the girl, she could imagine he would have regretted parting from her; but there had been nothing in his manner towards her to indicate any such devotion as would render easy the sacrifice of all his prospects of success. This episode of her son's life was a sealed book to her: about it she could only speculate. The part she had played in it lay heavy at her heart. It is hard that our convictions which are strong enough to bear us into action have a way of balking and weakening and turning coward when we are fairly in the field. Now, when the consciousness of duty fulfilled should have made her strong and helped

her to overcome difficulties, she found her moral
forces in a panic. She would have given a great
deal to have seen Barry's marriage in the light in
which she had seen it during that week when she
gave her husband no rest till he had consented to
make it possible.

"Mamma," said Lucy across the speechless
Phœbe, "don't you find Peyton looking thin? It
seems to me he has altered. He must have been
working hard."

"Let us call him here and ask him," said her
mother, laying her embroidery on her knee, and
giving up the problem of making Phœbe talk.
"Peyton, Lucy thinks you have been overworking," she said, raising her voice.

Peyton came across the piazza and stood before
them. Honor followed, for they were all on the
most intimate footing, and if Peyton was not a
cousin he ought to have been, for the frank affection
they all felt for him. He and Tartar and Barry
had been playmates from childhood. Lucy had
been a little younger, and not quite of the *camara-
derie*, while Honor had been the baby and play-
thing of them all. Peyton was as tall as Barry,
but not as well filled out. He was not thin, exactly; muscular, probably. His shoulders were a
little squarer than most men's, and he gave one the
impression of awkwardness; but he was not awkward, at least if awkwardness means want of ease.
He was easy. He had no trouble about the dispo-

sition of his limbs. He moved well enough. It
was chiefly when one compared him to Barry that
he gave the impression of being wanting in grace.
He was not, either, a handsome man. His hair
was a light, very light, brown; he had been one of
those tow-headed, freckled, little-nosed, blue-eyed
boys, of whom one wonders that anybody but
their mothers know them, there are so many of
them in every school and in every town and village. One is moved to admire the quality of
indefeasible individuality that belongs to all the
works of creation, that they are so known. What
made Peyton Edwards to differ from his many
little similar fellows it would have been difficult
to say. He did not shine in anything; he was
generally to be found in the middle of his class,
not by any chance to be mistaken for the head or
the foot; he was not especially anything but himself. But he was himself, and people that knew
him well, liked him, and people that did not, did
not think much about him. He was the Fidus
Achates of Barry Crittenden. Mrs. Crittenden,
who speculated a great deal about her children's
preferences, decided it must be because he was of
a neutral tint, which suited the gorgeous efflores-
cence of Barry, as a gay clump of hollyhocks
would choose, if they could be asked, a gray stone
wall for a background. It was possible she under-
rated him. She had a kind interest in him; but
how could any one, used to the contemplation of

Barry, see anything more than qualities to inspire
a kind interest, in him ? It was the habit of the
family to speak of Barry's affection for him as
something which reflected great credit on his (Barry's) kindness of heart. His devotion to Barry
explained itself.

The contrast between the freckled little commonplace and the young Adonis had decreased
somewhat as the years went on. The freckles
had disappeared and given place to a decent tan ;
the sinewy urchin had lengthened out into a muscular, if not graceful, youth. His hair was not
quite so sandy, and his mustache not a bad color.
His blue eyes had always been nice in expression,
even to those who thought they looked like everybody else's blue eyes. His nose partook of the
general neutrality of his features. If questioned
about it five minutes after parting with him, you
would not have been able to give any satisfactory
account of it. His mouth, what one could divine
of it under his mustache, was good, and his chin by
no means lacked firmness. He was silent but he
was not stupid, withdrawing but not hanging back,
shy but not shamefaced.

When he came across the piazza, in consequence
of Mrs. Crittenden's observation about his overworking, he stood by the railing before her without embarrassment, though with no bravado, and
answered the personal remark very simply.

"No, Mrs. Crittenden," he said, " I don't think

I 've been overworking, but I should have been if I'd done any more. It does n't hurt you, you know, up to a certain point. I think I've learned just where the point is, and I always stop this side of it."

"Does Barry know?" said Honor. "You ought to drive in a stake and not let him go beyond. He might injure himself. He begins going to the office to-morrow, and we don't want him broken down."

And then they laughed, as if Barry's laziness were a classic jest in the family. Phœbe reddened. She knew it was unreasonable that his own mother and sisters should not be at liberty to make jokes about him; but it was horrid to feel anybody could do it. Till now she had known more of him than any one else; now she seemed to know less, and have less right. Peyton saw the color spread over her beautiful face, upon which he was looking down.

"Barry 'll work hard enough now, you need n't be afraid," he said, and then he turned the talk away from the matter. Presently Phœbe looked up, actually looked up into his face, and anon said something of her own accord. It was the very smallest observation, a mere bubble in the ice of silence, but it gave Mrs. Crittenden a world of encouragement.

"These two silent people understand each other," she thought. " We are too diffuse, and drown out their faint possibilities."

She based upon this a re-arrangement of the
dinner-table.   Peyton sat by Phœbe, and Barry
took Tartar in.   It certainly was a good distribu-
tion, and helped the poor country girl very much.
She needed help.   What with their strange things
to eat and their strange ways of eating them, the
freedom and familiarity of their manners with her
husband, the strained and anxious character of
their manners with her, her natural reserve, her
unavoidable ignorance, her heaviness of heart, her
consciousness of blame, it is surely quite apparent
that she needed help.   It was undeniable help to
sit by one who would have been nearly as silent
as herself if they had left him alone, and who undoubtedly understood how silent people felt.   He
took care of her, too, in little ways that he could
not have done if he had been busy in talking the
strange nonsense about strange people that occupied the others.   A dismal certainty was creeping
over Phœbe, — a certainty that she should never be
at home here, that she was more out of place even
than she had feared.   She felt so dull.   Her small
powers seemed to be shrinking into nothing.   The
talk at the table no doubt was bright and vivacious, but nothing more; the easy chat of well-bred
people who know each other intimately and have
a hundred points of common interest.   She did not
know the names even of those they talked about.
She could not understand the allusions they made.
The language they spoke was not the language of

Malden, nor yet of high school Brixton. Her
heart ached, or rather it was numb. A deadly
sort of homesickness filled her for a home to which
she did not want to go. When she had come
away from Malden, it was with a feeling of shaking the dust off her feet. The events of the past
few months had embittered her recollection of
home. Companions and neighbors of her whole
life had stood aloof in her time of trouble; bitter
and sweet were bound up in her memories of the
little hamlet, but the bitter were stronger than
the sweet, and she could not turn to them with
comfort in this dreary time.

She was so afraid some one would see she could
not eat. Peyton saw, but she did not mind him,
and her mother-in-law, but she did not say anything.

There were two windows towards the west, in
the room, and the pink sky shed through them a
lovely light. Through the south windows came
glimpses of the orchard, and the tree-tops in the
ravine, and the blue hills beyond. The table, to
Phœbe unfamiliar with the details of such service,
looked glittering and gay, and almost magnificent.
The odors of the wine, the flowers, and the unknown dishes made it seem to her like a feast of
royalty. In plain fact, it was a nice little well-
served dinner, for which Lucy had decanted a bot-
tle of her father's best sherry which had considerable bouquet, in honor of Aunt David, and for which

she had gathered her prettiest flowers in honor of
her dearest Barry's coming back to them once more.
If it was a feast of royalty, it was the inner kind,
— the royalty of high natures and pure affections.
But whatever it was, Phœbe felt it was not her
place to sit at it.   She looked across, when she
dared, to Barry, to see if he had no look or word to
help her with.   But how could he help her?   There
was Tartar on one side and Aunt David on the
other, and such a fire of pleasantry to be answered
as left him no moment for her.   Honor was on her
side of the table beyond Peyton.   She was in a
very saucy mood, and was not sparing any one,
except Phœbe, whom she had forgotten, probably.
Even the father, careworn and severe, had a re-
laxed though half-cynical smile on his face.   Tartar was a great favorite with him.   The half of
the smile that was genuine was due to his pleasure
that she was their guest, the half that was cyn-
ical, to the fact that she could never be anything
else.   He had recently been growing a great respect for wealth, an unwholesome crop that is
pretty sure to spring up after a devastating finan-
cial trouble.   It was surely something to be cyn-
ical about, to have let a clever, handsome girl,
with half a million, slip through one's fingers, and
to have brought up instead such a lifeless, heavy
piece of flesh and blood as he was obliged to recognize as his son's wife.   They had been a pack
of fools.   He could not even look at her, but

turned his eyes away, and watched Barry and his cousin instead. Barry had a little flush on his cheek; he was merry, and his delicious mirth-provoking laugh interlarded the conversation liberally.

" Barry hath n't forgotten how to laugh," said Aunt David. Aunt David liked the little dinner; it was thoroughly good. She liked the best sherry and the flowers ; she liked the company. She even had an eye for the rose-flushed sky and the good view from the south windows. She was very well suited with her surroundings; and if she had a regret for the alliance rendered impossible by the presence of the passive bride opposite, she had the good sense not to show it. There was no cynicism apparent in the flattering, almost fond attention which she lavished on Barry.

" He hath n't forgotten how to laugh," she said. "My dear," to Phœbe, "doeth he alwayth laugh like that, even when you are by your two thelveth ?"

Phœbe looked up, and tried to answer steadily; it was the first word she had been required to say in public, as it were, for every one was listening now, and her monosyllables to Peyton had not counted before.

" Yes, I believe he does mostly, ma'am."

What was it in these very simple words that made Barry redden, that made Tartar suddenly bend over and begin to crumb into fragments the bread beside her plate, that plainly disconcerted

Lucy, and made Aunt David press her thin lips
together involuntarily, and begin vehemently to
talk about something else? Phœbe wondered.
She ran over the sentence in her mind : she parsed
it by the best Brixton method, she scanned it, she
turned it inside out, she tried to divine any hidden
meaning. She knew it did not sound like Tartar,
or Lucy, or Honor. Wherein lay the difference?
It was right, but it was wrong ; perhaps it was
mostly, perhaps it was that wretched ma'am.
She remembered with a sort of faintness that she
had never heard any one but the servants say
ma'am here. Her face grew red as she sat, with
downcast eyes, thinking it over. Why had n't
Barry told her? But then he could n't tell her
everything. He should n't mind such a little
thing, but he *did* mind ; she could see that. She
spent the rest of dinner planning what she would
say to him when they should be alone ; how she
would tell him he need n't be afraid, she 'd never
say ma'am again to any of his people, not even to
his greatest grandmother. Phœbe could be passionate, sarcastic, everything, in her imaginary
speeches, with all the greater freedom that she
knew she never would get them said in real fact.
When she came to wanting to say them, some
mysterious power raised the drawbridge of speech,
and she was left spell-bound, a moat of silence
round her.

It certainly had sounded provincial, that meek

little answer of Phœbe's to Aunt David. It was
not to be denied that besides the offensive ma'am
and undesirable mostly there was an intonation —
faint, it is true, but defined — that marked the distance between Brixton and the great city. Her
voice was so sweet that the ear once familiar with
the accent forgot it as anything offensive. Barry
had been·used to it for so many months, he had
forgotten the offense; hearing, in fact, no speech
that differed from it except in degree of provin-
cialism. But now, with Tartar's fine, clear tones
in his ear, with the subtly different voices of educated people all around him, he heard it, and he
reddened. He was not to blame for that. Nobody walks the earth who has kept himself from
reddening by an effort of the will.

When they were once away from the table, she
breathed freer. It was something to be out of
range of the eyes of that terrible old woman and
that no less terrible young one. Her immediate
relatives became almost friends in comparison. She
knew they did not want her laughed at, for their·
own sakes. She did not believe they would permit any disrespect in speaking of her; hard and
unloving as she believed the parents of her husband to be towards her, she knew they would in a
sense protect her against the world. It was therefore not with a fear that she was to be discussed
that she saw Mr. Crittenden go down the steps
with Tartar and turn in the direction of the gar-

den. The young lady had put her hand through
her guardian's arm ; he laid his own over it in a
caressing manner, unusual with him even with his
own children. It was quite understood in the family that Tartar was in high favor with him. He
was now taking her away to see his vegetables, in
which interest she was very sympathetic. Peyton did not leave Phœbe. They sat down on the
piazza. Presently Aunt David and Barry wan- .
dered away in the direction of the garden, too.
The old lady leaned upon him confidently. She
was talking constantly, and Barry was laughing
and animated. Lucy was playing a symphony of
Beethoven in the twilight of the library. Honor
fed her cats under a snow-ball bush which had
been their dining-room for many seasons. Her
mother gave audience to a departing seamstress at
the other end of the piazza.

"Shan't we walk to the gate?" said Peyton,
who had seen a longing look towards the little
cottage on his companion's face. She had in fact
been feeling she would fly there if she dared ; she
was homesick and unhappy, and that was her only
shelter. It was something to walk past it, and
she got up to go with him. Peyton looked about
him, as they reached the path, with an affectionate familiarity. The soft evening light made
the cottage rather indistinct through the trees,
whereas in the day it was only too apparent.
Mary Ann's dish-cloths were always in distinct

view from the piazza, and an indiscreet saucepan
set out to cool would be a picture from the parlor window. With different degrees of bitterness,
these anticipated trials had been dwelt upon in
the silent minds of the mistress of the big house
and the mistress of the cottage. But "dewy
eve her curtain draws over the world's turmoil."
The cottage looked dim, bowery, picturesque, in-
capable of dish-cloths and sauce-pans. Peyton
told Phœbe, as they walked slowly along the carriage road, that he believed he knew every inch of
the inclosure, and could draw a map of every tree
and shrub, and every angle of the fence. He
showed her where Barry and he had their rabbit
hutch, where they built their snow-forts, and
pointed out where the coasting was in winter and
where the little tents in summer. Phœbe liked to
hear the story of her husband's boyhood from
Peyton; she was willing that he should have
known him before she did.

They went to the gate and looked up and down
the road, and then sauntered slowly back. As
they neared the cottage, coming upon it from its
parlor end, where it looked best, Peyton glanced
with interest towards it, and said, how they had
changed it, how pretty it was.

"Won't you go in and look at it?" she asked,
hesitatingly.

He was very glad to go, and they went in to
the little porch. It was very dim there, and

they stumbled a little, getting inside the door. There Peyton stood, leaning against the post, while Phœbe sought the matches and made a light. He watched her while she carried the candle, with its pale light, to the table where the lamp stood. Her movements were graceful and free here on her own ground. The light sprang up warmly under her touch, and the pretty little room seemed anything but despicable to Peyton, with such a Juno as its permanent endowment. He came in, and they went around the room, moving chairs and tables judiciously to be able to do it, and examined the little ornaments, and the mirror frame that Lucy had painted, and the lambrequin that Honor had worked. They both looked pretty large for the room when they were standing up, but soon they sat down, and did the rest of their talking at a better advantage. It was a good while before Peyton glanced up at the clock and said he did n't know it was so late. Did n't she think they ought to go back now? A cloud came over her face at once, and the stiff, embarrassed speech returned.

"I don't think I need go back," she said, not moving. Peyton looked troubled.

"They — they 'll expect you."

"I don't think it 'll make any difference," she returned.

"I know, of course, you 're one of them," he said. "I should think — that is, if one can feel so about people that are not really one's own — that you will be very — much attached — to them in a little while. I 've been here so much, ever since I was a little shaver, I feel as if I knew them inside and out."

Phœbe did not offer any opposition, neither did she seem to acquiesce.

The trouble on Peyton's face did not pass away. " I 've always thought," he said, slowly, " that Mrs. Crittenden was the best woman in the world."

Still Phœbe did not answer, but sat looking down, passing slowly backward and forward over the lap of her dress a spray of honeysuckle that she held in her hand.

"She 's always just," he said, " and that is n't an every-day thing, you know. She has a good judgment like a man, and yet a soft heart like a woman." Phœbe probably thought of the domiciliary visit of the poor widow from Malden, for her lips grew tight and her forehead a trifle creased. Peyton saw he was not making a good thing of it.

" I suppose she 's reserved," he said, — " not one of those women that take an interest in everybody ; but once your friend always your friend. I think she would help any one she meant well to, consistently, in great matters and small, to the end of her life. I think consistency is a great thing, don't you ? So few people are consistent all the way through ; it takes a great deal more

character than to be anything else; you use up so
much in qualities that are n't generally noticed."

"Very likely," said Phœbe, not absent-mind-
edly, but absent-heartedly.

"It's difficult to say why you think different
people will like each other," said Peyton, awkwardly, getting up, with his head very near the
ceiling, "but I felt sure, from the moment I saw
you, that you and Mrs. Crittenden would be good
friends. You know Barry is like a brother to me,
and I could n't wish him better luck than to have
his mother and his wife get on together."

The paths of diplomacy are very thorny, especially in their earlier stages. This was Peyton's
first essay in social finesse, and he had no reason
to feel elated with his success. He felt very hot
and embarrassed, as he went out into the dark
alone and remembered what he had said. He was
afraid he had been more than questionably im-
pertinent: what possible right had he to force his
advice upon this unhappy girl, whose dignity
touched him instead of chilling him? He could
not explain to himself what had moved him to
speak, when in every other situation in life he
would have kept silence. But the feeling had
been too strong for him; even now he felt that, if
it were to be done over again, he would do the
same. He saw the trouble the poor young wife
was in, and the rescue that was held out to her.
How could he make her see and take hold of the

rope that was within her reach? It would have been impossible for him to speak to Mrs. Crittenden; it would be equally impossible for him to speak to Barry. Why it was possible for him to speak to Phœbe was one of those mysteries that one has to accept, and not solve, in the matter of reticent natures. When one thinks of the varied forms of misunderstanding that are possible in a world peopled with such varied tempers, temperaments, whims, wills, concealments, prejudices, and perplexities, it seems amazing, not that there is so much discord, but that there is anything else. It is difficult to decide whether the outspoken people or the inarticulate people contribute most to the general misunderstanding.

Peyton walked up and down in the shrubbery several minutes before he could get sufficiently over the sense of oppression that these thoughts suggested, to go into the house. He must let them go their way, he supposed, but it was a bad job. He only wondered that anybody lived in peace, since there are so many bad people in the world; what must be their condition, when these good ones seemed to have such difficulty in coming to an understanding!

Phœbe's reflections were not so general in their character, but even more oppressive. After Peyton went away, she moved restlessly about the small premises for a little while; then, with a wise instinct to seek employment as a defense against bad thoughts, went groping her way up the narrow stairs. There was a little work-basket in a corner, which she found without a light. There was comfort even in the touch of it. It was hidden work, — no one had ever seen it, not even Barry; but into those little garments she stitched her teeming thoughts. Sore and bitter ones had given way many times as she bent over the pretty cambric; so, with this charm in her hand, she went down the crabbed little stairs again. As she laid her hand on the latch of the stair door to push it open, she heard voices, and looking through the crack she saw Tartar and Barry standing on the threshold.

"Come in," said Barry, preceding her.

"It is irregular," returned Tartar, hesitating. "I should n't come till Mrs. Barry is here to receive me."

"Nonsense," cried Barry, a little annoyed. "Country people, in our position, do not stand on etiquette."

"Don't say anything more like that," said Tartar, rather seriously. "Do you know, it sounds bitter."

But still she did not cross the sill that divided the parlor from the porch, and only looked curiously into the lighted little room.

"Overcome your scruples," exclaimed Barry, taking her hand; "it is n't the first time you and I have been in this room together."

"No," she cried, with a merry laugh, following him. "Do you remember the day we brought the duck's eggs to Mrs. Flanigan, and got her to let us make an omelet on the cooking-stove that stood there? And oh, what a smell of soap-suds and cabbage! The windows were covered with steam, and the room was furiously hot. I shall never forget how ill I felt, and how the dreadful stuff she gave us to fry the omelet in flew over on the stove, and added to the bouquet."

"Yes," said Barry, laughing. "You got so white that I was dreadfully frightened, and took you out."

"And rubbed snow in my face, to revive me."

"No, by Jupiter, that I deny! Nothing so ungallant."

"I remember the snow distinctly."

"Well, then, it was Peyton who did it. It sounds like Peyton."

"Oh, Peyton!" cried Tartar, with an almost imperceptible chill of manner. "Peyton wouldn't have seen that I was white. Besides, he wasn't with us that day. He had gone back to school that morning; I remember it distinctly. You had two days' longer holiday."

"Ah!" said Barry, with a sigh. "Those were happy days, Tartar. I wonder if life will offer us anything better."

"Than duck omelet and Mrs. Flanigan? Oh, I hope so."

" Ah, come," said Barry, with the touch of sentiment that one must always expect when men
speak of their boyhood, " you can't make me believe you don't sometimes remember those times
with regret."

" I don't want to make you believe anything
of the kind. Of course *I* regret them, already in
the spinster sere and yellow ; but for you, in your
honeymoon, as it were, — oh, fie! "

Phœbe did not hear what answer Barry made
to this ; it was rather low, and was interrupted
by Tartar's sudden movement to investigate the
changes in the room.

" This surely is new," she said, — " this funny
little window in the corner."

" No ; don't you remember Mrs. Flanigan used
to keep her milk-pans outside? We borrowed
one without permission once, on some occasion, to
tie on Major's tail. It got a good deal damaged,
and I think the rupture between Mr. Flanigan
and his master was mainly due to the little misunderstanding which resulted."

" I remember ! I remember !" cried Tartar,
with a peal of laughter. " Oh, Barry, to *think* of
your living in Flanigan's cottage ! "

" Yes, to think of it," said Barry, with a frown,
walking up and down the very small space that
there was to walk up and down in, in that room.
" Time's changes, Tartar."

" Ah, well," said Tartar, mockingly, " it might

be worse. You might have had Flanigan's dinner as well as Flanigan's house to eat it in. Now I 'm sure Mrs. Phœbe does n't give you cabbage."

" Nor duck omelet," said Barry, stiffly.

" No, nor duck omelet, as I did. So, you see, your fate might have been worse. Ah, now I like that little fireplace. Whose idea was it putting those shelves above? Honor's, I 'm sure. Honor is such a clever little thing. Why, I really think I almost like Flanigan's parlor. It 's — the drollest little place. Barry, tell me one thing candidly " —

But Barry's candor was never put to the test, for outside the door came a reproving voice : —

" Tartar! you here! How doth it happen? Ith the Mithreth of the houth at home ? "

" No, aunt; this is irregular. Barry made me come in."

" Then I will make you come out."

" Ah, who ever made Tartar do anything ? " said Mr. Crittenden, advancing across the threshold. But Aunt David refused to follow him, saying she would not enter the cottage till its young mistress was at home to receive her. Mr. Crittenden gave a curious glance around, and silently followed her without entering further. Tartar pouted a little, and said they must go, notwithstanding the protestations of Barry, who would have detained her. And so their voices died away down the road. Aunt David was tired with her long walk through the vegetable gardens and around the grounds. The quartette who had started out to look at cauliflower and beans went slowly back, having seen some other things perhaps as entertaining.

Phœbe pushed open the door, after they had gone, with her work in her hands, and a burning color on her cheek. She sat down by the lamp, and worked a full hour before her husband's step crossed the little porch.

" How long have you been at home?" he said. " When I went to find you, just now, Peyton said he 'd left you here."

Evidently he had not been frightened about her, which was no doubt what she had been hoping during the hour she had been waiting for him. What woman is above hoping her husband may get frightened about her ? Desirable as confidence is, solicitude is more subtly flattering. Phœbe explained the circumstances of her return in a voice of which the tremor was not perceptible. Then Barry threw himself into a chair by the window, and smoked, but did not talk. By and by he tossed his cigar away, and sat gazing out into the darkness ; after a while, he got up and said it was bedtime, and he was tired, and, without further amplification, made his way up the narrow little staircase to his room.

CHAPTER IX.

MARROWFAT.

FOR two or three Sundays after their arrival in Marrowfat, Phœbe found many good reasons for not going to church, the principal, but least prominently mentioned, being that she had not any summer bonnet. Going to church had never been a well-defined duty in her mind. She had got farther and farther from it as she grew up. Logically, she could not see why she might not as well read a good book at home, when she had no nice bonnet to go in. Since edification was all that she had been instructed to look for, she felt she found it better in a chapter or two of the "Saint's Rest," in old brown calf and yellow pages with long *s*'s, than in the diluted platitudes of the worthy minister of the Congregational meeting-house at Malden. The brethren who found their way to that remote village were not generally of high cultivation or keen intellect. The sanctuary in winter smelled of hot iron, and made her head ache, and in summer glared with white paint, and produced the same effect. When she had her new clothes and the weather was fine, it was very nice to go and see how they compared

with other people's ; when she had not, it was not
clear to her why she might not stop at home
without offense. This was a great sorrow to her
mother, who was not logical. She considered it
your duty to hear a sermon once a week, whether
you had a good bonnet or not. If it did not do
you any good, it was your own fault; it ought to
do you good, and The Sermon was not to blame.
Preaching she looked upon as a sort of eighth
sacrament; one might almost say a unique sacrament. Phœbe, with a very earnest desire always
to do right, but with that unfortunate turn for
logical correctness which she must have inherited
from her father (since her mother did not even
know it when she saw it), could not accept the
dogma. If all you went to church for was to be
done good to, you'd better stay at home when
you found it did not do you any good; that is,
unless it amused you or pleased somebody else.

Therefore it happened that she had been three
weeks in Marrowfat before she went to church.
It was a warm, lovely June day, and she walked
with Barry under the shade of the wide elms, in a
perfectly satisfactory white muslin dress, and a
coarse straw bonnet, trimmed with white mull.
At her belt she wore a large bunch of the dark
red roses that seemed to have blown for her particular adornment. Barry had looked at her with
complacency; she knew she was all right. They
were rather late; that is, the bell had stopped

ringing, and the pews were all filled, and the clergyman was just entering from the sacristy, when they reached the door. It was an old stone church, with many vines about it, greensward, and fine trees. It looked much more agreeable to Phœbe than the bare and unadorned ecclesiastical edifices of Malden and Brixton, and she thought she should probably be well enough pleased to come often, if Barry wanted to.

The organist was playing a low and unobtrusive strain; the clergyman, having just entered, was on his knees, where, unfortunately, the congregation had not followed him. They were all ready to criticise the young couple who now walked down the silent aisle; very far down, too, they were obliged to walk. It was the one moment in the week when they would be most conspicuous. Barry felt it, and an unconciliatory hauteur straightened his shoulders. Phœbe felt it, and her color went and came in a very pretty manner. They were as handsome a pair as had ever trod that aisle. Marrowfat held its breath and looked at them. After all, it is possible to be too good-looking. This was the first glimpse they had had of Phœbe, for everybody had been hanging back, and no one had liked to be the first to call. They were prepared to see some one dowdy, or flashy, or commonplace. They were prepared to be deeply sorry for the family downfall.

For the whole story had been current for

months in the place. A journeyman tailor in
Marrowfat had married a wife in Greene County,
who had a cousin who had moved to Malden and
bought out the keeper of the village " store " two
years before; and there was not a detail of the
unfortunate matter that was not talked over the
counters of every shop in Marrowfat before it was
a month old. We never can be sure how much
our friends know or what they are saying of us,
and the Crittendens could not be blamed for hoping that distance and obscurity had hidden the
sorrowful truth from their neighbors. That Barry
had made a rash and undesirable marriage could
not be concealed, but the whole truth, surely, one
might reasonably have hoped need not be published.

But it had been published, illustrated and em-
bellished; and in the face of it here were Barry
and his wife walking down the aisle with their
heads up. If Barry had looked shabby, dethroned,
undefiant; if his wife had had mouse-colored hair,
thin shoulders, a dull skin, or a bad walk, this
story might never have been told, and virtuous
Marrowfat have added to its virtues that of a large
and liberal charity. It is easy to forgive acknowledged defeat; it is hard to forgive defiant success.
Barry looked a greater swell than ever, and his
wife was so much handsomer than anybody else in
Marrowfat that it was simple nonsense to talk of
ignoring the past. If one did not want to be

walked over by these young persons they must be
put down; self-preservation joined hands with virtuous indignation; to cancel the past would be to
sacrifice the future. Scarce a mother in Marrowfat but felt a bitter sense of injury as she thought
of Barry. Not only had he set the worst possible
example to her sons, but he had overlooked the
charms of her daughters; not only had he out-
raged public opinion, but he had disappointed private hopes. Society should hold him to a strict
account; Marrowfat was not to be trifled with
when it came to matters of principle.

It was an old town, with ante-Revolutionary
traditions; there was no mushroom crop allowed
to spring up about it. New people were permitted, but only on approbation of the old. It
was not the thing to be very rich in Marrowfat, it
was only tolerated; it was the thing to be a little
cultivated, a little clever, very well born, and very
loyal to Marrowfat. It was not exactly provincial;
it was too near the great city and too much mixed
up with it to be that; but it was very local, and it
had its own traditions in an unusual degree. That
people grew a little narrow and very much interested in the affairs of the town, after living there
a while, was not to be wondered at. It is always
the result of suburban life, and one finds it difficult to judge, between having one's nature green
like a lane, even if narrow, or hard and broad like
a city pavement, out of which all the greenness

has been trampled and all the narrowness thrown down.

The climate of the place was dry and pure: it was the fashion for the city doctors to send their patients there, and many who came to cough remained to build. The scenery was lovely: you looked down pretty streets and saw blue hills beyond; the sidewalks were paved and the town was lit by gas, but the pavements led you past charming homes to bits of view that reminded you of Switzerland, and the inoffensive lamp-posts were hidden under great trees by day, and by night you only thought how glad you were to see them. The drives were endless, the roads good; there were livery-stables, hotels, skilled confectioners, shops of all kinds, a library, a pretty little theatre, churches of every shade of faith, schools of every degree of pretension; lectures in winter, concerts in summer, occasional plays all the year; two or three local journals, the morning papers from the city at your breakfast table; fast trains, telegraphs, telephones, all the modern amenities of life under your very hand; and yet it was the country, and there were peaceful hills and deep woods, and the nights were as still as Paradise. Can it be wondered at that, like St. Peter's at Rome, it had an atmosphere of its own, and defied the outer changes of the temperature?

Marrowfat certainly was a law unto itself. Why certain people were great people, in its

view, it would be difficult to say. Why the telegraphs and the telephones, and the fashionable
invalids from the city, and the rich people who
bought and built in its neighborhood, did not
change its standards of value one can only guess.
But it had a stout moral sentiment of its own ; it
had resisted innovations and done what seemed it
good for a long while ; and when you have made
a good moral sentiment the fashion, or the fact by
long use, you have done a good thing. Marrowfat never tolerated married flirtations, looked
askance on extremes in dress or entertainment,
dealt severely with the faults of youth. All these
things existed more or less within its borders, of
course, but they were evil doings and not approved
doings.

In a certain sense, Marrowfat was the most
charitable town in the world ; in another the most
uncharitable. If you were to have any misfortune
befall you, Marrowfat was the place to go to have
it in : if you lost your money, if you broke your
back, if your children died, if your house burned
down, Marrowfat swathed you in flowers, bathed
you in sympathy, took you out to drive, came and
read to you, if need were took up subscriptions
for you. But if you did anything disgraceful or
discreditable, it is safe to say you would better
have done it in any other place.

It may be said that Barry, having dwelt there
all his life, should have known better than to have

come back there to live, with such a stain upon
him.   But in truth we are not apt to analyze the
atmosphere we breathe ; he had not realized the
severity of it while he was in good social health.
He had been a great favorite, an eminently
important person, man and boy ; it had always
seemed to him that the sun shone in Marrowfat
all the year round, and almost all the twenty-four
hours in the day.   The Crittendens had been as
important people as there were in Marrowfat.   If
there was any blue blood in the place it certainly
flowed in their veins.   Mr. Crittenden was approved for being a son of the soil, and for having
done credit to the soil in his subsequent career.
Mrs. Crittenden was approved for her many good
qualities, for her talents, and for her ready adapta-
tion of herself to the place.   The children were
approved for their good looks and good manners.
The family were in fact quite model citizens.
When their style of living improved with improving fortune, their neighbors were tolerant of
the change ; when Barry put on airs, they were
rather proud of him ; when Honor refused to
speak to the milliner's daughter at the rink, they
secretly sustained her.   It seemed impossible for
them to do amiss.   Mrs. Crittenden was indispen-
sable to all the clubs, book, musical, charitable ;
nothing could be done without her.   Her entertain-
ments were assured successes ; her ways of man-
aging were spoken of with respect ; her methods

with her children, with her vegetables, with the
languages, were equally superior. Her son was
the best match in Marrowfat, her daughters were
pretty, her house was always open in easy hospi-
tality. It was no wonder she was an important
person.

But now all \this was to be changed. That
amid the waving field of general approbation
there must have been some secret seeds of envy,
the harvest proved. Aristides must pay for his
title; one cannot be just and be called just and
have only glory always with impunity. It was
amazing, the rapidity with which the opinion
spread that Mrs. Crittenden was an overrated person, that she had made many mistakes in judgment, that she had brought up her children badly,
that the girls were assuming, that no words could
say what Barry was or what he would become.
It was plain, also, from the retrenchments they
were making, that they had been living beyond
their means. It was even rumored they were
heavily in debt; trades - people were vaguely
warned not to let their accounts run on too long.
It was evident that theirs was no longer a house
whence much amusement would emanate. Then
Virtue stepped in and said, "Is it a house where
one ought to go? Give me your hand and come
out with distinction, and give no countenance to
the doings of this young libertine."

When one can make a show of virtue, and vent

a long-cherished spite, and lose not even a whist-party by it, human nature cannot be expected to resist. It was a most fatal addition of fuel to this fire when Barry straightened his shoulders so defiantly as he went down the aisle, on the occasion of his first appearance with his wife. And Phœbe's two weeks' labor over that pretty muslin, — what a hundred pities that it hung so well; that her ribbons brought out the color in her beautiful skin to such perfection; that the roses at her belt were in such harmony with the ribbons, the muslin, and the skin! She became a danger to society, a flaming ship set loose amid peaceful vessels moored at anchor. A dreary beacon, a ship aground, beating and pounding on the bar, to warn people where destruction lay, — this was what she was to have been, in the anticipations of Marrowfat. Poor Phœbe! she little knew how dangerous to morals she was, as she turned over the leaves of the strange Prayer-Book Lucy handed her. Her heart thumped audibly against her Jacqueminot roses. She felt all the family despised her because she could not find her places; she hoped Barry would not look till she got right about the morning Psalms.

She had never seen people kneel down publicly before. The very faithful in Brixton used to tip their heads forward a little when the minister made a prayer. The prayers at Brixton were " oblique sermons," shied at heaven at an angle

that made them equally available for instruction
and edification to the hearers below: perhaps *that*
was the reason the people tipped their heads a
little forward when the minister shut his eyes and
lifted his eyebrows and began what was called his
prayer; they did not want to be hit. Here everything was new and strange. It would be saying
too much for Phœbe's intelligence and piety to
affirm that she was impressed by a ritual which
was presented to her for the first time, when there
was so much to agitate her in her surroundings.
The liturgy was pretty much lost upon her that
morning, but when the sermon began, she settled
herself to hear it with the feeling that now she
was *en pays de connaissance;* the firstly and sec-
ondly were like old friends to her and quite re-
stored her composure. The text was, " And let
all the angels of God worship Him."

As a sermon, it was nothing very remarkable;
nothing beyond a plain and well-defined instruction upon the subject of worship. The preacher
was not an orator, but he was an excellent thinker,
and never found any difficulty in getting you to
understand his thoughts. This sort of teaching
suited the young stranger; she listened eagerly.
It was a revelation to her to be told that she
did not go to church for any good it would do
her, nor even to set an example; but to pay to
Almighty God an act of service, a homage as un-
connected with these results as the sweeping of a

room would be with the making of a batch of bread.
Everything was to be done to his glory, " as for
God's laws; " but this was especially a thing to
be done for that and that alone. It *would* bring
a blessing, it *would* do you good, as all duty done
honestly would do; but that was a secondary effect, something given by the grace of God, not the
thing to be put forward as an object. If you
found, after years of church-going, that you were
not any sweeter-tempered for it, you must not
be any more discouraged than if you had been
learning Greek and did not find yourself any
farther ahead in mathematics because of it. Very
likely you would be able to get ahead much
farther for it because of the mental discipline,
but you would not expect it as a direct result, or
do it with that as a direct object. Greek is Greek,
mathematics are mathematics; worship is worship,
and not charity nor self-improvement. Your duty
to God as God is a distinct matter from your duty
to your neighbor and your duty to yourself.

The duty of public worship the preacher set
forth plainly as he saw it, bringing up the example of the older dispensation, of our Blessed Lord,
of the Christian church from its earliest breath,
of the heavenly pattern, where before the throne
unendingly

"Faint mists of seraphs rise and fall."

And he showed them, as he saw it (one cannot do
any more, and I suppose ought not to do any less),

that the great act of Christian worship is paid in the offering of the Holy Eucharist. He did not pretend to understand the mysterious strength of sacrificial service; in a certain sense, that is an intellectual sense, nobody had ever understood it, from Cain up to Kant. But, accepting faith as a faculty distinct from reason, "believing that he might understand, not understanding that he might believe," he could see the meaning of the chain of sacrifice, from the first sin in Eden to the Great Oblation on Calvary; coming on from thence to the last sin that shall offend the "most worthy Judge eternal," extends the Christian sacrifice "shown forth till He come," encircling the ages in its mystic round. From Eden to Calvary, from Calvary to Eden; the signet that clasps the chain the Great White Throne set up in the new heavens and the new earth.

The vacant plea of a memorial, a picture instead of a presence, a talk about a thing instead of the thing itself, had never satisfied Phœbe. She was either too spiritual or not spiritual enough to be contented with Protestant teaching on the subject of the sacraments. It was an unexpected comfort to her to find there was something she could take hold of in the very misty sea of Christian doctrine on which she had been drifting.

"If it means anything it must mean that," she said, almost aloud. She had spent so much of her life in listening to preachers engaged in rubbing

out the meaning of Holy Writ, it was quite a
surprise to see one stand up and write it out in
strong lines afresh, and teach in effect if words
mean anything they mean what they express.
The belief in the supernatural had been so faintly
emphasized, so detached from all contact with the
natural, in the teaching to which she was used,
that logically she rejected it, being, as has been
said, too spiritual or not spiritual enough to abide
in such an impalpable kingdom.   To such a mind
it was a great deal easier to follow the utmost
length of sacramental doctrine than to accept the
volatilized essence of a word as the point of un-
ion between God and man.   If you believe in the
supernatural at all, it is a great deal better to believe in it as the Word of God and the Church
Catholic teach it than as you in your ethereal
daintiness might wish that it had been arranged.
"Except a man be born of water and the Holy
Spirit," "Except ye eat the flesh of the Son of
Man," "Whosoever sins ye retain, they are re-
tained," are as easy to accept as "Ye are the
temples of the Holy Ghost," "This kind goeth
not out but by prayer and fasting," "Whatsoever
ye shall ask the Father in My name He will grant
you."   Why reject what the Christian world for
fifteen hundred years agreed to believe as the supernatural truth, while you accept a more subli-
mated portion of the same faith on the same
terms?   As against the scientists and hard deal-

ers in facts you can have little or nothing to say ;
you are not talking in the same language ; but if
you have the happiness to believe anything that
God has revealed, why can't you believe it all,
and do Him the honor of submitting yourself to
Him unquestioningly ?

These thoughts gave Phœbe a rapid sense of
satisfaction. She assimilated difficult truths with
the force of a young and healthy spirit.

When she went out of the church by Barry's
side, her heart no longer thumped against the Jacqueminot roses. She was happily so engrossed
with her new and satisfactory basis of faith that
she did not see that nobody came forward to speak
to them, and that Barry strode out flushed and an-
gry-looking ; for two or three people had looked
away when he caught their eyes, two or three
more he had seen whispering and looking at her,
and for once in their lives Honor and Lucy were
being permitted to walk home alone.

These and other little occurrences of the next
few days gave definite ground to Mrs. Crittenden
for believing that the current was setting against
them very strongly. It is hard to bear injustice
and insult for one's self, but I fancy no one will
deny it is harder to bear them for one's children.
Mrs. Crittenden could, perhaps, have nerved herself to see Barry punished for his wrong-doing,
though it would have been a bitter sight. But
he had sinned. He had made his bed, and he

must lie in it. He was working out his punishment, and it might be the best thing for him that it was sharp. It was a different thing when it came to seeing Lucy and Honor neglected and tabooed.

Who does not know what a daughter's triumphs are to a mother? One's own triumphs in youth are half lost by the greedy inexperience that does not know what a triumph is and when to be satisfied, and by agitation of nerves and uncertainty of judgment; it is generally more hazy than brilliant. But with matured judgment, with calmed nerves, with an egotistic pleasure refined from selfishness, with romance stimulated by the prose of one's own fate, with base calculation mixed with purest sentiment, a woman watches the career of her young daughter with a satisfaction that the daughter misses. She feels no self-reproach at her pleasure, no uncertainty as to the result, for such love is always full of hope: it is the purest and most unselfish romance of which a woman's heart is capable. But turn the chances, and give her, for success, failure. What compares with that for sharp distress? The calmness of nerves is gone, the mature judgment has quite failed her, the injustice is a great deal more stinging than if she had the inner consciousness of some desert, which people always have when the injustice is personal. The better woman she is the more she suffers; the tenderer her heart, the livelier her imagination, the more unreasonable her sufferings. " These sheep, what have they done ?" What she could have borne for herself with heroism, she fails to bear for them with even passable dignity or patience.

CHAPTER X.

HONOR'S WOUNDS.

"MAMMA," said Honor, coming in from the post-office one morning in late June, with her hands full of letters and her cheeks flushed and an angry light in her eyes, "I have something to tell you."

Mrs. Crittenden had grown to dread what Honor might have to tell her; she laid down her work, and said "Well?" in a patient voice.

Lucy, who had been reading aloud, put her book on her lap, and looked up too. They were sitting on the piazza, which was covered with a tangle of roses and honeysuckle, all in bloom. Honor looked charmingly pretty in her simple muslin dress and round hat. She threw down the letters, of which there were quite a number, as if they were of very little interest, and, sitting on the arm of a piazza chair, began pulling off her gloves.

"I don't think you will believe me when I tell you: the Meadow Club had their first meeting yesterday."

"Impossible!" said Lucy, quickly. "Why, *we* got up the Meadow Club. I was thinking only this morning it was time we started it again for the season. It's the fourth year now, you know, and we always have to give it a start to begin; but this year I really had n't thought about it till to-day."

"Well, you 're saved the trouble, then. It 's started, and we are left out."

"How absurd, Honor! It does n't seem self-respecting, it does n't seem quite nice, to think such things possible," said her sister, reproachfully.

"It 's less nice to have them happen," retorted Honor, sharply, stretching out her gloves to their greatest length in her two hands, and holding them across her knee.

"*What* is n't nice? Pray let us have your woe," said Mrs. Crittenden, taking up her work again, and trying to seem unmoved.

"It is n't nice," cried Honor, with passionate tears springing to her eyes, "to be left out of everything, to be snubbed by everybody! This morning, when I came out of the post-office, the Merryhews' carriage stood there, and I went across the sidewalk to speak to Fanny and Sue, who were waiting in it. They seemed a little embarrassed, — I did n't know why; but while we talked Fred Warden came up and joined us, and in a moment he said to me, 'Why were n't you at the Meadow Club yesterday? There was such a large meeting, — everybody was there. I looked around for you.' At that Sue and Fanny colored up, and I saw Fanny give him a look, and he got so confused. Then I said I did n't know there had been a meeting, and Fanny said, Oh, it was quite informal; they did n't mean to have the Club very large this year, — just among themselves. This only seemed to make it worse, and Sue tried to say something, in her stupid way; and I was so blind with agitation that I could n't look at any of them. Then Fred went blundering on, and began to ask if they were going to the Burleighs' tonight, who it seems are to have a party, and what time they were going, and how many would be there. Everybody was going, they said, so glad of something else to talk about; and then I got away before they could ask me if *we* were going. I think Fred wanted to walk home with me, but I would n't look at him, I would n't let him come near me. I hate him. I hate them all. I want to go away from this horrid place. I won't, I *won't* stay here any longer! Mamma, what do they mean by treating us so? How dare they do it? How *dare* they do it?"

And poor little Honor flung herself down on the piazza floor beside her mother, and, burying her face in her lap, sobbed passionately.

"You are tired with your hot walk," said her mother, disengaging her hat with hands that trembled, and smoothing back her hair. "It is too hot for you to go for the letters in the morning now. I will send one of the women."

"I will never go again," sobbed Honor. "I won't ever go out any more. I never want to see a soul in Marrowfat as long as I live. I want to go away. Oh, mamma, mamma, take us away! What is the use of staying here to be snubbed — and snubbed — like that?"

"Oh, my baby, that's a trifle," said her mother, bending over her. "Why do you mind a thing like that?"

"It isn't a trifle," cried Honor, "to be left out of a club that you got up yourself, and not to be invited to a general party at a house where you've visited all your life! Lucy mayn't mind; she's above such things, perhaps; but I *do* mind, and they're not trifles to *me*."

Lucy looked as if she did mind, though; her questioning eyes had been on her mother's ever since Honor began her story, and her sensitive face showed all the pain she felt.

"I don't understand what it means," she said, falteringly.

"Ah," said her mother, still smoothing down Honor's hair, "these are things that are happening every day in the world. We have been fortunate never to have had them come to us before. Just do not think anything more about it. It seems, as Lucy says, not self-respecting to care at all for slights like these."

"But I can't help caring. I can't think about anything else. I shall always be wondering what is coming next. It is n't as if it were a big place, where you could get away from people ; but it is all or none here. You run up against people who have been rude to you all the time. Everybody knows whether you 're invited or not, and everybody watches you. Mamma, mamma, I wish you 'd go away."

" Well, I am sure I gladly would," said her mother, putting the girl's arms, off her lap, and rising to get the letters. " I am sure I gladly would, to please you, if we had the money. We have n't the money, and so we must stay and make the best of it."

She took out her own letters from the package and went away to read them, feeling she could not bear a word more now.

She had a good deal of the same sort to bear as the summer went on. The gayety was all in the hands of a young set, who seemed to have no compassion and no principle. Lucy and Honor were as much excluded as if they were not living in the place. The intimacies of years were undermined ; not of course in a moment, but one or two slights brought coldnesses and misunderstandings, and Honor was on the lookout for neglects. Tartar was not there to fight the battle for them. She was of too much social importance and had too much force to have been ignored. But beyond that little visit in the last of May they saw no more of her all summer. Lucy was easily crushed,

Honor was too young and hot-headed to make any effectual resistance, and Mrs. Crittenden could only submit to what had befallen her.

As for Barry, no one knew what he felt; with all his genial ways, he was deeply reserved. He worked early and late at the office, however, and made his fatigue an excuse for the rather unconvivial character of his conduct at home. Phœbe probably did not know what was going on outside the fence that bounded the Crittenden domain: she could not be expected to guess that it was something new that so few carriages came past her humble door, and strange that so few people took the opportunity of making her acquaintance. Barry had agreed with her that it was best to dine at home on most days, and she had a good deal to do in making the dinners acceptable to his rather fastidious taste. She had a great deal of sewing to do, besides, and little as the house was it was not a trifle to keep it in good order, with such a stupid maid as Mary Ann, who could not even set a chair back as she was told. That Barry was not morose, that Tartar did not come again, that her sisters-in-law did not pay her too many visits, that her mother-in-law let her alone a good deal, and that she had to see her father-in-law only once or twice a week at dinner, were so many things to be thankful for, and, added to her constant occupation, good health, and her interest in thinking over the new creed presented to her, made her, perhaps,

the most contented member of the family group.
She eagerly imbibed the habits and manners of
those who surrounded her, and took good care to
copy the dress of her sisters with as much accuracy as was possible with her purse. She went to
church quite regularly, whether Barry went or not,
looking dangerously handsome, but not at all conscious of it, and much more interested in finding
the places in her new Prayer-Book and in digesting
the very strong teaching of her new faith. Once
or twice some friend of Barry's had walked home
with her when she was alone; but these friends
found so little coquetry combined with her beauty
that they were not encouraged to try it again.
They, however, did not cease to extol her attrac-
tions before their families. Discussions about her
became, in fact, almost as much a part of the Marrowfat Sunday dinner as the roast-beef itself. The
rest of the week was comparatively peaceful, as
she was rarely seen save on Sundays. The more
the fathers and husbands and brothers praised her,
the more the mothers and wives and sisters condemned her.

CHAPTER XI.

A DAY IN TOWN.

THE summer, as to weather, proved very hot, and no rain fell for many weeks. The vines dried up around the piazzas of the big house and the porch of the little one. The lawn grew crisp and brown, and dust flew up in one's face as one walked over it. The days were sultry and the nights oppressive. The bread-winners came home fagged from the city, and the eaters of bread at home received them with spiritless languor. Honor and Lucy missed their pony-phaeton and pony more than ever when after sunset the carriages began to appear, to catch the faint breezes on the road. Mrs. Crittenden looked at her pitiful garden, and thought almost bitterly of the faithful old Michael who had been mowed down by the scythe of retrenchment, now fighting the drought on the premises of a prosperous neighbor. Mr. Crittenden was more doggedly economical than ever, and more unreasonably apprehensive that they were going to total ruin. Small things and great seemed combined to make the summer intolerable. But the drought alone was fearful. One got a feeling at

last that if it would only rain one would never
complain about anything else.

At last it did rain, lightly to be sure, in the
night. The air was a little cooled and the dust
laid and the sun faintly shaded by clouds when
people got up in the morning. They had so long
been doing nothing that the change inspired them
with plans. Those who had carriages ordered
them and went about to make visits and give invitations and do errands ; and the rest of the population went to town to do the shopping that had
been so long neglected.

Among these latter was Phœbe, who had only
been once or twice before, and to whom it was a
great event. The day proved a very delightful
one to her. They had gone in an early train, and
Barry had detailed a clerk from the office to show
her the way about the shops ; she had made some
unequaled bargains, and had invested her small
capital most successfully. Then Barry had met
her at a restaurant, and they had taken luncheon
together. He had expanded, once out of the
smothering moral atmosphere of Marrowfat, and
the excursion had been really a little honeymoon.
The luncheon was the work of a much more advanced artist than Mary Ann, and it was delightful to the housekeeping soul of Phœbe to have
known nothing of its previous history, and to have
no responsibility about the disposition of its remains. They sat by a window, where the air

came in very pleasantly through tåll coleus and
dracænas and blossoming plants, which had not
been permitted to feel the drought that had with-
ered the greenery at home. The people about
them were all strangers ; the little tables were
charmingly neat and well served ; the waiters' ob-
sequiousnesses were as good as a play to the innocent Phœbe.

"I 'll tell you what I have in mind, Phœbe,"
said Barry. "Another year we 'll cut Marrowfat,
and come to town and be free. We 'll take a little
flat somewhere, 'up in the sky, up in the sky,' and
get out of the way of people and do as we dern
please. When we want to be amused we 'll go to
the theatre, and when we want to be convivial
we 'll come here and get our dinner. It 's only a
question of finance. Save your pennies up for
that, my dear."

Phœbe did not answer, but he saw by the shining of her eyes that she was thrilled with pleasure
at the prospect. They went to look at some pictures and into one or two shops that were shows
of magnificent unattainableness, and all the time
Barry talked of the flat, and of the happiness of
getting away from people and being where nobody
would know them. Phœbe told him how much
she thought they would have to pay for a servant,
and exactly what per diem would be needed for
the table. She asked questions about gas, and he
promised to inform himself. Rent was the great

item, and the next day, he said, he would go to
some agents and find out. It seemed rather early
to canvass the matter, as they could not possibly
leave Marrowfat till the following spring,' unless
the sky rained briefs and the flood of success softened the father's heart. But the thought gave a
motive and a hope, and the two young people
walked the hot pavements with more buoyant
tread because of it.

They went back to Marrowfat in the afternoon
train, in which all the business men and shopping women went back. With the sight of the
first familiar face came a shade over Barry's. He
bowed stiffly and carried Phœbe's parcels with a
less *dégagé* air. On the ferry-boat, he took her
outside among the carmen and the nursery-maids,
hoping to escape contact with his townsmen. But
once on the train, they were surrounded by them.
Phœbe's inward blessedness added to her ordinary
beauty. She was not tired nor hot, as the other
shopping women were. Their presence did not
annoy her, because she did not know they were
Marrowfat people who had not called upon her.
One or two elderly gentlemen came up first, and
Barry not very graciously presented them. They
took the nearest seats, and talked to her a great
deal. Encouraged by the conduct of these heads
of families, the young men came up too, and before
the train reached Marrowfat they were standing
three deep around her seat, presenting what Mrs.

Corbin, sitting alone with her bundles in the rear of the car, characterized afterwards as " a disgusting spectacle."

Phœbe did not know that Mrs. Corbin and her bundles were there; she did not know it was irregular for an Ex-Judge and an Ex-Commodore to be talking to her, when Mrs. Ex-Judge and Mrs. Ex-Commodore had not been to see her. She only knew Barry and she had had a very happy day together, and that down in her tightest-tied-up bundle there was a tiny gown, all lace and cambric and embroidery, that warmed her very heart to think about. She talked naturally and happily, but not very much, and she looked most dangerously handsome. The Ex-gentlemen shook Barry's hand warmly at parting : upon their words, they thought to themselves, he was not to be blamed. Their elderly compliments had had as much effect upon Phœbe as elderly compliments ordinarily have upon the average young girl. They had made her a little uncomfortable, and filled her with a vague wonder whether these gentlemen knew how old they were, and how grizzled and unpleasing. The young men all seemed to her vastly below Barry, and not nearly so nice as Peyton Edwards ; but since they were his friends, of course she must be as well-mannered and amiable as she knew how to be. When they got off the train the most persistent of them carried her bundles, and led her to his dog-cart, before which were horses harnessed tandem, and which was altogether the most conspicuous seat she could have occupied. But when she found that she would have to go alone, there being no place for Barry, she declined, and went away with Barry through the fast-dispersing multitude.

She did not consent to his proposal to take a hack; had he not told her there was a motive for which to save her pennies? But when they got half-way up the hill, Barry looked so scowling she regretted the economy. Crowds of carriages were passing them; the rain of last night had all evaporated, and they were powdered with dust from the gay equipages, whose inmates looked out with the fine scorn of luxurious comfort upon the toiling pedestrians. Barry was loaded with bundles; there was even a basket of peaches that was materially heavy.

" Why in thunder did n't you give these things to an expressman ? " he said, impatiently.

" That would have cost as much as a hack," said Phœbe, simply.

" Bother the cost ! " he said, trying to shift them into less prominence. But bundles are bundles; they are a mathematical fact, and not a chemical combination, which by the heat of your furious disgust you can resolve into more portable elements. Assort and pack them as he would, they still remained an ungainly armful.

" I can't think what you wanted of all these things. Women are never happy unless they are getting the house full of trash from shops. I wish you 'd only told me that you had such a lot of parcels."

Phœbe looked hurt; she did not tell him that the parcels had not increased in number since they were in the city, but were identical with those he had carried cheerfully for her there. Mrs. Corbin, now in her comfortable carriage, with her own bundles beside her on the seat, thought them looking very far from happy as she passed them.

" He is tired of her already," she ejaculated, "and she is already spoiled by the flattery of those unprincipled men."

Mrs. Corbin did not make a secret of these discoveries; by noon the next day it was well known in Marrowfat that Barry and his wife did not live happily together.

CHAPTER XII.

LUCY HEARS THE STORY.

By a later train that day, Mrs. Crittenden and her two daughters had gone to town unpremeditatedly, being tempted by the change in the weather. They returned in the same train that brought the others, and found themselves in the rear of the same car, with a dozen people whom they knew seated near them. After the exchange of a few greetings, they were virtually quite as much alone as if they had been on their own piazza. The events of the last few months had increased the coldness on both sides; it was as difficult now to approach any of the Crittendens as it had at first been to treat them with neglect.

Honor was tired with the day in town and a little flushed with the heat, and possibly the contact with so many of her former friends. She certainly did not look as pretty as usual. Lucy had a worn, unyouthful expression, which had been growing lately on her face; it stung her mother to see it. Looking bitterly at the two, she did not wonder that, social reasons apart, the young men preferred her daughter-in-law, at this moment, to her daughters. There is nothing so successful as success. A good heartache from a love affair, or a deep grief, sometimes adds depth and pathos to beauty; but beware of care, disappointment, chagrin, anxiety of the ordinary kind, if you have control of a young girl's career. There is nothing ages so fast and so surely.

Honor buried herself in a book, and did not look up to receive the perfunctory salutations of the gilded youth of Marrowfat who passed through the car. Lucy saw them or not, as happened, and returned them gravely and distantly. No one stopped to talk to them. The circle round Phœbe was too conspicuous not to attract the notice of the most indifferent spectator. Mrs. Crittenden saw the whispering heads of some matrons in her neighborhood, and knew but too well of what they whispered. Lucy's eyes met hers once or twice in a troubled, questioning way. Poor Lucy! *must* she know? Mrs. Crittenden had fought bravely to keep her in the dark, but it began to force itself upon her that this was no longer right. Concealment is fatal to those "set in families." When one member suffers, all the members must suffer with it; bandages and ligaments and all the muffling in the world will not keep the secret of the wound from the rest of the body. Lucy must suffer for Barry's sin, and she had better do it intelligently than blindly. Her first contact with evil of this sort would come cruelly near;

but things must work themselves out. We cannot pick and choose for our children, this trial now, that chastisement a little later on, such and such an experience by and by. The great wheel of their lives has been set in motion by a higher hand than ours, and we must patiently submit to see its workings.

And so that night, as she sat alone in the library, she called Lucy to her from the piazza. The lamps had not been lighted. The slow, dull heat had returned, the temporary freshness having passed away with the effects of the short-lived shower. The house was still, the air was stagnant ; the servants, even, sitting about the kitchen steps in the rear, fanning themselves with their aprons, had not the spirit to be noisy in their petulant complainings. Lucy sat down beside her mother and put her hand in hers. It was hard to begin the story, but once begun it was an inexpressible relief to the mother. She did not spare anything, from the first hearing of the news to the last feeling that she had had that day in the cars when she had seen in such strong light the social gulf that Barry's marriage had put between them and their little world. And when she described the harrowing doubts that had beset her lest she had done wrong in using all her influence to effect it, Lucy's quick breath and tightened grasp of her hand as she whispered, " Mamma, how could you ever have doubted ? " lifted a weight from her heart. Lucy would help her bear this burden that had seemed so intolerable. Lucy said few words, and those very low-whispered ones; but her mother felt the beating of her heart and the hot trembling of her hand, and was thankful for the darkness that hid the shame and pain in her eyes. At last came the question that she dreaded:

"Mamma, do you think that he loved her, and that he would have done it of himself?"

"That, Lucy, you know as much about as I do. When the secrets of all hearts are revealed I may know, but not before. I shall never get near enough to Barry to ask him; he will never of his own will approach anything so painful. Sometimes I think he never could have left her, there is so much to make her beloved; then, again, I watch in vain for any sign of the lover. I appeal in vain to my knowledge of human nature. Barry is a sealed book to me in these days. I don't know whether he is one of those men to whom love is impossible without respect, or whether the tenderness of his early passion would cover the frailty of virtue that to most men is unpardonable. All experience is against the probability of a man's valuing what is forced upon him. And yet he had an alternative; he was not forced into it. It was made possible for him to go away. On the other hand, did he do it from duty, — from the sort of conviction that you and I have, Lucy? Your father would tell me that such a view of duty is just a woman's notion : and we have never thought Barry likely to take a woman's view of duty; happy if he took a man's! No, my child, it's all a riddle to me. I can only watch with a sore heart the working out of what with perhaps rash assurance I at first said was the right thing to do. Your father is against me in it, and every day hardens his convictions and weakens mine. I have put it out of my power to win Phœbe's confidence, by my unhappy failure of charity when her wretched mother came to me. I am her enemy, and I am not Barry's friend, apparently. I have spoiled life for you and Honor, and the courage of my convictions seems to have left me just when I needed it most. You must help me, Lucy, — help me, and forgive me if I have done you and Honor harm. God knows nobody ever meant to do right more earnestly. I thought I knew what it would cost."

"And if you had known, mamma, you would have done it. If you had it to do to-morrow you would do it again. I shall never think that you *could* do anything else."

And so Lucy helped bear the bitter load. A new light came into her eyes, and the worn, anxious look left her face. She had a mission, to help Barry, to soothe Honor, and above all to aid her mother to bear courageously the penalty of doing right. Perhaps no discipline could have been as good for her as this was. It gave play to all her

virtues, self-sacrifice, tenderness, high conception
of duty, while it corrected some of her mistaken
enthusiasms, and supplied her with the wholesome
though bitter tonic of practical common sense.

After all, parents do not always know what is
good for their children, and it is just as necessary
to submit in an humble spirit to their children's
discipline as to their own.

11

CHAPTER XIII.

LEFT BEHIND.

IT was February; damp snow below, wet fog above. Little rivers ran parallel with the side-walks, where there rose little mountain-chains of snow banks, as yet undigested by the thaw. The air was full of splash and drip, and a smell of moist wood and moist earth and moist everything. The country was at its most unlovely point, the "awkward age" of the year. The "getting about" was so bad that nobody got about. The Crittendens' door-bell did not ring once a day. But some changes had taken place in the household since the August drought. The cottage was shut up, and the third floor was now the home of Barry and his wife and the little boy who had been born to them in December. The draughts, and the leaks, and the necessity for stoves made the cottage a more desirable residence for gardeners than for gentle-folks. Phœbe had consented for the baby's sake to give up her own will, and Barry found himself so fretted by the discomforts of the little shanty that he would have made a much more decided abdication of independence than this without complaint.

Virtue was its own reward, however. Shortly after the change had been made another was determined on. The successful termination of one or two important suits gave Mr. Crittenden an impression that he was not nearly so poor as he had thought himself all summer. A good deal of money in his hand is apt to change the views of even the most prudent man. No doubt Mr. Crittenden ought to have invested it all in government bonds, and gone on in his path of retrenchment unmoved. But instead he considered that his girls had had a very dull summer and that seven o'clock came much too early for comfort at this season, and he proceeded to find them a charming and not inexpensive suite of rooms in town, whither with much dispatch and some rejoicing they went for the winter, leaving Barry and Phœbe to keep house alone.

This was delightful, and Phœbe was most happy till the fogs and the snows and the thaws seemed to make it a necessity for her husband to spend two or three nights in every week with them in town. Barry's spirits improved very much about this time. These little tastes of town invigorated him. He appeared to have thrown off the incubus of Marrowfat condemnation. His sisters were enjoying themselves, Tartar was constantly with them, the atmosphere was a fresh one, his ready popularity made him happy again. People are not critical in a large city; they want to be amused, and they do not ask questions. Barry was unencumbered; he was "small change" for dinner parties; he was always in demand; he had so many invitations that he had a feeling of great virtue when he waded through the slush every other night, on his way home to his wife and baby.

"It is n't every man would do this," he would say to himself as he kicked the snow off his boots at the door, on some dismal nights when it was pitch dark at six o'clock. Yet he liked to do it; he liked to feel he was doing better than most men would do. He was not bitter about it; he was quite cheerful. He enjoyed the baby; the house, when he got to it through the slush and fog, was quite as delightful as any city house could be, his little dinners were above criticism, and his wife always handsome and not reproachful. If it had not been for the importunity of the givers of dinners and the getters-up of theatre-parties it is quite possible he would have come home every night without feeling bored. Still it did heighten his spirits to taste the wine of social pleasure again; it did please him to be desired and approved.

A most absorbing interest, too, arose at this time. Somebody got up some theatricals, and found the Crittendens useful. Honor was delighted to be asked to play, and Barry was "roped in," according to his own account very much against his will, but he did not seem to make great struggles to get free. The rehearsals were endless ; every page of the three-act drama must have consumed about a week of time, if everybody's studying, rehearsing, costuming, consulting, journeying, were summed up accurately together. Barry professed great disgust of the whole thing before it was over. "If he were ever caught in such a scrape again !" But he did not seem to think he could be excused from anything, not even one of the three suppers which succeeded the final and not very triumphant representation of the play. Phœbe ought to have admired his sense of duty very much. " When you 've once undertaken a thing you 've got to see it through."

It is needless to say that the days were very long and the nights very dark to the young wife left at home. But she had her baby, she was · very busy, and she was not inclined to dwell upon the thought that she was ill-used.

At last, however, there came a day so dark that it made all these look light, when she recalled them. Barry had come home looking unusually animated and eager. She had a feeling that something had happened to rouse him beyond the ordinary. She longed rather apprehensively to know what it was, and wished that she had the ability to say plainly to him, What is it that has excited you so much ?

Evidently he had made up his mind not to reveal his matter till after dinner. He caressed the

baby with unusual fervor, he praised the dinner
freely; there was compunction with his fervor,
surely. Phœbe's appetite faltered fatally; what
was coming to explain his mood? At last it
came, after the dinner had been taken away, and
the baby, and they were sitting alone by the
library fire.

" What should you say, Phœbe, if I went away
for a little while? Could Master Baby take care
of you for a matter of six weeks or two months?
He looks to me capable of it. Let me tell you all
about it. We've had a certain turn of things at
the office. These railroad matters have occupied
my father pretty closely, and a telegram yesterday
settled it that he's got to go across. Then came
the worry about leaving my mother and the girls.
Going abroad is what they've all been longing
for, for years, — here was the chance. Mamma
had a thousand minds about it, but Honor only
one, and I believe Lucy was ' unanimous!' So
the fact is, I've been racing over town all day
like mad, have arranged everything: given up
their apartments, got state-rooms, written letters,
settled matters at the office, and done the work of
twenty able-bodied men. Father growls, but I
think he likes the idea, and there is n't a doubt
but that the change will do them all good. They
had got in a rut, and the girls would have a beast
of a time this summer if they stayed at home."

" But you," said Phœbe, faintly, — " I don't
understand."

" Oh, well, I had n't got there yet. You see this is the way it stands. If I don't go with them my father 's got to come back at once. If I go I can take the first steamer home after it 's settled, bring back the papers, and attend to the matter at this end of the line, and leave him to a holiday of several months. There is enough there to require his attention and to give him a feeling that he 's right to stay; in fact, if he did n't stay I 'd have to. Somebody 's got to be on hand there as well as here. You see, it 's an important matter, and we have just got to give up our individual interests, and take hold of it. I don't like to ask you, Phœbe, to stay so long alone, but I don't see how it can be helped. I 've thought it over on all sides. It seems the best arrangement I can make. Father needs the rest. It would be hard on him, at his age, to make that voyage and come directly back, and probably have to go again in six weeks' time. Whereas if I go with him, get all the ins and outs of the matter the little while I 'm there, and come back, I can intelligently conduct the case here, and bring things to a successful issue. There 's a good deal of money in it and a good deal of glory, and I like to feel my father trusts me enough to leave things on this side to me. It 's just the place where, if I hung back on the score of leaving you, he could reproach me with my marriage. I 've counted on you, Phœbe, to help me, and I know you won't mind, for such a little while."

Such a little while! If one night was long, what would sixty be. A terrible sinking of the heart made Phœbe's lips white, but she managed to say, " I can see that it is best for you to go."

" That's right," he said, stooping down and kissing her. " I knew you 'd look at it in that way. I don't mind telling you now that my mother opposes it, and thinks I ought not to leave you alone, with the baby so young and all that. I told her I would put it before you, and if you did n't think it best there should not be a word more said about it. But I shall be proud to tell them you 're not the woman to stand in the way of your husband's business interests."

" And private pleasures," said a voice within her. Her heart had grown so stony heavy it did not seem that it could sink any lower. That he was going would have been bad enough, but that he was going with such spirit, with such ill-concealed pleasure in the change of scene and prospect of amusement, made it almost more than she could bear. Once having got over the bad business of telling her of it, his relief made him more communicative than his usual habit. He drew upon her sympathy in all his plans; he expected her to see how great the advantage to him was, how much he would gain by the experience. All the details of preparation were delightful to him, and he seemed to think they would naturally be the same to her. He was the sort of man who makes a good traveler, loving travel, being systematic, observant, self-reliant. He had never had enough of it, and had resented that part of his fate always, and in other days been inclined to reproach his parents with not giving him a year abroad before settling him down at the study of the law.

Phœbe was not unreasonable: she repeated these facts over to herself; she added to them that he had been working hard for several months; that he was stimulated by the prospect of pleasing his father and showing himself a man in business matters. He was going with his family, too, who were in every way agreeable and companionable. It was but for a short time, as the world counts time. She was safe, well provided for; the baby was perfectly healthy. It was in no way an unjustifiable request that she should stay contented at home while he went abroad on a legitimate call of business. It was not unjustifiable, but oh! —

Your inarticulate natures have a good deal to bear in the way of imposed attributes. If a woman does not say she is unhappy, it is so much more comfortable to think she is happy, that those near her get in the habit of concluding that she is; if she does not scold, that she does not mind; if she does not draw a dagger, that she is not jealous; if she does not complain, that she is satisfied with what is being done; if she listens silently, that

she is wholly sympathetic. Now Phœbe found it
not the least of her trials that she was talked to as
if she were his elder sister, or his aunt, or almost
his mother, by this eager youth on the threshold
of his adventure in the world. And not only by
him, but by the others, who came home for their
last day and night, to settle up matters for their
absence.

"Is n't it nice for Barry?" whispered Lucy,
counting on her sympathy.

"Does n't Barry look like a prince in his new
ulster?" cried Honor. "Phœbe, you won't mind
if we don't tell people that he 's married!"

"If Barry keeps his mind on his business, he
may make something yet," said her father-in-law
to her as he went in to dinner. As he rarely said
anything to her, she concluded it was meant to
indicate he approved of her for not putting anything in the way of Barry's going. Only her
mother-in-law was silent and watched her nar-
rowly. "You are a little pale," she said, when
they were alone in the nursery.

"Oh, no," said Phœbe, with a rush of crimson
to her face.

"You must n't let the baby keep you awake at
night," said the mother, with foreboding, seeing
where the wound was, and that she could not
offer sympathy. "Let Mary Ann take him, if he
bothers you at night. You know young mothers
must get sleep enough."

It was a very bright-shining day, that last day
at home. The sun shone with brilliant effect
on the fresh snow that had fallen the night before. The sky was unnaturally blue, it seemed to
Phœbe. It hurt her eyes to look out of the window. Sleigh-bells sounded from the road with a
jingle that fretted her nerves. They were all to
go in a late afternoon train; their steamer sailed
the next morning. It had at first been planned
that Barry should stay at home, and follow them
in an early morning train. But some doubt arose
about somebody being seen at the office, whom
Mr. Crittenden did not think he would have time
to see if he had the charge of the family's getting off. So it was decided Barry should go with
them and spend the night in town.

This decision was arrived at just before they
sat down to their early dinner. It was not an uncheerful meal. Honor's spirits were wild. Lucy
was quiet, but probably happy. Barry was too
busy to be depressed; every few moments he
thought of something to tell Phœbe, which he
had forgotten. The father and mother were full
of care and plans, but the journey was a hopeful
one; they took all their dearest with them; for
them there was no parting. The sunshine gave a
stimulus to their spirits; the evergreens outside
the windows were sparkling like so many mam-
moth aigrettes; the hills were white against the
brilliant sky of blue. They were all hungry and

healthy and hopeful — and going. Phœbe alone was heavy-hearted and unhungry and to be left behind.

"Oh, by the way," cried Honor, "what have you done about Aunt David's state-room, Barry? Has she made up her mind to submit to the extortion, or does she take the other one?"

"Yes, yes," said Barry, absently, — he was making an addition to his already endless memoranda, writing on the table between his plate and Phœbe's, — "that's all settled. Don't bother me, Honor, till I get these things written down."

"Just think, Phœbe," said Lucy, "of Aunt David's consenting to go at four days' notice! She is like a girl in her spirit and energy. She will be the youngest of the party, I am sure. Was n't it hard upon her, though, to break up her winter quarters, and go off on a sea voyage in midwinter! But she can't deny Tartar anything."

"Tartar would have gone without her, if she had n't consented," cried Honor. "She has just followed because she did n't want to be left behind. No great credit in that. Nobody wants to be left behind!"

Mrs. Crittenden's eyes involuntarily sought Phœbe's face: it was so white she almost made the blunder of starting up to go to her. But Phœbe had not looked up and had not seen her solicitude. She sat still, her eyes cast down, her agitation showing itself only by the pallor of her face and the deep breaths she drew. It showed itself, however, only to those who looked, and nobody looked but Mrs. Crittenden. The rest were all so busy.

It was rather an irregular meal, Barry leaving the table two or three times to look after last things, and Honor dancing to the sideboard more than once to supply the place of the maid, who had been sent up-stairs for something suddenly remembered.

" Oh, horrid old Marrowfat; how glad I am to be going away from it! " she cried, starting up as her father left the table.

The next hour was a very busy one. The last things to be put in the valises, the last orders to be given to the servants; expressmen, hackmen, next summer's gardener; a real-estate agent to know if the place would possibly be in the market, a man with a forgotten bill of butter eaten six months ago; the reporter of the " Chronicle " to write up a local item; a laundress who wanted a recommendation; a poor man whose family had developed pneumonia; the carpenter to see about the parlor shutters; the locksmith to tighten the hasps of one of the steamer trunks. It was a racking pressure; the afternoon sun was sinking, the brilliance fading from the snow, when the hour for starting came.

"Come," cried Mr. Crittenden, impatiently

(every one was at the end of his or her patience),
" there is no time to be lost if we catch the train.
The sleigh is at the door."

Phœbe stood half-way down the stairs on the
landing-place, with the baby in her arms. Barry
was up-stairs, the rest were below. The girls ran
up and kissed her good-by, and caressed the
placid baby. It was the instinct, probably, of not
taking the baby too near the outer door, where the
cold air rushed in, that made her stand there and
allow her father-in-law to come up and give her
his cold kiss and a half mocking good-by to the
little heap of white cambric in her arms, but she
did not say so, or explain herself. She went down
a step to meet her mother, whose kiss was not
cold, and who whispered in her ear, —

" Good-by, I will take care of him for you."

Then she had some right in him ! But she did
not answer. They might as well have been saying
good-by to a statue on the landing-place. They
hurried out and into the sleigh, and the horses
shook their bells restlessly, but still Barry had not
come. His father called out for him impatiently,
almost angrily ; the hall door stood ajar, and the
icy current of air was forcing itself into the hall.
Phœbe stood instinctively holding the baby's
head against her shoulder with her hand, but she
was not thinking about it much. She was listening for Barry's step above, and hearing his father's
voice below. There was indeed not a moment to
lose.

"Yes, I'm coming!" he called out from the upper floor, and he came down hurriedly. "Phœbe, you'll have to see to the locking of my desk; I can't get the key out. Confound the hurry! It all comes of going so many hours before I had arranged to."

A sense of suffocation came over Phœbe as his step reached the stair on which she stood; a crowding of too much into a space that would not hold it.

"Good-by," he said, taking her in his arms and kissing the baby and her alternately. "Good-by, good-by."

He held her closely, and she clung against him, going down step by step, till they reached the hall. Her lips moved, but she could hardly make him understand the only words she could speak:—

"Don't forget — baby."

He laughed lightly. "And how about you?" he said, giving her a final fervent kiss at the door, as his father called him harshly from outside. He had laughed lightly. Barry would laugh so when he stepped into the boat to cross the Styx; but his face had been pale and his kiss fervent. He pulled the door shut after him; it closed with a heavy noise. Phœbe, staggering against it, leaned listening till the sleigh-bells passed out of hearing into the road, and were lost. Then, with a low cry that it is to be hoped the servants did not hear, she caught the baby against her breast, went flying up the stairs to her own room, locked the door, and, panting, put the child into its cradle, flung herself upon the floor beside it, and burying her face in the soft blankets rocked backward and forward in her oppressive anguish. She fought her battle alone; the baby went to sleep, rocked by her sorrow as he had been borne by her pain, and equally unconscious. The servants gathered together below, and chattered over the going in the idle twilight.

And in the fast-rattling train, Barry no doubt got over his pallor and his fervor, and possibly even the mother's foreboding heart grew lighter. It is so much easier to go than to stay, to be active than passive, to be a man than to be a woman.

CHAPTER XIV.

ISOLATION.

AFTER all, to a reasonable being in fair health there are few troubles that are unbearable. That first night was bad enough, and the second little better; but soon the sorrow settled down into a habit, and was worn accordingly, and not taken into the hand and inspected hourly. Then she resolved stoutly to make the best of it, and not to hurt the baby by fretting. Making the best of it involved keeping herself busy and scrupulously attending to every smallest duty of the household. Things had been left entirely to her discretion as to the housekeeping. She had been told to keep as many of the servants as she chose; to use whatever rooms she liked; to act, in effect, exactly as if the house were hers.

On the third day after they had gone she roused herself to look into the situation and make her plans. It pleased her to feel she was doing discreetly with the matters left in her charge. She was saving money, if the rest were spending it. Barry's baby had a right to a home; she was merely staying in it to take care of him. If there

12

was a touch of bitterness in these reflections, they
gave her the nerve she might have lacked to dis-
miss the unnecessary servants and place things on
an economical footing. The cook was reduced to
a general servant, and Mary Ann kept for the
baby's nurse. All the best bedrooms were shut
up, except the two on the third story which had always been Barry's. The parlors were cleaned and
clothed in their drab coverings and locked; the
dining-room alone was open. The furnace was
put on half rations; the butcher and grocer were
made to understand that the family was almost
extinct; the gas-bill was nearly nominal. All these
changes were not effected without effort: but your
true reformer is he who has not much to lose, and
who "sits loose to the world," as the pious old
books say. A dash of recklessness helps one
through some trying domestic situations wonderfully. The whole matter seemed trivial and un-
important to Phœbe, aching with her real sorrows,
and she carried it through with so high a hand
that it was necessarily successful. The most vital
element in the management of servants is not to
be afraid of them. Phœbe did not care in the
least whether Mary Ann stayed or went, or
whether the cook resented her reduction or not;
she had at heart almost a feeling that it would be
agreeable to her if they all went away, and left
her and baby alone in the third-story room,

"Rolled in one another's arms, and silent in a last embrace."

She rather invited anarchy: she was in a mood to have welcomed change. And so the cook meekly took her increased work and decreased pay, and Mary Ann ,made herself agreeable to the baby and filled many minor offices in the house without a murmur, and the butcher and grocer were as respectful as when the bills were huge. Whether this was the perversity of fate or the perversity of human nature out at service is not quite clear. At all events, it was so, and Phœbe's days, once started, rolled on without household change or friction.

She never went out except to take an occasional walk on the loneliest road she could find, or to go to church. Often the baby made it impossible to go to church ; she never felt easy to leave him so long with the flighty Mary Ann, but she never stayed away without a fretted feeling. She had given up hoping that any one would help her and hold out a hand to her in the path of faith to which she was drawn. They were evidently not a proselyting people, these people to whom her instincts were leading her to join herself. One day her baby had been taken to church and brought to " the illumination of baptism, with God's grace preventing his election, and by an artificial neces-.sity and holy prevention engaged to the profession and practices of Christianity." She had had such deep thoughts they might almost have forced their way out into words. But when the service was

over and they were coming away, the clergyman
had shaken hands with her cordially and common-
placely, and had said they had a fine child, and
that he had behaved remarkably well. His words
and manner were somewhat unsacerdotal, though
sufficiently civil. It would be difficult to know
what she had thought he ought to say or do, but
he certainly had not done it, whatever it was.
And from that day she grew dumber than ever,
and knew she could never speak to *him*. And to
whom could she speak? Between her mother-in-
law and herself there was a gulf fixed; Lucy was
a little afraid of her, and never knew exactly what
to say to her on any subject; and to Barry nobody
would ever think of talking about such things.
So, one by one, the chances had slipped away from
her, till she had been left in material as well as
fancied isolation.

Living " in a corner of a wide house " is necessarily dreary living. The stairs resound so when
you go up them at night, the doors slam with
such an echo, the winds blow with such insinua-
tions, the blinds have so much to say, the nightly
solitude is so peopled with suggestions. The light
from Phœbe's room shone across the snow very
late at night sometimes. But the baby's good
condition showed that she was not fretting unreasonably, and if she sat up late it was to sew for
him, or to write letters to her husband, or to read
some book that took her thoughts away from her

own trouble. No young wife could have behaved better than she did ; and if the two months were long in passing, they did pass at last, and she found herself in possession of a letter that told her, when this came into her hands her husband would be half-way across the ocean on his way home.

Barry was not a fluent letter-writer. He said very little generally, and did not say that little with an air of voluntariness. One had a feeling he was writing up his books, doing what had to be done, getting square with his conscience. But it was his characteristic, and Phœbe had steeled herself against being hurt by it. His sisters always joked about his dispatches, and she knew she had no more to complain of than his family had had for years. This letter, however, that told of his coming home had a few unusual words in it that gave her a thrill of joy. It was better than all the diffuseness of other people. This he must really mean, or why should he have said it ? He was surely glad that he was coming back to her, no matter what or who he left behind him.

The letters of the others had naturally had many stings in them, notably Honor's, who, happily for her sister-in-law's peace of mind, did not find time to write very often. Tartar occupied a very prominent place in Honor's occasional letters, and Barry's good spirits and great popularity were strongly dwelt upon.

"You must n't mind if he comes back to you a little spoiled," she wrote, "for between mamma's and Lucy's coddling and Tartar's cousinly devotion he is made entirely too much of at home, and when we go out it is positively revolting. You'd think the women here (in Nice) had never seen a man worth looking at before."

Lucy's letters and her mother's were so devoid of such observations, and so full of soothing sentences about dear Barry's natural anxiety to be at home, that she distrusted them entirely, and found them much worse than Honor's naive truth. But here he was, almost back again : three days more, and she could see for herself how spoiled he was, or how glad to be beside her.

It was not till she knew that he was away from Tartar that she realized how great and how constant the strain had been of knowing that they were together; she had been fighting the thought all the time, and resisting the impulse to imagine scenes and incidents that were torture to her. But now she had fought her battle, and she knew she had fought it well, and the sense of victory over herself and of a truce with fate was very soothing.

CHAPTER XV.

A DIDO OF TO-DAY.

It was a stormy day in early April, the day after Barry's letter had come heralding his return. The little household was in busy flutter. Two women were undressing the parlor chairs and sofas, and washing the windows, notwithstanding the persistent splashing of raindrops on them. Mary Ann was busy below in some unusual work resulting from the great occasion. Phœbe, in a state of keen, expectant happiness, was " minding " the baby in the little room always called Barry's study, adjoining their bedchamber, on the third floor. It was a pretty little corner room, with two windows, an open fire, an æsthetic mantel, and some nice engravings. It had never been much altered since Barry's bachelor days, and nothing ever spoke to his mother's heart of the past as did this place. To Phœbe this association had not been pleasant, of course, but she rigorously forbore to ask questions or to propose changes. She did not know why that picture had the knot of faded pink ribbon tied above the cord, nor why those two pipes crossed over the desk must not be taken down, nor the particular value of that wisp of dried grass in the Copeland vase in the corner. She had endured the sight of these inanimate incentives to jealousy all through the lonely winter. Now she quite defied them, and felt as she dusted them that familiarity had robbed them of their sting. Nothing, it seemed to her, could sting her to-day, she was so content. She felt she had earned her peace. She knew she had behaved well; she looked over the battle-field and felt it had been a sharply-contested fight.

The rain outside and the peevish spits of snow that occasionally mingled with it did not depress her. She looked about the room, and put it, in imagination, in the order in which it was to be on Thursday. In the good weather which was sure to come to-morrow it was to be swept and cleaned, and the windows were to shine like crystal. Mary Ann should spend two hours on the brasses of the fire-place, and she with her own hands would lay the fire that would blaze up in his welcome. There should be flowers in those glasses and fresh ribbons for the curtains; and baby should lie there in his berceaunette with his prettiest blanket over him. It was a pity it rained so to-day, and she could do so little. At any rate, she could put the closet and shelves in order and re-arrange the books in the little book-case in the corner.

This took all too short a time, and still the baby

slept. Many times she went over to him, and touched the swinging cradle with a light hand, and moved a blanket this way or that, and gazed fondly at him, and went back to her work. It was a very hard part of her discipline that when she was disturbed about her husband she loved her baby less rather than more. Instead of clinging to him and finding comfort in him she felt her heart turned hard to every one, even him, and only held him by an instinct that seemed no higher than that of self-preservation. She looked at him with cold eyes when her heart was hot with jealousy; she cared for him with perfunctory hands when her mind was filled with forebodings and distress. But to-day she was happy in the sight of his beauty and health. She began to feel that he would be a bond to bind her husband to her. They two could unite in love and interest and effort for this child, who belonged almost equally to both. She felt for perhaps the first time as most ordinarily happy mothers feel always about their first-born children.

Her instinct, however, was not to muse and brood over joy or sorrow. So after a few minutes given to these thoughts, leaning over the cradle, she lifted herself up, and said, " What shall I do towards getting ready for Thursday ? "

Her eye fell upon the desk that stood beside the window. She remembered the circumstance of the key refusing to turn in the lock the day her husband went away, and that she had noticed, when she had shut it up and locked it, that it was in great disorder. She had never looked into it before or since. Barry had always carried the key in his pocket, and it was no doubt owing to the obstinacy of the lock that day that it was not there now. At another time she would have thought of this, and reflected that she might better not look into what had never been offered for her inspection. But she was too happy to-day to have such thoughts. It was something she could do for him. It was impossible to be doing anything with any other motive. Whatever she did, even down to her little cares for baby, was indirectly done with the feeling that it was for him, for his child, who represented him. So very light-heartedly she went to fetch the key and unlock the dusty desk.

The key was cranky again, but her fingers were strong and her intention was deliberate. In a few moments it turned and the doors opened. Oh, what an untidy place! Phœbe loved order and neatness and thrift, but she thought it rather a manly attribute to be regardless of all these. She laughed softly to herself as she said, " Oh, Barry, this is just like you! " There were keys and pipes, cigars and visiting-cards, note paper and wrapping paper, bills and family letters, cheek by jowl in the most *dégagé* manner. The shelves were literally heaped with such elegant trifles, the pigeon-holes stuffed with papers which were doubtless as incongruous. She cleared the shelves first, wiping and dusting them very carefully, and arranged the contents with some regard to fitness of companionship. Evidently the desk had not been emptied for a couple of years. There were letters and bills as old as that, and one knows what an accumulation of such things can be acquired in two years. She assorted the letters and filed the bills. Happily the bills were receipted, and the letters were mostly from men, or in the handwriting of his sisters and mother. She did not read the letters, of course, but tied them up in decent order, bundle by bundle, as she did her own. When this was all done she put them back neatly in piles as they belonged. The shelves did not look half full; it was a pleasure to see what a little order would do. Barry would know where to lay his hand on everything. In future she would ask him to let her have his keys and keep things in place for him. What comfort, what a saving of time and temper, it would be! He would have had ten minutes more for his good-by to her if he had not got embroiled with this disordered desk the day he went away.

Baby moved a little uneasily. She left the contemplation of the well-ordered shelves and went to him. He did not wake, only turned and fretted for a moment; then twisting his head down on the pillow, and moving his lips in the imaginary bliss

of nursing, sank again into repose. He was a
beautiful child, inheriting apparently all the magnificent health of his father and mother. He had
a full but delicate mouth, chestnut hair that lay
in soft rings upon his forehead, lustrous eyes and
wonderful lashes, and a fine creamy skin with
warm tints. There was a little moisture on the
chestnut rings, and she turned back the blanket.
She lifted the pink hand : the fingers closed
around one of hers ; it was like undoing the ten-
drils of a vine to get them loosened without waking him. So! She laid the rose-tipped hand back
and stooped down and kissed it lightly, and then
with a half sigh turned again to her work.

But first she put a stick of wood on the fire ;
then she looked out at the unseasonable storm,
which was turning to hail at the moment, and
wondered if the invisible buds on the trees below
the window would be chilled to death by it, and
whether "the wonders under-ground," the up-
starting, up-pushing forces of the spring, would
be put back by it. It was hard to fancy the sun
shining to-morrow, but it would shine ; and on
Thursday it would be spring.

And then she went practically to her work.
Any one who has ever cleared out a man's desk
with a tenderness for the man who owned it can
understand the charity with which she collected
overturned boxes of new pens from among the lit-
ter of old ones, and the care with which she dis-

criminated between time-tables two years old and those of recent date. All memoranda in his handwriting were sacred. She was a good deal in awe of everything that looked like business papers. Here was a crumpled slip of legal cap with mystic words like these upon it: —

"3 Meeson & Welsby, 140; 5 C. & P. 23. See Tidd."

She lifted it with care. What might not depend upon it? Baby's inheritance to the extent of thousands might be damaged by its loss.

But here was something that did not look like — business. It was put away in one of the upper pigeon-holes of the desk, far back. She could not remember whether, when she first opened the desk, she had taken away anything from before it. She rather thought not. It was an envelope, and it contained a paper. On the face of the envelope Barry's initials were written, and in the corner at the left, "February 2, 188-." It was Tartar's handwriting, and the envelope, which had never been sealed, was marked with her monogram. Phœbe's heart tightened with the old pang. She held it in her hands. What had Tartar had to say to him on February 2d? That was just the week before the plan for going abroad was started. What had Tartar had to say to him? She had a right to know. If men had been writing notes to her, Barry would have thought he had a right to read them, if he had found them lying in his way. She had never looked at any letter of his before that he had not given her to read; but then she had never had in her hand one written him by Tartar. The temptation was new; the circumstance of her present happiness and confidence made it strong. She said to herself, " I ought to be ashamed of myself for doubting him after what he said in his letter the other day. I *am* ashamed, and yet I do doubt. If I look at this, it will stop the pain, it will clear everything up. There is nothing in it; *I know* there is nothing in it. If I put it back without looking inside, the thought will torment me. It will spoil the pleasure of his coming. It is best to make an end of the suspicion, even by doing something that may hurt my self-respect a little. But why should it hurt my self-respect? I have a right. It is not as if I had had no cause for distrust. I *have* had cause, though I have put away from me the recollection of it. I want to end this forever. Perhaps this will be the last time that I shall have such a feeling." Still she did not open the letter. She held it in her hand, with her eyes fastened on the inoffensive words upon the envelope, her lips pressed together, her whole face inscrutably changed. The baby roused and began to fret. She went to him and bent over him, and tried to quiet him, not harshly, but woodenly, without feeling or tenderness, as if she were thinking of things in which he had no part. He refused to be quieted,

but twisted about, and put up his struggling little
arms. "Come, then," she said, for he was hungry;
and taking him out of his soft bed, she wrapped
a blanket about him and sat down near the fire.
He nestled close, seeking with hungry hands and
with eager lips, like a little animal guided by the
scent of food, the breast which she made bare for
him. She settled him on her arm, and drew the
blanket over him, but paid no further heed to
him. He lay looking in her face with the half-
speculating but satisfied expression in his eyes
that one often sees in a nursing baby's; but she
turned away and did not answer them. Finally
the wide-open eyelids began to droop, the eager
lips drew less and less eagerly, and the satiated
baby slept. She put him back again in his cradle,
and settled the blankets over him, and shaded his
eyes from the light, turning back to put the ruffles
of the little pillow smooth under his shoulder, and
to wipe away with her handkerchief the white drop
that hung on his bright red lip. Then she pushed
the handkerchief into her pocket and drew out the
envelope again, going towards the window as she
did it. She held it in her hand, not looking at it
any more, but gazing with fixed eyes out upon the
dreary, rain-soaked scene. The shutter, loosened
from its fastening, came banging against the window with some caprice of the ill-tempered wind.
She mechanically put up the sash and stretched
out her fine white hand and arm into the cold

rain to fasten it back. A great rush of chilly air came into the room before she shut the window down again. She turned, with hard eyes, to see if the noise or the chill had disturbed the baby's sleep. No; he had health in his veins, and she had fire in hers, and neither of them felt the icy breath that had come in.

Should she read it, and put herself out of pain? For that it would put her out of pain she confidently told herself. An honorable instinct forbade her to read what was not meant for her to see; but against that honorable instinct a hundred good reasons marshaled themselves. How could a poor little instinct hold out against this host? The fight was a hot one, but was not very long. She pulled the paper from the envelope. For a moment there was a glare before her eyes, but from the blur presently the words came out. There was neither address nor signature, nor any date. It was unmistakably Tartar's hand; the initials on the paper were as unmistakably hers.

Phœbe read: " Without disguise and without excuse, I have acknowledged my love for you. Concealment between us in the past was fatal; in the future it will be impossible. You have taken it out of my hands by your abrupt words last night. Why could you not have been silent, when speaking could no longer do anybody any good? Ah! what we have before us! This is only the beginning. If I see you to-morrow, as you ask, remember never to ask it again. It cannot be wrong to say good-by to you, for it shall be good-by, though we may meet every day for years. *Remember, it must be good-by.*"

Phœbe had been reading, standing by the window. Her eyes went two or three times over the words before she mastered them. A feeling of illness overcame her, and she made two or three staggering steps towards a chair, in which she sat down. There was a tight, dreadful feeling across her chest, and her breath seemed stifled and pressed back into it. All the color went out of her face. Then it was true, — all her fears, all her doubts of him. All his lightness of heart at going away meant that. All his staying in town through the dreary winter meant that. All his weariness and *ennui*, his commonplace answers, his silences, his unlover-likeness, meant that ; and all his fond words in his last letter to her meant covering it up and blinding her. She had struggled with herself and reasoned herself for months into believing that it was just the change that comes over all men after marriage. No, it was a worse change than other women have to see. She had lost him. The love on which she had staked everything was gone, ended, dead. For the moment, she did not feel jealous or angry. If he had been there, she might almost have thrown herself at his feet and implored him to give her back his love. She would have sued him for it as she

13

would have sued Heaven for her child's life, struck
with mortal illness.   The grief that desolated her
would have made her forget everything else.   The
thirst that consumed her would have dried up all
lesser feelings.

The Carthaginian queen stretching out her
arms to the ships fading from sight on the "endless sea" was not struck with a suddener, more
appalling sense of helpless bereavement than poor
nineteenth-century Phœbe, sitting, stunned, by
the æsthetic mantelpiece in Barry's little study.
Human nature is much alike in all ages.   You
cannot do more than love a man entirely, whatever
century you happen to be born in.   You cannot be
more than desolated, whether it be by command
of the gods, to which your Æneas is not dis-
inclined, or solicitation of the world, the flesh,
and the devil, which your Barry does not resist.
There are diverse ways of taking your loss, — as
diverse as the temperaments of women from those
distant times till these.   By far the least hard is
the heroic treatment, if one's nerves and creed
permit.   Who would not rather Dido's swift
sword and flame, and the chance of getting square
with Æneas in the other world, and giving him a
piece of one's mind in Hades, than the prolonged
torture of a deserted woman nowadays, like the
Madonna carried in procession,

> "Smiling and smart, .
> With a pink satin gown, all spangles,
> And seven swords stuck in her heart"?

Ah, we see our Æneases sail away from us sometimes, we know that they are gone forever, while in their places stay with us some shadowy, strange, unreal things that wear their shapes, with whom we have to live, for whom we have to smile our smiles and curb our tongues and bear our burdens. All that was easy to do before is hard and hateful now.

As Phœbe sat motionless with the letter in her hand, looking at the smouldering fire without seeing it, some far-away anticipations of the life she would have to lead came over her, succeeding the first agony. It would be only two days before she would be obliged to meet him, to treat him as nearly as might be as she had treated him before — before what? His treachery? Had he meant to desert her? Had he meant to do what his fate had made him do? No, surely, he had never been a coward, he had never been cruel. It was simply, destiny was too strong for him. He had loved his cousin all his life; he had been diverted from it by some misunderstanding. His cousin was the one to whom he belonged; his wife was the usurper. Then what a sharp pang came, and with it a rage of anger, a fire of jealousy. No; he might have loved Tartar, — she had played with him, had thrown him off, perhaps, in the old days; but he had loved her, Phœbe, in that strange, delirious time, that was so full of bitter and sweet to remember, and Tartar had robbed her. She was desolate no longer, but maddened.

If she could have hated him steadfastly it would have been easier. She did hate him, in bitter gusts and tempests of feeling, but she yearned for him so passionately that her hatred melted again and again at some chance recollection, and she only hated for ever and ever the woman who had lured him from her.

How do people live through days like this? It gives one a respect for the human brain and the material part of us to know that they seldom dissolve or go into chaotic disorder under such pressure.

When Mary Ann came up to tell her mistress that her dinner was ready, the girl started, and asked, looking blank, if she were ill. As Mary Ann's perceptive powers were of the lowest order, there must have been some conspicuous change to call out the question. Phœbe turned her face away from her, and said she was not ill, but only tired ; she had the feeling, which she did not arrange into words, that she was then putting on the mask which she would never take off again as long as she lived. When we are very young, everything is going to be " forever." As we grow older we find that it is possible to outlive Æneas himself and the sword of despair, and even the flames of annihilation. Middle-aged anguish says to itself, " This will wear out." It is by so much less a stimulant.

CHAPTER XVI.

PEYTON EDWARDS.

TOWARDS evening the rain turned to snow. The ground was chilled enough to bear a thin coat of it. It looked a winter scene when Phœbe pushed her way out of the heavy, slowly - moving front door into the early twilight. The snow had ceased to fall, but the chill of it filled the air, which was damp as well with the long day of rain. The sky was dull with monotonous clouds: it was all most dreary. There are some states of mind in which one cannot stay in the house; Phœbe had gone out because it seemed as if she could not draw another breath in the stifling atmosphere within. She longed to walk and tire herself, and get rid of this pain which was to last forever, and which had just begun. She had no purpose in her walk, only to walk, and that not slowly. She had waited for the twilight because she did not want to be seen by any curious eyes. Since Mary Ann had recognized the trouble on her face, she did not want any one else to have a chance to see it.

The houses along the road are just beginning

to be lighted: at the door of one a young wife stands waiting for her husband, coming down the walk on his return from town. Poor Phœbe turns away with a bitter pain. At another, a nurse sits in the window with a white baby in her arms, who drums upon the pane, while a carriage turns in at the gate, and an eager pair lean forward and wave salutations to the baby.

The stage comes rolling down the road; people are getting out at another expectant cottage, — guests, valises, welcomes, kisses. The light from the door shines across the snow, — such a babble, such merriment. Sore-hearted, she wonders what they can find to be so happy about.

She passes an old house that stands but a little way back from the street. The great trees in front of it, now bare, do not protect it from the passers-by, nor the dry, brittle hedge on which the snow is lying. A light streams across the wide piazza; between the pillars of it is a window, through which one sees the peaceful picture of an old lady reading by a lamp. The street is quiet here, no one is passing; Phœbe leans against the fence and gazes in. It is a face she knows well and has often seen in church, and thought of when she was in trouble: a sort of benediction that blesses the eyes that look on it, — serene with love of God, tender with love of man, cheering, self-forgetting. Ah, Phœbe wonders, as she looks, was that peace bought through suffering? Is that power to bless its price? She knows that in the churchyard, hard by, lie more than one beloved who have left her. But they left her *that* way. One might be the better for sorrow, but not *this sort.* She thinks of the children that rise up and call, this calm woman blessed, of the troops of friends that gather round her old age, of the silent influence she has, of the honor in which her town's-people hold her. Was it

> " The not unpeaceful ending of a day
> Made black by morning storms " ?

She longs to speak to her, to ask for her pity, her prayers. But the calm saint reads on by the peaceful household lamp, and poor Phœbe goes away uncomforted.

She turned down another street and went towards the churchyard, of which the gate stood open. The church itself was shut, not resembling in all things the God whom it professed to represent, who neither slumbers nor sleeps. It looked dark and cold. She tried the door, but it was fastened against her. If she could have found sanctuary there for a little while, and in the silence and dimness have cried to God before that altar! Well, she was not sure that it would have done her any good. She sat down on the step a while till she grew cold, and then, remembering scornfully that she had a body yet to be taken care of, she got up and walked through the snow to the graves that lay so still under the still, bare trees and the still, dark sky. "To mortals no sorrow is immortal." At least, she thought, there is cure here. She wished that her baby were lying here dead, and she beside him. She thought of the many paragraphs in the papers, that she had read with horror, of poor mothers who had drowned, or burned, or butchered their children, and then themselves, when the furnace of domestic misery had become too fiery hot, and their tortured nerves had reached the point of madness. She did not mean to kill herself; she knew she was not mad; she almost wished she were, — that would be one way out of it. What way *was* there out of it for long-living, healthy, strong-suffering, silent Phœbe?

But it was cold. Her feet were wet, and her skirts draggled with the snow and slush. Her sense of neatness felt the outrage, even at her high tragedy pitch. She left the cold graveyard and the colder church, and went out again at the gate, more desolate than she had come in. Outside the gate there was a street lamp, and in the halo of this she stood for a moment irresolute. Presently, out of the misty dimness beyond it, came the sound of a man's step, and she started uncomfortably. The side street on which the churchyard opened was without houses; it was a lonely spot, though near the heart of the town. Before she could get out of the range of the lamp the step was beside her, — an amazed exclamation, and she was face to face with Peyton Edwards.

" What are you doing in the churchyard ? Has anything happened ? " he said, in a direct way, for it was impossible to talk conventionally in such a spot, and with Phœbe's face and dress testifying so loudly to her abandoned misery. She did not answer, but turned silently towards home, and he walked beside her.

" Nobody is ill ? " he asked. " You have n't heard bad news from — them ? "

" No," she said, slowly.

" There 's something wrong," he went on, after waiting a minute or two for her reply, while they made their way through the slush and mire. " I should think you might speak to me. You know they 're like my own people."

"I am not your ' own people.' I 'm nobody's people," she thought ; but she only said, " I 'm not, though."

" Well, I 've always felt as if you were, any way," he answered. A sort of sob rose in Phœbe's throat. She had always trusted Peyton Edwards. He had seemed more like a friend than any one else in her new, strange home.

" I 've had a lonely time," she said. " I have n't had a soul to speak to since they went away."

" I was afraid so. I 've thought about you a great deal," he answered. " I 've just come from the train, for it 's been bothering me all day, and I made up my mind to come out and see how you were getting on."

" You did n't come for anything else ?."

" No."

" You have n't heard anything ? " she asked,
with a suspicious glance at his face, which the
corner lamp under which they had come showed
her.

" No," he answered, straightforwardly. " I
sent around to the office this afternoon, but they
said there was no news. Barry has n't written
to me since he went away."

Phœbe did not speak.

" I suppose Barry 'll be coming home pretty
soon ? " he asked.

" He 'll be here on Thursday," she said.

" Thursday ? Then you ought n't to be looking this way."

She did not answer, and they walked on for the
length of a block in silence.

" Is n't he well ? " asked Peyton, at last. " If
there 's any trouble, I wish you 'd tell me."

" It 's *my* trouble," she answered. " May be
you would n't think that counted."

" I do think it counts. I 've thought about you
a great deal. I felt Barry ought not to have
gone."

" Then you knew, I suppose ? "

" Knew what ? "

" Oh, it was n't just his leaving me alone."

" Well, that was all I blamed him for ; the baby
being so little, and you a stranger here, and — and

— the place and the people being so — new to
you."

" I understand. Oh, I did n't mind that. As
long as it was all right between him and me I
could stand all that."

" Well, I hope it 's all right now. You 're not
the kind of woman to fancy things. You don't
need me to tell you how Barry feels about you."

" No, I don't need any one to tell me," she said,
between her teeth.

Peyton looked anxiously towards her, for it
crossed his mind that her loneliness might have
worn upon her nerves and rendered her morbid, if
not absolutely unsound mentally. He remembered
how young her baby was, and how much of a
strain there had been upon her for the whole past
year. Silent and unmistakably manly as he was,
there was an acute understanding in him of
women's sufferings, and an acute tenderness, too,
well understood by the little girls who swept the
crossings that he passed daily, and the women
who scrubbed the halls and stairways of the down
town offices which he frequented. His heart was
tolerably hard towards men, but very soft towards
women who were " down on their luck." And it
was not necessary that the objects of his sympathy
should be good-looking always, either. By this
time, with their halting slow talk, and steady,
though rather quick walk, these two people who
were not in the habit of talking about their feel-

ings, got inside the gate, and well on towards the house.

"You think I'm crazy, I suppose," said Phœbe, abruptly, as they approached the piazza steps.

"No, not that altogether," he answered, hesitatingly, for it was so exactly what he had been thinking that he could not honestly deny it, and he had not the readiness to dissemble.

"I've had enough to make me," she said, "but I don't suppose I'm the kind that goes crazy. All along I have been blaming myself for everything, but now I know I have been badly used."

"Well, I can't tell "—

"No, I know you can't. I didn't think I could ever talk to anybody about such a thing as this. But — won't you ring the bell? Mary Ann has locked the door."

While they waited for the opening of the door they stood without speaking, Peyton not looking at her, but with silent, deep thoughts, no doubt, and a clouded face. When Mary Ann, quite out of breath, got the door open, Phœbe walked in first, and reproved her for not having the hall lamp lighted. Mary Ann always had a good reason to give for what she did and what she omitted to do. It was the baby who was fretting, and wouldn't let her lay him down a minute, ma'am. Phœbe left her in the full tide of her explanations, and shut the library door, and so cut off the stream.

The library fire was burning, and the room looked comfortable by its blaze, but there was no lamp lighted. Phœbe took off her bonnet and cloak and laid them on a chair in the corner, then went to a jar that held matches, and, stooping down, lighted one at the fire, and went over to the lamp. Peyton sat down. He did not look into the fire or about the room, nor did he follow with his eyes the movements of the tall, beautiful young woman whose unknown trouble was occupying all his thoughts, but stared before him at nothing, and was as silent as a Sphinx.

Certainly he was not sympathetic looking; why did Phœbe and the scrub-women and the crossing sweepers pick him out from all the crowd of handsomer, more genial, more amiable-looking men? People in trouble have an instinct that rarely leads them wrong. When Phœbe had lighted the lamp and put the shade on it and turned it carefully to the right height, she sat down, too, and gazed before her some minutes without speaking. Her hand was in her pocket, as if she held something there on which her thoughts were centred. She tried to speak several times, but failed; then with a slow, determined gesture with the hand that lay upon the arm of her chair, she said, —

"I 'm going to show you something that I found to-day. I don't believe you 'll think me crazy when you read it. I suppose you know the writ-

ing; perhaps you know more about what's past
than I do. It isn't new to me, but it's"—

Her voice choked. She pulled the envelope
from her pocket, and taking the paper out of it
handed it to him. He got up and went towards
the light to read it. The writing he certainly
recognized. A slight flush mounted to his forehead, but faded as he read. In fact, he turned a
stony gray; his face was no longer expressionless
and neutral, but showed that he was enduring a
pain sharp enough to need much self-control.
Phœbe did not move her eyes from him, but with
parted lips watched the effect upon him of what
he read. A look of satisfaction came into her eyes.
It was not imagination, then. Poor Phœbe had
had so many struggles with herself against doubts
that she could not prove that it was in a certain
sense a satisfaction to find she held a proof that
gave so much pain to some one else. Her companion did not speak for some minutes. His eyes
went over and over the words before him; he
seemed to hunt for escape from some most painful
conviction. When he first attempted to speak,
his voice failed; his failure to control himself
seemed to make him angry. When he spoke
again, it was quite distinctly.

"Where did you find this—note?" he said,
still looking at it, and not at her.

"In Barry's desk, that I was putting in order."

"It has been there—since—since before he
went away?"

" ,There is the date of it," she said, getting up and giving him the envelope.

" You don't often go to the desk? " he asked, slowly, after a few moments' pause.

" No, never before. He always kept it locked. At the last moment the day he was going away, there was great hurry and confusion ; just as he was locking it, while they were calling to him from down-stairs to come, the lock broke ; he had to leave it or be left. He told me to take the keys out and attend to it. I suppose for the moment he forgot — what was in it — or thought I would not likely look."

There was a silence. Phœbe sat down again, but Peyton stood motionless, his eyes fixed on vacancy, the hand with the letter in it hanging at his side, his face pallid.

" I don't know anything about the past," she went on slowly, at last. " I don't know whether he could have helped that part of it or not — but — going away together " —

" The envelope was not sealed," he said, as if he had not heard her, looking down at it.

" No ; she has handed it to him some time. They were together every day ; I knew that. So many nights he did not come home. And this was just the week before. the sudden plan to go abroad. I never knew she was going till — till that last day at dinner."

Peyton seemed hardly to hear her, but to be carried on by his own thoughts.

"Damn him!" he said, suddenly, under his breath, crushing the paper that he held in his hand, and throwing it from him.

"Damn *her!*" said Phœbe, setting her lips together and lifting her burning eyes to his. A shudder passed over him; he walked two or three times across the room, then stopped before the mantelpiece and leaned against it.

"Don't speak so," he began, in a husky voice. "A woman ought to say her prayers" —

"I shan't say any prayers for her."

"Well, she needs them" —

"I hope she 'll need them more and more; I hope" —

"Hush," said Peyton, hoarsely, lifting his head. Phœbe and he looked each other in the eyes for a moment; and then Phœbe, with a sort of sigh that was half a groan, leaned back in her chair and looked away from him. It was a bitter, miserable consolation to know that some one else was enduring the pain that she was, — some one stronger, and some one whom she had respected. If jealousy and the wound of treachery could make his face so ashy and his eyes so fierce, she need not feel ashamed for herself. She got up and went across the room and picked up the paper that he had thrown from him, and smoothed it out and put it back into the envelope.

At this moment Mary Ann rolled back the door that led into the dining-room, and appeared in the entrance with the baby under her arm, announcing tea. At this interruption the two who were so far away from thoughts of commonplace comfort or discomfort experienced the wholesome . though hateful shock of recall to actual life. Peyton's first impulse was to go away, but he submitted when Phœbe said, " You 'd better stay."

They went to the table; it was as small as it could be made, but was still far too large for the two people who sat down to it and the slender meal set forth upon it. Phœbe's hands shook a little as she poured out the tea. Peyton set down his cup, and scarcely tried to drink it. He took some things to eat upon his plate, but did not eat them. He sat looking before him in a fixed way, not attempting to speak. Mary Ann chirruped to the baby, which was the only conversation that enlivened the meal except the apologies which she made for bringing him down-stairs. He just would n't go to sleep, she said, and it was the cook's night out, and tea could n't be kept waiting any longer. It may have surprised her that these apologies did not have any interest for Mr. Peyton Edwards or her mistress; she gradually grew more reticent, and chirrupèd in a whisper to the baby when she passed him. She had set him down on the sofa and barricaded him in with pillows. He goo-ed at her with placid interest, and struck aimless blows upon the pillow before him. The baby in his wide unconsciousness and

14

the nurse in her narrow ignorance made a strange
contrast to the two others of the *partie carrée.*
When at last these latter moved away into the next
room, Mary Ann in haste clattered the tea things
off, with kind consideration for the cook's outing.
The baby set up a little whine for his mother;
she took him in her arms and walked about with
him for quiet's sake.　Mary Ann, with more apologies and more whispered chirrups, went off to her
own supper.　Peyton stood looking into the fire
as if there was no one in the room beside himself.
Once or twice he started as if to speak, but
stopped, walked two or three times across the
room, and stood again beside the fire.　The com-
mon-place tea and Mary Ann had turned the key
on his utterance and on Phœbe's, and they could
no more go back to the mental attitude of the
hour before than they could make it six o'clock
instead of seven.

　The baby fell asleep uneasily, and lay across
his mother's knees, a heavy weight.　Mary Ann
came back and tiptoed about the room, not to
wake him.　At last the slender meal was all out
of sight, the windows barred, the light turned
down, and the large, empty-looking dining-room
left to its night's repose.　Then Mary Ann, with
slightly curious glances, came into the library and
held out her arms for the baby.　Phœbe put him
in them, wrapped his blanket round him, drew
an end of it over his head, and opened the door
for her.

" The hall is cold : be quick," she said.

Mary Ann looked back furtively while her mistress was closing the door; she wondered what they were going to talk about. She need not have wondered. They were not going to talk. After a while Peyton got up and told her he was going; he would see her in the morning. This was a relief; it would be easier to talk to-morrow. After he was gone she turned down the lamp, and drew her chair close to the fire, and sat down and bent forward towards it and tried to warm herself, for she was strangely cold. She began to think after a while that she was going to have a chill. All that wet snow in the churchyard and in the streets and the damp night air and her terrible excitement would be so many deadly enemies to the poor little mortal who took his life from hers. The baby, — she almost hated him as she got up from her low seat and went to find some medicine, and a shawl to wrap herself in. She was denied even the luxury of brooding over her trouble, of desperately risking herself. And finally came the voice of Mary Ann : the child would not sleep; there simply was not any use in rocking him; he just would not. Then setting her teeth together she followed the nurse up-stairs, and spent the first night of her great desolation with a fretting baby-in her arms, and spongia and aconite in alternation with despair and jealousy.

CHAPTER XVII.

BARRY'S RETURN.

BUT before Thursday the baby got over his croupish attack, and Phœbe was not seriously the worse for her chill. They were well endowed physically, both mother and child, and it takes a great deal of mental anguish to undermine a good country constitution. Phœbe had spent nineteen years in a fine climate, with calm and uneventful days alternating still and peaceful nights; she had been much in the open air; she had not been idle either in mind or body; she had had no quarrel with her simple life, but had been happy in it. She had inherited from a robust father fine health and power of endurance. It would take a good many months of such nights and days as she had just passed through to make her permanently ill.

Peyton had come out once each day to see her. There was not much that he could say, but he seemed to have a care of her, and she clung to him in thought as her only earthly friend. He telegraphed on Thursday morning to her that the steamer was in, and again that the passengers were landed, and on what train it would be possible for Barry to go out to Marrowfat. After this came a telegram from Barry himself, saying at what hour he would be at home. So there was no uncertainty and no long waiting.

The day had been a fine and clear one; the sunset was just reddening the sky and bronzing the bare trees and the brown earth, when Phœbe from the library window saw a carriage drive into the grounds. She held the child tight in her arms; her breath seemed to stop. She saw Barry burst open the door of the cab and leap out, with an eager look up at the house. She tried to go forward and open the door, but there are some things we cannot do, even if we try. Barry had to open the door for himself, which no doubt was a little chill to his enthusiasm. In the hall, by the entrance to the library, stood Phœbe, white and quiet, with the baby in her arms.

" Well! " he cried, with eager joyfulness, dashing at them and enfolding them in one embrace. He kissed Phœbe again and again, and then the baby, and then Phœbe. He looked brown and well, with a fine color in his cheeks, and his eyes dancing with pleasure. You could not fancy a happier-looking man; so handsome, too, in his traveling clothes, so distinguished, so broad and high and manly. " Well! You are n't glad, I suppose! " he cried, as he gave her another kiss and another.

" The door," she said, faintly, gathering the

baby's blanket up when for an instant he released her. "I am afraid he'll feel the air."

Barry turned back and banged the door shut in the driver's face, who was bringing in some things that had been left in the carriage.

"Bother the man! he's got to be paid, I suppose," he exclaimed, plunging his hand into his pocket and tossing him a coin while Phœbe retreated into the library. He did not wait for the change, but telling the man to leave the things in the hall, he followed Phœbe into the library, and threw his arm around her.

"It's rather rough on a fellow," he said, "not only to have to open the door for himself, when he's come a journey of three thousand miles to see his family, but to be told the first thing to shut it after him. But no matter!"

"Baby's had a threatening of croup," said Phœbe, rather huskily.

"He has? Bless the little man, he doesn't look it."

He caught the child in his arms, and threw him up, and looked at him with pride and pleasure, and kissed him again and again. "There isn't another child as handsome in the world," he said. "And he's grown tremendously. You rascal, sir, I ought to have brought you a set of razors and a pair of riding-boots." He smothered him with kisses after this flight into the future, and then he gave him back to his mother, and put his arm

around her waist, and drew her head against his
shoulder, as if it were she, and not the child, after all, that he was most glad to have again. "It
seems a year," he said fondly, "since I went
away." Then he held her off from him and looked
at her. "But you're not looking exactly well,"
he said. "You're pale."

"Baby's kept me awake," she said, evasively,
looking away.

"Why do you let him? Turn him over to
Mary Ann. I'll set all that right," and he took
her in his arms again. The fact that she was holding the baby made some excuse for his not having
his caresses returned. You cannot caress a person
very much without the use of your hands. When,
therefore, Mary Ann appeared shyly in the door,
Barry hailed her with a bluff greeting, and told
her to take the baby for a little while.

"Don't let him get cold," he added, as the girl
carried him away. And then he turned to Phœbe,
and with his arm around her waist and both her
hands pinioned by his walked towards the fire-
place, where a gay little fire was crackling. Phœbe
had grown paler and paler. This was infinitely
worse than a captious, cold, or constrained greeting. The thought of its falseness never left her
mind, nor the conviction of his nature's shallow-
ness and easiness. It was such a cruel travesty of
the past; it was so torturing to the hunger of her
heart. It takes a good deal of cold to chill the

circulation of some people's blood, and it took a good deal to chill the circulation of Barry's hope and confidence, but by and by he began to feel indefinably the lowering of the temperature. He had thrown himself into a chair before the fire, and, stretching out his arm, tried to pull Phœbe down upon his knee. But she resisted, standing back by the mantel, and saying, " I must go and see about baby."

" Well," he cried, in a tone of pique, " that's pretty soon to desert me, don't you think?"

" Why, you," she said, embarrassed, " you'll want to go up-stairs yourself. Don't you want to wash your hands before dinner, and — brush your hair a little?"

" What! do I look such a savage?" he said, with the confidence of a handsome man, pushing his hand through his brown hair. He got up and stood beside her, close to her. It seemed as if he could not keep away from her, cold or kind. He began to look about for some explanation of her lack of warmth. Perhaps it was unpreparedness. He knew she was reserved and undemonstrative; possibly she had not received the warning of his coming, and the shock to her nerves of his sudden appearance might account for her pallor and silence.

" Did you get the telegram?" he said.

" Yes," she answered. " The last one just an hour ago."

"The last? Why, I only sent one."

"I know: but Peyton Edwards telegraphed me after he went away this morning that the steamer was in the bay, and then later that you had probably landed."

"Peyton Edwards? You don't say. I did n't even suppose he knew that I was on the way home. I wonder that he did n't come down to the wharf to meet me."

They were standing before the fire, which had deepened into a broad blaze. Barry was looking into his wife's face in the interested way in which we look into the faces of those from whom we have been parted for a length of time. As he said these words, carelessly, scarcely thinking that she heard them or would note them, a sudden rush of color came over her face. She was thinking, "When will he know why he did n't go to meet him?" And when she felt the hot blush on her face, and saw that her husband was startled by it, her thought was, not that he would have any unworthy suspicion of her or of his friend, but that he would in it read the truth. She felt as if the story were printed on her face, and forgot (as people unused to deception often do) how much more she knew than he did. The blood receded, and she grew pale again, and her eyes were troubled and downcast. Barry scrutinized her face keenly for a moment. Then his glance brightened. It was impossible to doubt her (or his own empire, either).

"Come," he said, "if you insist on my ablutions, I will go up with you."

But he did not put his arm about her again, and he went up-stairs after her, both of them laden with shawls and bags and books, that the cabman had left in the hall, and that the flighty Mary Ann had failed even to lift from the floor.

"Where are all your servants?" he said, on the way up.

"I have n't got any but the cook, and she's busy with the dinner, and Mary Ann can't leave the baby."

"What's become of the waitress?"

"Oh, I concluded to do without her."

"Why this parsimony?"

"I 've been trying to economize."

Barry laughed lightly. "Well, we won't do any more of that," he said. "Affairs are marching very well. We 've made a good thing of it. Even my father can't find anything to grumble at, and I am more than satisfied. I tell you, Phœbe, that little fellow in his cradle up-stairs will have a better start in life, a good deal, than his father had."

"I don't think you had much to complain of."

"Oh, there are starts and starts. I mean the boy shall have some advantages that I 've always felt the need of."

"People always say that."

"I know: but it 's well for the race to go on improving."

" Only nobody can see the improvement. The ones that don't have any start always get ahead."

When they were at the dinner-table (it had been tea when she was alone; now it had risen to dinner, and was served in courses as long as the baby would lie still), Barry again reverted to Peyton Edwards's telegram, and with similar results.

" It was very good-natured in him to see about the steamer and send you word," he said, — " very. I must look him up to-morrow."

Again the strange color and pallor and agitation followed each other on Phœbe's face. Barry would have been more than mortal if he had not felt a sudden sharp suspicion cross his mind. But he was a man of the world. He went on carelessly, with no change in his voice: —

" Has he been out lately ? "

" He was here — this morning," returned Phœbe, her voice gathering strength, for this was not what agitated her.

" Ah ! And what does he have to say ? What has he been about lately ? I suppose he 's working like a dog, as usual."

" No, I should n't think so. But I don't know. He would n't be likely to talk about business to me."

The thought of what he did talk about, the only thing of any kind regarding which they had exchanged a word, made her flush guiltily again. Would Barry see it all? Would he ask her in the next breath how she dared to speak to another of their relations to each other? This was her thought and dread, and only this.

Barry had seen enough for this time. He changed the subject, and went into details of his journey and accounts of the family party left abroad. His mother was not looking well; traveling seemed to tire her, while it freshened up his father wonderfully. Honor was as gay as a bird ; she kept them all in fine spirits, was admired everywhere, and as willful as ever. She declared she never would come home, and he almost believed she would keep her word. She hated Marrowfat with a hate unprecedented. Lucy was sweet and good as ever ; mended everybody's gloves as well as tempers, carried out all plans but her own, kept the peace between Tartar and Aunt David, and was the good fairy of the party. Phœbe could not find voice to ask any questions ; she felt as if she were choking while Barry talked about his life of the past two months so easily and carelessly. He grew a little absent-minded as he talked, and his brow knit. He was leading back to the subject which was uppermost in his mind, and he wished to reach it naturally.

" By the way, I must n't forget," he said. " I 've got a little package for Peyton from Tartar. It 's in my valise, I think. Help me to remember it in the morning. I 'll take it over to him."

His keen and angry eyes did not miss a shade

of the change that came over her face at these
words. She did not attempt to look up, but sat
with her head a little bent down, a deadly, sickly
pallor taking the place of her ordinary coloring.
She was thinking of that deep imprecation, that
fierce "damn him," that Peyton had uttered when
he first discovered Barry's treason. What would
their meeting be? She wished that she had died
before she had told him anything. What good
was his sympathy compared with all this peril to
Barry and to him? She had never sinned much
in giving her confidence to others; why should
her first fault of unreserve have such a punishment? What would she give to unsay what she
had said! How could she prevent or postpone
this meeting? It seemed to her that anything
that could put it off a while would be so much
gained; just a few days till Peyton should have
cooled down a little. Alas, she remembered that
people like Peyton do not cool down; they are always at one heat. What Peyton meant to do half
an hour after the letter was in his hands he would
go on meaning to do, and doing, till his steady
heart stopped beating. He would always be good
to her; he would always be hard, though just, to
Tartar; he would always be unrelenting towards
Barry. Time could not change him nor years wear
out his first impression. Still, she wished that she
could hold them back from meeting: her hand
was feeble, but she stretched it out to retard the
crash a moment longer.

"Don't fail to remind me," he said, as he dropped the stopper in a decanter, and took up his glass.

"I don't know — but I think — that is — I believe — he is going away to-morrow — you would n't see him if you went" —

"Oh, I 'll send him a dispatch to-night, and get him to wait over a train. It would be too bad to miss him. I wonder where he 's going."

"I think it 's — Washington, but I can't be sure. I have forgotten what he said about it. I — think he goes quite early in the morning."

"That will be all right. He 'll wait for me."

Barry's tone was generally confident; this time it was a little more than confident. Phœbe knew that he was angry; all his good spirits and vivacious talk could not conceal it. There was no more warmth, and there were no more caresses received or rebuffed. The baby gave a rough, barking cough, and she had to go in haste up-stairs with him. Barry was left to spend his first evening at home alone. He walked up and down the room, pulling at his mustache, and drawing his brows together in perplexed thought. He was not of a suspicious or unloving nature; it was hard for him to make up his mind that he had ground of complaint against either wife or friend. But this looked so amazingly like it. When he went away, Phœbe and Peyton had not been on any terms of intimacy that would have made it seem probable

that he would come out to Marrowfat to see her.
They had not met more than half a dozen times;
the last year there had been a great diminution of
the frequent visits of the old days. Perhaps he had
come out to see some one else in the place, and had
only called at the house in passing. No: Barry
ran over in his mind all the people whom he could
have had occasion to come to see; they were all
away. He had not an intimate friend in Marrowfat. Barry remembered once, just before they
went abroad, Peyton, in speaking of the dullness
of the winter and of the changes in the place, said
he had not a friend left there but themselves. It
would have been difficult to account for even one
visit, but there had been many. Two telegrams,
after having seen her this morning! And no word
to him; not even a clerk sent down to the steamer
to get his news, if it were impossible for Peyton
to go himself. But all this, all Peyton's part,
could have been easily remanded to that deep
vault of unclaimed property, of unexplained omis-
sions, that all generous-minded people keep open
all their lives, and never trouble themselves to de-
scend into unless at the request of some anxious
owner. "Always trust your friend" had been
Barry's maxim through life, and he had been perfectly satisfied to follow it. But a wife is a different thing. She belongs to you, while your friend
belongs, perhaps equally, to a great many others.
While you know she has no material rights that

are not subordinate to your right over her, there
is a vague uncertainty about your title to her inner life that naturally makes you less easy than
if you held it in fee simple. If any one had told
Barry yesterday that he would to-day be doubting his wife's unquestioning devotion to him, he
would have been much amused. But this coldness, those hot blushes, that mysterious agitation
and eagerness to prevent a meeting, — how could
they be explained? Barry would have been more
than mortal if he had not been suspicious, and he
certainly was *not* more than mortal, not any more.

The evening was not a pleasant one to him.
The last eight or ten, when he had been seasick
and bored and chilly, were agreeable in comparison. He wrote his dispatch, but when it came to
sending it found himself at a loss for the direction.
He knew that Peyton had changed his hotel; he
was just doing so when they went away. What
one had been decided on he had never known, or
had forgotten. It was useless to send his dispatch
to Peyton's office. He could himself get there in
the morning before it; if Peyton had gone it would
do no good; if he were there he could better judge
what ground he had for complaint if he met him
without preparation. As for asking Phœbe for
the address, he could more easily have done a much
more difficult thing. Though good-natured and
genial, he was as reserved in one sense as Phœbe
herself. He could not talk about what he felt,

though he could talk endlessly about what he did not feel. He did feel this unexpected doubt most uncomfortably; in fact, most damnably, he admitted to himself. He could no more have gone upstairs and opened the subject with her or spoken Peyton's name than he could have taken her by the throat and made an end of it and of her on the spot. He was unprepared for either step. So he went up at bedtime, and scarcely looked at her when she came into the room and told him that she had known he would not want to be disturbed, and so had had the baby's crib moved into the adjoining room, where she would probably have to sit up and watch him through the night. His hoarseness had increased, but she was giving him very frequent doses; if before midnight it did not yield to treatment, she thought they ought to have the doctor. Did he think so?

He thought she knew much more about the matter than he did, he said, and he should be satisfied with whatever she decided, unpacking his valise, with his back turned to her while he did it. He had the conviction that the baby's illness was merely her defense against him, and he was quite resolved not to take any notice of it.

"I will send the cook and Mary Ann, if I have to send. I know I ought not to disturb you."

He said, coolly, perhaps that would be as well; he was pretty tired. Disturb him! He wondered if she did not think she had disturbed him enough

15

already. He counted all the hours strike till five o'clock, when he dropped into an uneasy sleep, during which he successively fought a duel with Peyton and suffered shipwreck in mid-Atlantic. Out of this he was awakened by Phœbe's muffled opening of her wardrobe door at eight o'clock. He said something very cross, and did not even ask how the baby was. Phœbe took what she had come in for and went out, telling him, when she got outside the door, to ring when he was ready to have his breakfast put upon the table.

When he came down to the dining-room he found her there, ready to pour out his coffee. This soothed him a little: a man is always the happier for feeling he is being served by the woman whom he ought to be serving. He showed his ameliorated state of feeling by asking how the baby was. The baby was better; she had not had to send for the doctor. As if that were any news to him, who could hear the lightest movement in the room adjoining, and who knew perfectly well that the baby had not even coughed since half-past ten o'clock! It was all a put-up job, that croup, and he hardened again as he thought of it.

He hurried off in the 9.15 train, feeling hot and angry when he thought how certainly he should miss Peyton if he were really going to Washington, and how long it would be before he could have any definite light shed on what disturbed him.

To think of bearing this suspense for a week or a fortnight put him in a very bad humor. He knew himself capable of behaving as well as any other man in this position, if the uncertainty were not too protracted. Now, by daylight, he said to himself, he did not suppose that there really was anything for him to resent in their relations to each other. He was disposed to be reasonable. He knew that he had left Phœbe alone for a long time and under rather trying circumstances. He must not wonder if Peyton had had some nonsensical views about protecting her, and all that. It could not be anything but duty; it was impossible (by daylight) to associate Peyton with anything but a stolid pursuit of the "stern daughter." And Phœbe, perhaps, had not understood him; was embarrassed, frightened. It was equally impossible to think of Phœbe as anything but — perfectly devoted to him.

On the cars he was at once surrounded by gentlemen glad to welcome him back. Some newspaper paragraphs about the success of the business interests that had taken Mr. Crittenden abroad may possibly have contributed to this welcome. There is a great deal of human nature even in the provinces; the Crittendens were rising into notice again. Mr. Crittenden was a good deal spoken of among railroad men. It would be his own fault if he did not make a good deal of money in the course of the next few months. So Barry was slapped on the shoulder and shaken by the hand, and familiarly welcomed by all the solid 9.15 men on the train. It made him feel quite like his old self. He was not so stupid as not to see why the tide had turned, but as long as it had turned, why, that was enough. He was too good-natured to be critical. Human nature is human nature; he would not exactly forget the past, but he would not rake it up. *Hic jacet:* he would perhaps keep the moss scraped from the stone, but he would not do anything so unhandsome as to go below the surface and dig among the bones; he knew they were there, but there let them lie. The experience had done him good; it was incorporated into his life; he had got all out of it that it could give him, — that was enough. Such was Barry's easy philosophy, and so he met the welcome cheerfully and with his old jolly freedom of manner.

The 9.15 train is the banker, the head-of-the-house, the out-of-business-looking-after-investments-man's train. These gray-beards are not always the discreetest. Among them was one who never thought of Barry but as the possessor of the handsomest wife in Marrowfat or a much more extended district. To do him justice, he seldom thought of him or her at all, but when he did it was in this relative position and in this light.

"Ah!" he said, leaning towards him from the seat behind and speaking in his ear, "you were a brave man to go away and leave your handsome wife alone !"

He did not speak so low but that another elderly person of valor, sitting beside Barry, heard him, and added jocosely, "Mason thinks you 'd better leave her in his charge, next time. We old fellows are much more responsible than these younger ones. Now I can recommend Mason, and Mason can recommend me, eh ?"

And then they both laughed, a senile laugh, that sent Barry into a hot rage of resentment and jealousy. It was a perfectly random shot. Neither of them had probably seen Phœbe during her husband's absence, and had not thought of her after the little local gossip about her being left alone had subsided. It was in very questionable taste to speak of her in this way to her husband, but good taste does not seem the natural result of advanced age in men, and in men living in the country especially. Barry flushed so perceptibly that they both saw he was annoyed. The conversation was abruptly turned upon something else. In a moment more the express train had drawn breath in the depot, and bankers and book-agents, lawyers and laundresses, had made a rush-and-tumble exit, and were plunging pell-mell to the ferry-boats.

Naturally Barry got rid of his aged neighbors ; but the new deal did not help him very much. He was joined on the ferry-boat by a couple of young men, who, having been at a german the night before, were rather late in getting down to business. They greeted him cordially.

"You've been back a week or two, haven't you? No? I've seen Edwards on the train several times, and I thought he was going up to see you."

And a look of well-bred inquiry. The look was perfectly accidental, but of course Barry thought it was a studied insult. His young friends found him so stiff and irresponsive that they moved away, and agreed between themselves that foreign travel had not improved his manners.

Barry hurried to Peyton's office. Phœbe was quite right. He had gone away in the eleven o'clock train for Washington; stay indefinite, object unexplained. Barry made sharp and not very civil inquiries of Peyton's confidential clerk. The young man, not pleased with his manner, answered more unsatisfactorily than he would have done if he had been spoken to with greater suavity. The impression Barry got from him was that the journey was a mysterious one; it looked more like a flight than a journey, to his jaundiced eyes. The clerk admitted that there was a possibility that Mr. Edwards might be gone for weeks or even months. This, to any one who knew Peyton's business habits, was astounding news. Barry was not to be blamed for feeling it meant a great deal. He wanted to knock the clerk down for giving him such intelligence and for having such cold blue eyes ; but they were not quite valid excuses for doing so, and he went away with a curt snarl that made the man's cold blue eyes flame fire, as he looked after him.

Once in his own office, the press of business after such an absence drew him away from himself. He spent four hours in close and engrossing consultation with men who had been awaiting his return with anxiety. Large interests were at stake, and Barry found himself lifted into a place of unusual authority for one of his years. It stimulated him, naturally. He felt himself equal to it, and knew his business life was opening up great vistas of promise. A healthy, honorable ambition stirred in him. For four hours he forgot Phœbe and his paltry jealousy ; forgot everything but the work for which his powers were expanding. It was not until he neared home in the fast-flying train that the morning's doubts reasserted themselves, — still in a modified way. He was somewhat ashamed to remember them, but they came upon him with little sickening rushes of conjecture, and then died away, and then came on again. He felt as if he could almost hear the little devils spitting and hissing in his ears. He grew more and more irritated by his return to such low vexations, when he remembered Wall Street and his life there. He resolved to think of that exclusively, and to let his life at home shape itself as it would. He would not prejudge any one. He would give Phœbe a fair chance to show herself an affectionate and dutiful wife. If she did not, it was time enough then to look into matters. As long as he could keep his temper everything else would keep. And he resolved to keep it. There was no hurry.

He found Phœbe quiet and undemonstrative, as the day before. She looked even paler, but she was not as agitated. Something seemed to have reassured her. A gay little devil pierced Barry's ear with the whisper that she had had the intelligence that he and Peyton had not met. The conversation between the two was rather forced at dinner. After it, one or two people came in on business. Phœbe went up to the baby, and did not come down again. When Barry, at ten o'clock, went to his room he found that the baby had developed a little hoarseness, and Phœbe in her wrapper was anxiously bending over him. His crib was still in the adjoining room, and he was wide awake. Mary Ann was sleepily making the last arrangements for the night, and went away asking if there was anything more wanted in so tired a tone that only a brute could have had the heart to keep her up any longer.

" Why don't you call that girl back and let her take him ? " asked Barry, as he saw his wife move an easy-chair up to the crib and sink down in it.

" She is half asleep already; what would she be

by two o'clock?" answered Phœbe, leaning her head back wearily and putting her hand through the crib rails to pat the baby.

"It's all nonsense, this sitting up to watch him. He has no more croup than I have, and you are only injuring him by all this coddling. It is simple mismanagement, and you will soon have your hands full if you don't make up your mind not to spoil him so."

The undermining the principles of a baby of three months made Phœbe's lip curl, but she did not reply, and softly pushed shut the door with her foot after Barry's exit, which was final for the night.

The baby did not have croup, nor even any more hoarseness, but he lay awake a long time and looked at his mother with much interest. At last he slept; then she crept to the sofa and covered herself with a shawl, and went to sleep too. Healthy people cannot stay awake continuously, even if they are in trouble. Barry probably slept also, but he got up in a bad humor, and came down to breakfast later than he had meant to come. He would again have to take the 9.15 train, and it would be the loss of an hour in Wall Street, which he did not like. He rather longed to be in Wall Street again, to get out of himself and his fretting doubts.

CHAPTER XVIII.

A BUTTON OFF.

In the dining-room Phœbe was waiting for him. She sat by the fire reading the paper, but when he came in she got up without speaking and went across the room to ring the bell. The cook brought the breakfast, but Phœbe put it upon the table herself, moving about the room silently. Barry was not in the habit of thinking of her beauty, but he furtively studied it now while he pretended to read his paper. He could see what those old duffers meant; she was very different from ordinary women. He thought at that moment he would have preferred a wife who would have commanded less general attention. But out of humor as he was, he was just enough to remember that it was not her fault that she was striking-looking, and that he must put her standing with the old duffers out of the question and confine himself to her relations with Peyton, which was his only quarrel with her at the present moment.

Breakfast was very quiet. Mary Ann had been left up-stairs with the baby, and the cook drew the line of her concessions at waiting on the table, so Phœbe quietly left her seat and changed Barry's plate for him, and got him hot cakes from the pantry, where the cook had brought them, and "waited" upon him without any sense of degradation. It was what she had been used to doing all her life at home, besides cooking the breakfast and sometimes making the fire when the "hired man" overslept, and it was in no way a trial to her.

But in his present condition of ill-humor it was gall and wormwood to Barry to see her doing it, and being reminded of the different social place which she had occupied. It seemed to make all his doubts possible to recall the past. He rather curtly told her he wished she would engage another servant at once, and have things a little "in order." She said, "Very well," and flushed painfully. It was difficult to imagine things in better order than they were, except in the matter of service. Probably no man in Marrowfat had sat down to a better breakfast or a daintier looking table. The whole house was a miracle of neatness. Phœbe had only this outlet for her restless misery. She had not allowed herself an hour of idleness yesterday, she had promised herself this solace again to-day; she literally could not sit still and think. Now she must go out and get another servant, who would take this occupation away from her. There was no longer any need for economy, if what Barry had told her was true.

She wished it were not true. All the good that she could possibly have been to him was wasted if he were to be rich.

After breakfast Barry went into the hall and brought in his ulster: a button had come off. He hesitated to ask Phœbe to do anything for him in his present humor, but he said, " I wish you 'd tell Mary Ann to put this button on at once."

She took the coat and went into the library, and from a corner closet took out her work-basket and opened it.

" You 'll have to hurry," he said, ungraciously, following her.

She evidently meant to, for her fingers shook a little as she hunted for the thread and thimble. The black thread she wanted was not there: she laid down the coat, and went quickly up-stairs to get it. Barry glanced at the clock and saw there was plenty of time. He knew that she would hurry. He walked uneasily around the room. His eye fell on the open work-basket which she had left. A letter lay face downward in it. He gave it a snip with his fingers and turned it over. His heart seemed to turn over sharply as he saw the writing. It was Peyton's, and the letter was addressed to Phœbe. The clerk in the post-office must have been in the devil's employ, for the clear stamp on it glared up in his very face. There was no ambiguity. It was mailed in the city, Station A, at ten o'clock the day before; the last thing Peyton did, probably, before he took the eleven o'clock limited express for Washington. Barry did not touch the letter after he turned it over with his finger. He stood and looked at it till he heard Phœbe's step on the stair, and then he turned his back and looked out of the window. She hurriedly entered, and he heard her swift needle drawn in and out of the coat. But he heard something else. He heard her crush down the lid on her basket. That roused the dumb devil in him into speech. He turned to her just as, having fastened and cut the thread, she held the coat out to him. His eye fell on the basket; it was covered, and she had pushed it, accidentally or otherwise, a little out of sight.

" I see you are corresponding with Peyton Edwards," he said. " I don't ask any explanation, but I leave you to judge whether it would be wise to offer one."

He paused and stood looking at her, a dark fury in his eye. She did not raise her eyes nor attempt to speak.

" I don't ask an explanation," he said, slowly, " because between husband and wife, in ordinary circumstances, it would be an insult. But I suppose one would hardly say that our circumstances are ordinary. I don't think that a woman who has once given the world ground to doubt her discretion can complain if she is warned to be at least decently careful in her conduct."

With this stab he turned and left the room. The hat-stand was just outside the door. He did not omit because of his wrath to brush his hat, select his cane, take out his gloves. Not a sound came from within. He was too furiously angry to trust himself to glance back. He held the hall-door open for an instant, said, " You need not wait dinner for me to-night," shut it sharply, and was gone.

If he had looked back, he might not have gone so quickly. Even very healthy people can come pretty near fainting when they are stabbed deep enough. The poor young woman's face turned ashy white. . She leaned back in the chair in which she had been sitting upright. It is doubtful whether for a few moments she knew clearly what had happened. It was a whole half hour before she got up from her chair, and seemed to try her strength by walking once or twice across the floor. She sat down again, evidently waiting for the physical ability to do what her not-baffled mind proposed. It was not long in returning to her. She had apparently been coming to some decision, which was stimulated by a glance at the clock. She got up, took her work-basket, one or two books that lay on the table, and glanced around the room in search of something else she wanted. She rang the bell, and the cook came.

" Mary Ann 's forever about coming down to her breakfast," said this functionary, out of humor.

r

"Yes," said Phœbe, whose voice sounded as if she had not used it for a good while. "I am going up-stairs, and I'll send her down to you. It's my fault. When she comes, help her bring up the smallest of the two trunks that stand near the door of the lumber room. I am going away rather suddenly, and shall have to take her with me. You will have to get along for a day or so alone. There won't be any dinner to get to-night. You may give me my luncheon at half-past twelve. Don't let Mary Ann waste any time down-stairs."

The sudden marching orders delighted Mary Ann, and were not unpleasing even to the cook, who loved a return to her ancient solitary reign occasionally. Phœbe locked herself into her room. The baby slept. With swift hands she assorted the contents of wardrobes, drawers, and closets. Her brain must have worked with great rapidity, for the work she did between ten and half-past twelve o'clock was very considerable. She never seemed to pause or doubt, or have a misgiving or a regret. Mary Ann was a little afraid of her, she was so quick and her eyes shone so, that was the only drawback to her pleasure in the unexpected outing.

A little after twelve Phœbe sent Mary Ann down to bring her luncheon to her. She glanced around the rooms. They were in perfect order. The trunks stood packed and strapped. The baby in his fresh dress lay happy in his crib, his

cloak and cap and veil lying on the bed ready to
put on. Phœbe went to a drawer in her wardrobe,
took out a roll of bills and counted them over: here
she showed her only sign of perturbation or distress. The use of money suggested a field of anxiety to her to which she was not accustomed. Her
hands shook, and she went over them again with
agitation. Yes, forty-seven dollars. That was all
right. It had seemed a good sum to her when she
had counted on it for some little indulgence. *Now*
it was doubtful whether it would go very far. It
was a secret hoard. She had never told Barry of
it. It was a legacy, and she felt sure he would
laugh at the idea of a legacy of forty-seven dollars.
An old aunt had died since she came away from
home, who had left in her will a sum of money to
be divided between her nieces and nephews. The
dividend was not princely, to be sure, but it had
given a good deal of satisfaction in the remote
country homes to which it had found its way, and
it had been a ray of light, a rope of safety, a beacon of hope to poor Phœbe that morning when
she had first remembered it. She had blessed
Aunt Abby's memory many times that dark day.
She took out another purse, that in which she kept
the ordinary money, for household purposes and
all that, and taking out from it a little key and
some small memoranda, wrapped it in paper with
the change left in it, and put it in her drawer.
She forced herself to eat some luncheon when it

was brought: her manner had a resolution in it, as if something external to herself were carrying her forward. The cab came while she was still trying to eat. Mary Ann, very much excited by the prospect of adventure, caught up the baby and began to put on his cloak. There certainly was not a moment to lose.

When, a few moments later, Phœbe passed over the threshold of her husband's house, and shut the door after her, a bright spot burned on each cheek, but nothing in her eyes or manner indicated that she felt the deep significance of what she was doing, or was overcome either by sorrow for what was past or by terror for what was to come. The baby, in his wide-eyed unconsciousness, gazed out of the carriage window at which his nurse was dandling him, and showed neither interest nor apprehension of the fact that he had turned his back upon the only legitimate home that the world offered to him.

16

CHAPTER XIX.

HAGAR.

It was the second night after Phœbe's flight from home. Midnight was just striking from the city clocks. From the fifth story of a great hotel she looked down upon the gas-lights far below her in the streets. There was a dull, slow rain against the pane; a mist filled the space between her and the gaslights below, and above it was all dark. Mary Ann, no longer in high spirits, slept on a little cot beside the bed in which the baby lay. The room was small, and hot, and littered with the contents of the open trunks. There was no shade for the little flaring jet of gas; there was no glow in the little ashen fire which had made the air so suffocating. There was discomfort and homelessness in every inch of the cheerless place.

Phœbe sat down by the oval white marble table, and pushing a little space free put her elbows on it, and leaned her face down on her hands. Yes, it was true, — something must be done, something promptly, or she had failed. In her lap lay her porte-monnaie, and in it were the remains of the fast-melting forty-seven dollars. Her ignorance of traveling expenses had made it a shock to her to discover that she could not get far away from home with that amount of money. Here they were only at Albany, and there would be but thirteen dollars left after the hotel bill was paid, if indeed that did not swell up and even swallow the thirteen dollars. It made her feel faint whenever she remembered the bill and thought of the possibility of its exceeding her estimate of its amount. There had been so many things that she had not thought of, — the porter, the express, the fire, and last, not least, the doctor for the baby. The hoarseness had come back, and she had had a great terror of his being ill where she could not get a doctor. It was on account of this attack that they had not pushed on at once. Evidently they could not travel very fast with a delicate young baby, and evidently they could not travel very far with such a slender purse. No, Phœbe admitted to herself, a crisis had come : her first plan must be abandoned ; she must do what she could, and not what she would. The fiery strength with which she had started had long since failed her; her purpose was not weak, but it was leaden, and sunk her to the earth. She moaned as she laid her head down on her arms upon the marble. Oh, that she and her baby were indeed at rest, indeed hidden out of sight ! There was no rest, there was no hiding ; she could not get far enough away from people's eyes. How they looked at her wherever she went; how impossible it was to disappear! It had seemed so easy when she had planned it. It was like a nightmare, — eyes, eyes, wherever she turned, following her, meeting her, looking down upon her from heights and up at her from depths. She felt as if Hagar and Ishmael must be written on their faces. She had made sure, when once they got away from the little strip of territory where her name and face were known, that she could sink out of notice, and be no more an object of interest to any one. But porter, hall-boy, waiter, gazed; commercial travelers, clerks, men and women, old and young, shot glances, inquiring, admiring, deriding, what not. How did she happen to be traveling alone? How did she happen to have such appealing eyes and such an agitated manner when anybody attempted to get speech of her? She was too handsome and well dressed to be unnoticed; the baby was appareled like a little prince, and was beautiful. Mary Ann thought the interest they awakened very flattering. She did not fail to encourage it as far as she was able.

It was no use: slipping away and not being seen was impossible. The whole thing was at an end. All she could do was to cheat fate by changing her mind. She had been awake so many nights she was almost like ordinary women for nervousness and unreasonableness. She wanted to cry, but she was too frightened, too close drawn into herself; a kind word would have broken her

down, but that did not seem likely to come, seeing
Mary Ann was rather afraid to speak to her, and
the baby did not know how.

It was not her way to sit down and think over
things forever. She had been cabined and con-
fined in this little room so long she had been
forced to do more of it than was natural to her.
Now she must end it and resolve upon something. She got up, walked restlessly to the window and back; gazed down from the dizzy height
into the narrow misty street below, then to the
baby's bed, and then back again. By this time
her resolution was taken. She went to a trunk,
pulled it out, and began to rearrange and repack it
carefully. A few stitches were needed on some
of the baby's clothes. She took out needle and
thread, and stood close by the little gas jet and
mended them. Her own traveling-dress she
brushed carefully, and she even pulled out the fingers of her gloves and examined them. It was
plain she was afraid her occupation would not last
her the night out; she was quite right. At four
o'clock she had to lie down beside the baby and
consider that there was nothing else to do. She
felt a shuddering horror of the dark and silence
and covered up her eyes and tried to get asleep.

As soon as it was dawn she waked Mary Ann
and told her they were going away; she must
get up and dress. She dressed herself, and went
down to get her breakfast in the great, gray,

empty dining room, where the million subtle scents of as many savory meals slew appetite and filled one to repletion. One or two sleepy, stolid-looking travelers were breakfasting; the waiters seemed to blink and their steps to resound in the bare, empty room. The clerk at the desk where she went to pay her bill looked sleepy, too, and indifferent. The bill was not quite as large as she had thought possible; she had fifteen dollars instead of thirteen wherewith to meet the world. There were yet so many things to think of, — the hall-boy, the luncheon, the railway tickets, the chamber-maid.

While Mary Ann went down to get her breakfast, and the baby lay on the bed and amiably shook his rattle in the air, she counted out a certain sum and laid it by itself, hurried into a valise the few possessions of Mary Ann, put that young woman's bonnet and cloak beside it, and taking out her watch counted the moments till she came back.

"I am afraid you are late," she said, in a voice in which there was a little agitation audible. "Your train goes in fifteen minutes. Put your bonnet on as quickly as you can."

Mary Ann looked bewildered, but obeyed.

"The baby," she said. "Shan't I dress him before I put my cloak on?"

"No," answered her mistress, looking at her watch, and not at the woman. "You are to go

home this morning. I — have thought — that is
— it seems best — for you to take this first train
to New York. When you get there you can find
your way easily to the Marrowfat train. Any
policeman will tell you, but I 've written it all
down here in case you forget anything. Here is
the money for your ticket; there are crackers in
the bag for your luncheon."

" But " — said Mary Ann, too dazed and helpless to button her cloak — " the baby — who is to
mind the baby " —

" Oh," said Phœbe, desperately, putting the
bag into her limp hands and almost pushing her
towards the door, " don't stop to think about the
baby. You really have n't a moment to spare.
The hall-boy is waiting outside to take you to the
depot and show you where to get your ticket.
Remember to keep it in your porte-monnaie. And
here is your return ticket to Marrowfat from the
city. Put that in the other side. There, good-
by ; you really must not stay another minute."

Mary Ann cast a mute, distracted look towards
her little charge on the bed, but had not the composure necessary to ask for a last embrace of him.
She grasped the bag and the porte-monnaie, and
impelled by the stronger will of her mistress went
out of the door without another word. Phœbe
gave the waiting hall-boy directions about the
train and the car in which he was to put the pli-
ant Mary Ann. It was all done so promptly and

so assuredly that the poor girl did not get her breath till she was in the cars and fairly on her way to the city. There was but one form of words which came to her relief. " Well-I-never," she began to murmur at Greenbush, and at Spuyten Duyvil she had not got any farther, but only emphasized the expression of the same idea, if Well-I-never may be said to be the expression of an intelligent idea.

CHAPTER XX.

BARRY had said he would not come home that evening; he was even more vindictive than he promised, for he did not come home on the following. It was a satisfaction to him to know that he could in this silent way express his feelings of indignation. He shrunk from another interview. He felt ashamed of himself for what in his anger he had said to his wife, but yet in a way he was ashamed of feeling so. He said to himself that he ought to have said more, that he could not punish her enough; and yet his heart told him he had done a cruel and unmanly thing when he taunted her with his own wrong-doing. He was by turns furiously jealous and sickeningly repentant.

But away from Marrowfat the whole thing weakened and lost coloring. He hated the idea of going back and having the uncomfortable sensations revived. He was not pacified, but he was diverted. His natural kindliness of nature was glad of the reprieve; his habitual feeling of what others owed to him only consented to it as a reprieve. When after the pressure of an exciting

day in Wall Street he concluded to go up town
and dine with a friend, he thought to himself he
was acting very handsomely in not locking himself up in a hotel room and brooding over his
wrongs, or even blowing his own or Peyton's
brains out. He felt few men would have done
better. He even went to the theatre that night;
and though there was a weight on his spirits that
made him vaguely uncomfortable, there was no
noticeable depression in his manner or expression.

When it approached evening on the following
day he found himself instinctively dreading the
renewal of the disagreeable experiences which going home involved. He knew that with it he
must take up matters where he had laid them
down. He did not say to himself that he doubted
his doubts or was suspicious of his suspicions when
he was away from Marrowfat, but it was about
the truth. Still, when he thought of it he grew
angry again. He yielded to the importunities of a
friend who urged his staying with him that night.
He wrote a dispatch to Phœbe and then tore it up.
It would be well for her to look for him, and she
must bear her disappointment as best she might;
it would be a wholesome lesson to her, and would
show her what even the faintest disloyalty to him
would always cost her. He grew angry as he
allowed himself to think of it; he always grew
angry when he thought of it; his only safety
was in keeping it out of his mind, and the only

way to do that was to have his mind full of other things. Wall Street answered very well during the day; and the club and the theatre and two or three old friends stood him in stead for the evening. But the night, "the dead, unhappy night;" he was not so successful in the matter of the night.

When the third afternoon of his absence wore away to train-time he had many misgivings, but he had begun to feel he had carried the punishment far enough, and that it would be unmanly to be longer unforgiving, or at least unbending. And at his heart there was a little uneasiness lest his silence should have caused a wound too deep to be healed by the palliation which he was prepared to offer. Yes, he would go home ; a train later than usual was the compromise with his pride which he decided on. She would have one full hour of thinking that he was not coming. It would be very wholesome.

This train brought him to Marrowfat a few minutes before seven. There were none of his friends on it, so he had the time for reflection. It was dark and sloppy when he got out of the cars, feeling sore and ill-used, but yet in a certain sense relieved by being here, with no chance for retreat possible. It was not pleasant to meet Phœbe under the circumstances, but it was pleasant to feel he was manly enough to do the right thing, whether it was what he liked or not. Self-approval was very necessary to Barry; when this failed him he collapsed. Splash, splash, through the mud, — phaugh! what a night for a man in his social standing to be coming out to a dreary country home! What a life he led! What privations he had suffered for the past year! And all for the sake of — what, and who? Not many men would have done as he had done, as he was doing; certainly, not many men. When he thought of the luxury and ease, and, what was more important to him, the dignity and good form, with which his life would have been conducted but for this marriage, he did not grow bitter; he grew better tempered, because he thought so well of himself. He said to himself, The money is coming, and that will restore everything, and all will yet be well if Phœbe will but prove herself all right, and explain away the dark circumstances that he was not to blame for demanding an explanation of. As he neared the house he began to feel an assurance that she would make such an explanation.

The gate was closed, which he thought unnecessary. He pushed it open, and went through the damp grass to see that it was fastened back and would not come shut again. He looked up to the windows of the rooms they occupied on the third floor. There was no light. Neither was there one on the first floor. All was as dark as if no one lived in the house. This did not please him.

People knew he was at home again, and it did not look well for a man who was something very important in a syndicate to be living like a journeyman tailor in a back shop. Phœbe's economies had become detestable to him. He knocked the mud off his boots, and fumbled about for the knob of the door. The door of course was locked : he did not blame her for that, but he had to hunt again for the bell handle, which when found he pulled very sharply once or twice. After an unreasonable time of waiting, a faint glimmer appeared in the fan-light over the door, and some one said, "Who 's there ? "

Barry said who was, in a very irritated tone. Then an exclamation, and some one began undoing bolts and bars which seemed to have no end. He rather uncivilly pushed against the door before the last chain was dropped. The cook said she was doing her best, if he would please wait a minute longer. He waited, not because he pleased, but because he could not help himself. The cook stood back and let him pass, and set down her candle on the floor while she replaced a few of the household defenses.

"Why don't you have a light in the hall?" he said, angrily, setting down his hat and taking off his coat.

The cook said she was not expecting anybody, and it did not seem worth while to be burning out gas for nothing. He threw down his coat and pushed open the library door: there was no light nor fire there; it felt very cold and damp, as if the furnace fire had not been lighted for some days. By this time the cook had fastened the door and taken her candle up and set it on the table.

" You 'll be wantin' somethin' to eat," she began.

" Naturally," he returned, shortly.

" There is n't a happoth in the house," she said, well pleased that her economies should be recognized.

" What 's the matter?" he asked, sharply, turning to her. " Has Mrs. Crittenden had her dinner ?"

." Mrs. Crittenden !" ejaculated the woman, throwing up her hands. " Why, she 's been gone these three days ! Bless you, has anything happened her a-gittin' to you? Why, I made sure she and you was having a foine time together in the city, after her bein' so lonely all the winter. And hearin' no word from either of yez, I never laid in nothin' from the butcher nor the grocer, nor the iceman even. I just let 'em come and let 'em go, and scold and fume as much as they liked. Do yez live on nothin' yerself, they said. I told 'em it was none of their business what I lived on as long as I done my dooty."

Barry's back was turned to the woman, and she did not see how pale he grew at her first words. Her final ones (and a great many had intervened, of no great literary or statistic value) seemed to demand some kind of a response. She could put some tea, anything, on the table, and send Mary Ann up-stairs to tell him when it was ready.

"Mary Ann!" she cried, throwing up her hands again in genuine amazement. "What is the man talking of! You did n't think she 'd left the baby behind her, and her a-nursin' of him yet! Why, Mary Ann 's went with her. You had n't been an hour out of the house when such a pullin' out of trunks and a packin' up of clothes begun as never was. And they was off in the noon train. Mary Ann, indeed! Why, Mary Ann was as pleased as Punch, and never so much as passed a remark about my being left alone, and not a soul in the house day in day out, to speak a livin' word to."

All this time Barry was walking, dazed and speechless, up the stairs. The woman's voice rang after him with clear distinctness in the still and empty house. He longed to get to his own room, to turn the key, to think, and to adjust himself to this unexpected situation. She went on talking about his tea, about her economies, about Mary Ann. He shut the door when he got up-stairs, and struck a match and lighted the gas. There was a chair near him, and he sat down in it; possibly he felt a little weak and ill for the moment. Of all the surprises of his life, this was the most complete. He did not know exactly what he thought or felt. He did not for a while

ask himself what it meant ; he only said over and
over to himself, Could it possibly be true ?   Later
on he was racked with the doubt whether her going meant guilt or indignation.   But he had not
yet begun to weigh things, to decide, to define.
All he could say or think was surmounted by
amazement.   Phœbe gone, the child gone, the one
spot on earth of which he felt himself in sure and
stable possession a blank to him.   No word, nothing ?   It was impossible.

After a while he got up and began to look
about for a letter.   He had not asked the woman,
but if she had had any message she would have
given it to him.   Indeed, as she had thought they
were together, there could have been no message.
He began vaguely and abstractedly ; he grew feverish and frightened as he went on.   He pulled
open drawers and closets ; he searched in boxes
and on shelves.   All were in order ; everything
showed a recent definite arrangement.   Everything told one story.   The going was final.   If
there had been haste in her going it was directed
by an intention so definite that nothing escaped
it.   Of the child's possessions there was nothing
left that could be packed into a trunk; only the
crib and a chair or two of his remained in either
of the rooms.   Of Phœbe's own, everything was
gone that had been hers before marriage ; everything was left that had been given her by her
husband or bought with his money — gloves half

worn, handkerchiefs, veils, scraps of lace and ribbon, a new dress or two, all arranged in perfect
order, and laid by themselves as if with gravest
intention. In her dressing-table drawer lay a
package containing her wedding-ring and the few
pieces of jewelry he had ever given her. It was
not even addressed to him. In another package
was her porte-monnaie and little account-book,
with a hurried entry in pencil on the day of her
going. The change in the pocket-book agreed
with the statement of household expenses up to
that day. He looked through her writing-desk.
There was nothing there but paper, pens, stamps,
some bills, not a scrap of her writing, not a letter
that belonged to her except — the slim package of
Barry's own while he was away.

Could all this have been the work of three
hours? Was it possible that she had had no intention of going away from him till he had said
what he did to her that morning? Barry did not
know what he believed, what he apprehended.
He walked up and down the rooms feeling stunned
and helpless, like a person recovering from a pros-
trating illness, or getting over a long debauch.
He felt feeble in will, weak in judgment, incapa-
ble of continuous thought.

By and by the cook came up, bringing a tray
of things for him to eat. She made an exclamation at the coldness of the room, and went down
on her knees upon the hearth and scraped to-

17

gether the remnants of some half-consumed wood,
and succeeded in lighting them.

"It's no matter," he said, wanting to get rid of
her.

But she saw he was in a great deal of trouble,
and she was clumsily sorry for him. She had
liked her mistress very well, but, like a true Irish-
woman, she liked her master very much better.
So she set out his tea with considerable clatter,
and made a nice fire, and lighted a lamp, and tried
to cheer him up with a good deal of rambling conversation, which he did not seem to hear. Indeed,
she was surprised at the things which she made
bold to say to him, and which he did not appear
to resent or even understand. He had always inspired her with much respectful admiration ; now
her principal feeling was that of admiring pity,
and every one knows to what length Irish admiring
pity is capable of going. He humbly wished she
would go away. He did not know what made her
stay ; he could not eat anything she had brought
him. He had swallowed the coffee and felt a little
nerved up by it, but not to the point of asking
her questions which he knew beforehand she
could not answer. He looked so wretched that
she could hardly tear herself away from the sight,
and yet was so irresponsive that she was finally
obliged to do it. She took the tray away, and,
promising the fire a little more wood in the course
of half an hour, went down the dark stairs into

the dim kitchen, filled with the emotions that we seek in the drama. While our servants have to go to funerals and are driven to make the most of fires and robberies and their friends' misfortunes, we go to the theatre to get the same sensations, or find them in highly-wrought fiction with even less effort. It is not the least trying of the inequalities of fortune. The cook could no more have given up the contemplation of the third-story drama than you or I would be likely to give up voluntarily the contemplation of Salvini in the third act of Othello. She soon found an excuse for tiptoeing up the stairs again, and tapping at the door of the little study.

"A letter, sir, that's after comin' from the mail. May be you'd be wantin' it."

She put it into his hands at the door, and so arranged matters that he could not very well shut it in her face; by which means she commanded for the next ten minutes a certain though imperfect view of the stage and its agitated actor. If one cannot have a front balcony seat, one is sometimes thankful to catch a glimpse between the flies. Barry forgot his audience; he devoured the direction on the letter with kindling eyes. It was addressed to Phœbe, and was in the abhorred handwriting of his childhood's friend. The postmark was Washington, the date was obliterated. He ripped the envelope open with no paltering of conscience about the act. It read as follows : —

My Dear Phœbe, — I reached this place last
evening. I leave to-morrow for St. Louis. A letter addressed to the Southern Hotel will find me
there till after Tuesday. Then my next address
will be the St. Charles, New Orleans.

Yours sincerely, Peyton Edwards.

This letter acted like the application of a battery to a comatose person. Barry's eyes seemed
to burn holes in the paper as he looked at it. He
clinched his hands, ground his fine white teeth together, uttered some passionate exclamations, and
walked about the room angrily. At this moment
there was a ringing at the kitchen bell, which
seemed to the cook too cruel an interruption to be
borne. She was consoled only by the thought
that it might be another letter, equally electric,
or at any rate that she would not be long away.
She would make short work of any ordinary
visitor of her own, and would return on the
legitimate and flat-footed errand of bringing up
more wood. So she tiptoed down in all haste, and
left Barry walking up and down the room quite
unconscious of her interest and attendance. Her
return was flat-footed, breathless, prompt.

"I 've come to tell you," she panted, supporting
herself by the door-post, for she was no longer
young, and such rapid journeys up and down
the stairs, not to mention these exciting scenes,
were exhausting to her strength, — "I 've come to

tell you Mary Ann's after getting back this minute."

" Mary Ann!" exclaimed her master, turning sharply round. " Where " — and he stopped short, facing the lean, keen-visaged, curious Irish-woman, and realizing in an instant the full ignominy of his position.

The woman dropped her eyes; she was keen enough to know that he must be ashamed to ask questions of his servants about his wife. "I thought you'd likely want to know how she'd left the mistress and the baby " —

" Yes, send her up."

" She'll come in a minute; she's sort of upset like. She ain't used to going about by herself; she's kind of childish, is Mary Ann. I'll give her a dish o' tea, and let her rest a bit, and then mebbe she'll be able to come up."

"She must hurry, then," said Barry, desperately, " for I'm going out."

This gave the cook a fright, as one would feel, in the most exciting moment of a tragedy, to think of the gas being turned off, the curtain dropped, and the audience told to go about their business. She hurriedly said Mary Ann would certainly come up, if he would wait a bit. She'd see herself that no time was lost about it.

No time *was* lost about it. In a very short space, Mary Ann stood before her master in the doorway of the little study, with the tears scarcely

dried upon her cheeks, her bonnet strings untied
and fluttering, her hair agitatedly awry, and her
cloak unbuttoned, but not taken off.

When she saw Mr. Crittenden, she began to
cry afresh ; what for, it would be difficult to say.
The sight of her rather unnerved her master ; he
hated tears from any source. She was young and
presumably innocent, and she affected him very
differently from the elderly and inquisitive and
most unbeautiful cook. He did not feel the degradation to be nearly so great to have to learn from
her the last news of his wife. Besides, he had so
constantly seen her with the child in her arms,
she seemed at a little less impossible distance than
the other.

" Well, Mary Ann," he said, suppressing a rising sob, roused by the thought of the baby and
the sight of her agitation, " don't cry ; that won't
do any good. How 's — baby, and where have you
left him ? "

That only made her cry the more ; what for,
who shall say ? For Mary Ann had not been a
very absorbed nurse, and had frequently found
herself much wearied by her duties, and had given
warning more than once. It was a good while before she could calm herself enough to say when
she had parted from her mistress. Indeed, she
hardly knew where ; she had very little memory
for names. She bethought herself at last of the
written directions her mistress had given her, and

hunted for them in her pocket, and gave them to him, a little the worse for much study and consultation with conductors and policemen and benevolent persons on the way. They were written out in Phœbe's clear, strong hand; even muddle-headed Mary Ann could sail by such a chart, it seemed. Barry studied it for a moment.

"When did you go there?" he said.

"To where? To the big hotel, do you mean?"

"Yes, the hotel in Albany."

"Oh, the day we went away from here; we got there in the evening. The baby got hoarse, — that's the reason we stayed there all next day; she told the doctor we was in a great hurry, but he said it would n't do to take the baby out."

"Tell me: the day you went away from here, what did you do till you took the train for Albany? Did you go anywhere, to any house, or meet anybody anywhere?"

"Oh, we met lots and lots of people everywhere, but nobody, I think, that spoke to us. We went right up in a carriage to the depot where that train started from, and stopped there till it went. The baby was that good he never fretted onst all the way a-goin'. You would n't have knowed there was a baby in the train at all."

And Mary Ann began to cry again.

"Well," said Barry, walking up and down the room, "and while you were at the hotel, did — did anybody come to see your mistress?"

"No," said Mary Ann.

"Did she send for anybody, write notes, go out anywhere?"

"No," returned the girl, rather bewildered. "She was always takin' care of baby. She was in the room all the time but when she was down to her meals. She might have wrote notes while I was asleep; I can't say as to that."

"And what did she say to you when she told you to come home?"

"She did n't say nothing but just that."

"And when did you know she meant to send you back?"

"After I'd got my breakfast, this morning. She just told me I was to go home, and she give me my ticket, and there was n't anything for me to do, for she'd packed my things up unbeknownst, and she put the bag into my hand and just whizzed me off before I knew what it was all about."

And Mary Ann, at the recital of her wrongs, began to cry again. "And she never told me whether I was to stay here after I got here, or whether she did n't want me no more, or anything about it. She just sent me, that was all. She might a-told me, I should think."

"And do you know how long she was to stay at the hotel?"

"I don't think she was goin' to stay at all; I think she was goin' right away. She had all packed up the trunks last night while I was asleep.

There was n't anything left out but baby's cloak and cap."

"What place did she talk about? Where do you think she meant to go?"

Mary Ann could not remember, though she tried. She had heard her ask at the office for a time-table; she had heard the clerk tell her the hour that a certain morning train would bring her to a certain place, but the name of the place she had forgotten. Barry repeated to her many routes, the names of many cities. At the naming of Montreal and Canada she showed interest.

"I should n't wonder if that was it," she said. And that was as near as Barry could get to assurance of any kind. He came to a sudden conclusion; there was no time to be lost; the last train to the city left the depot in fifteen minutes. When for the second time that day Mary Ann was treated to the surprise of a sudden separation from her employer, she found herself better prepared to meet it under the sheltering wing of the cook in the comfortable Crittenden kitchen. Her "Well-I-never" echoed harmlessly among the pots and pans of that well-scrubbed region. The cook could not hear too much of her recent strange adventures; together they sat up till "all hours" of the night, and talked "about it goddess and about it," till, like their betters, they scarcely knew what was truth and what was speculation.

CHAPTER XXI.

RACING AND CHASING ON CANOBIE LEE.

BARRY's first telegram was sent to the hotel at
Albany. He could not tell if she had registered
in her own name or not; but it seemed she had.
In due course of electricity came the intelligence
that Mrs. Crittenden had left the hotel on the
previous morning. His next was to Malden, sent
in the name of one of his clerks, to know if she
were in the place. The answer was prompt. She
was not living there. His third was addressed to
Peyton Edwards, and contained a demand for intelligence of the whereabouts of his wife. From
Washington came the information that he was not
there; from St. Louis the same. After a couple
of hours of desperation, consultation with detectives, and all the unwisdom of a maddened man,
a dispatch arrived from Peyton at St. Louis. He
had just reached there, and had found Barry's dispatch. He knew nothing of Phœbe; had looked
for a letter from her, but was disappointed. "Try
Malden." An hour after, another: "Try Brixton. Answer." Another, after another not much
longer interval, evincing the keenest anxiety:

" Let me know at once. Avoid publicity. You may be sure it will be all right."

It began to be borne in upon Barry's mind that his wife was not eloping with Peyton Edwards, though the detectives did not see his grounds for confidence. If he could have cleared up the mystery of her possessing money enough to go away, he would have dismissed the theory of Peyton's complicity in her going. But her money statements were so accurate and simple. She had had no friends to apply to for funds. She had left behind her every piece of jewelry that would have brought her anything. If she had gone on the spur of the taunt he had thrown at her, he could not account for her having enough money to make the journey to Albany. If she had had it long in contemplation, then Peyton was at the bottom of it. But in his heart, somehow, he felt a growing conviction that he had sent Phœbe away, and that Peyton had not enticed her. He dismissed the detectives, gorged with his money and sworn to keep his secret, threw to the winds Wall Street, Syndicate, and Fortune, boarded the first train to Albany, and, with a heavy heart, set out to find her.

At Albany he could strike no clue. The only thing was to follow the nurse's suggestion and look for her in Montreal. Then there was simply nothing to help him. He spent two days in pursuing phantoms; came back from Canada despairing and angry, with suspicions again aroused against Peyton. In this state of mind, he hurried to Chicago, led by a clue chance threw in his way. An official to whom he spoke in the railway station remembered a lady, with a child in her arms, buying a ticket for Chicago some four days ago. He recollected her perfectly: large, handsome woman. Could not tell the color of her dress ; something dark. Did not see the child's face ; thought it was asleep; wondered why she did' not have a nurse for it; she looked "smart" enough dressed to have one. She looked like a lady. She acted as if she did not want people to see her. She pulled down her veil when he looked at her. He should know her in a minute.

Barry kept track of this lady without much difficulty. She was a noticeable person and did not want to be noticed. It was very plain she was getting away from somebody. He traced her step by step to a third-rate boarding-house in the outskirts of Chicago, was treated to screams and hysterics from the other side of a thin partition, and finally, with many misgivings but with desperate resolution, forced himself into the presence of a stout, flashily dressed woman of thirty-two, with a great deal of frizzed yellow hair, who swooned with joy to find he was not her pursuing husband, and who clutched in her arms a sickly girl of three, apparently the bone of contention between the ill-assorted pair.

After this he had no way to turn. He had given up all theories, to the one engendered by this clue, that Phœbe was on her way to St. Louis to join Peyton. He telegraphed to his office for news; was answered by replicas of telegrams of Peyton's from New Orleans, where he was now apparently pursuing the even tenor of an honest way, and where Phœbe was not likely to be by any ordinary mode of locomotion, with a croupy baby in her arms, and with very limited experience in making connections and studying out schedules. Peyton's dispatches were not suave. They were rather peremptory; but the language was ambiguous enough not to be readily interpreted at the office. He wanted to be answered; he advised Malden; he almost demanded discretion. Barry sulkily put the dispatches in his pocket; he had no intention of giving any answer to them, but because there was no other plan put before him he accepted the counsel they contained, bought a ticket to Malden, and, haggard and worn-looking, took his seat in the train that with many changes and turns and much provincial deliberation would bring him to Malden by the coming on of dusk.

CHAPTER XXII.

GRAY SHINGLES ON A WET DAY.

THE spring rains had swollen the brooks and gullied the roads about Malden. The mud was deep, the air was raw. Phœbe got out of the train with a sickening weariness of the dreary scene. It was not raining, it was just "misting;" and though it was not cold enough to prevent the snow left along the edges of the fields and in sheltered spots from melting rapidly, the air seemed more chill than winter. The stage-driver even walked up and down the platform, and beat his heavily gloved hands together to keep them warm. He opened the door of the stage for Phœbe with a little nod of recognition.. He did not look more interested and surprised than if she had been away a week instead of a year. She had not wanted to make a sensation; she had longed to steal back in the night and not be seen. But this coming back by midday, and being nodded at as if it were not the deepest wretchedness that had brought her, — this was even worse than active curiosity. It seemed to her such a note of the life to which she had returned, stagnant, common-

place, uneventful, low. She had gone away from
it in bitterness; she had come back to it with
loathing. Nothing but the direst necessity had
forced her to it. If there had been any other
shelter for her she would have taken it. But
these few days of battling for life among strangers,
with a weight of helpless care in her arms, had
cured her of her bold hope and steadfastness. For
the child's sake she submitted to give up, to seek
the only refuge that was open to her, and steeled
herself to endure the most repugnant life she
could imagine. She felt beforehand the taunts of
her neighbors; she knew that she must work hard,
live low, forget the past, endure the present, re-
nounce hope for the future.

No wonder that her face was stern and set as
they jolted along the muddy roadway that led
from the station to the little village. The driver
looked back askance at her, and concluded not to
make any conversation; he leaned forward on his
elbows, hummed a Moody and Sankey tune, and
drove on stolidly. There was no other passenger.
Phœbe had the back seat and the " buffaloes "
quite to herself. The baby was wrapped in a
traveling-shawl; the fine cloak had gone two or
three days ago to a greedy shop-woman, who paid
her a third of what it cost. Phœbe did not look
any too grand to be riding in the Malden stage.
Her dark dress had a little mud on it, and the in-
definable shade of careless and constant wear.

She had wound a blue veil around her bonnet to keep it from the rain.

It was a strange coming back, she thought, looking at the baby in his crumpled cap sleeping on her arm, which ached. She had sometimes had dreams of how she would return to Malden with her beautiful boy and her devoted husband. She had felt it was not altogether unpardonable that she should have such dreams, considering her humiliations. She had fancied how, in some prosperous future summer, they would drive over the hills in an open carriage, making all the journey from Marrowfat in that luxurious way; she had even seen in her mind's eye the sash and the sailor hat, and the soft brown curls of the pretty boy; there should be a maid in a white cap, and a man possibly with a silk hat and a band around it and a buckle. She did not go the length of a livery, but the velvet band would be so possible, even if they had grown only moderately prosperous. Phœbe was economical even in her dreams. She had always had the picture in her mind of their arrival at the gate of her little old home. It was always towards evening of a June day that they arrived: everything about the house and yard was looking its best; her mother, proud and smiling, was standing at the gate to welcome them; the little cavalcade filled the roadway, Barry, handsome, merry, and sunburned, with a dog or two about his feet, stooped down, uncovered, to kiss his mother-in-law; the man stood at the horses' heads; the maid held up the boy, who shouted in delight; and always at this moment passed Mary Carpenter and Letitia Gregg, who had said the bitterest and hardest things about her.

And *this* was the way she was coming home: outcast and forlorn, and alone forever but for the baby who lay a dead weight in her tired arms; the June evening, the fine carriage, the attendants, found their fulfillment in the damp April drizzle, the lumbering old stage, the grizzled, psalm-singing driver. Poor Phœbe! she could not cry, she did not want to cry. She was hard and bitter and resentful.

She knew every barn and hay-rick they passed. That pump, this stile, — she had not thought of them since she went away, but they were as familiar as if she had been seeing them every day. The dreariness, the weariness, of it; and underneath all the wound that had brought her back to it.

In the drive from the station to the village, Peterson's half-witted boy tending the cattle at the farmyard gate, and old Nancy Briggs wrapped in the faded plaid shawl that she remembered so long, were the only human beings that they passed. The village was silent as a graveyard. The "store" door was shut, but a mist on the panes of its one window and a "team" hitched outside showed that the tide of commerce was still flowing through the little hamlet. Half a dozen silent, spitting, steaming male figures were undoubtedly seated around its sulky stove. The driver stopped at another rival mercantile house; this was new since Phœbe went away. Here the mail-bag was left; a small board over the door said Post Office. The man stayed a good while inside; he came out puffing at a very bad cigar, the smoke of which floated back into the stage for the remainder of the way, and made Phœbe ill and angry.

The last house was passed that lay between the village and her old home. Her heart began to beat, and the tears that had refused to come for so many suffering days were gathering in her eyes. Beneath all the revolt at coming home and the certainty of misery there, there had been a yearning to throw herself into her mother's arms and weep out her despair. She knew that the comfort would be short-lived; that more wretchedness than solace would come from telling out her griefs to one of so different a temperament from her own. But the impulse was deep as nature and old as Holy Writ: "as one whom his mother comforteth."

It required all her force of will to keep back the flood of tears that the mere thought of meeting her mother brought. The horses climbed the little ascent slowly; Phœbe scarcely dared look out. At last, with a jolt, the stage stopped before the gate, and the driver called out Whoa! in a loud voice intended more to rouse the inmates of the

house than to check the horses, who scarcely
needed any invitation to stop.

The house stood near the road; below this road,
in front, the land dropped away suddenly, and a
wide stretch of pasture land, several miles' perhaps, lay out in view, bounded by bare-looking
hills, now covered with mist, in the distance. At
the right of the house lay a patch of garden; adjoining it the barn and out-houses. At the back
of it the hill rose so suddenly that the house lost
a story in consequence, and was built up against
its base. The hill was covered with bushes and
trees, now dripping and bare and brown. The
house looked very old and very small; it was un-
painted, and its gray shingles were dark with the
soaking rain. It did not look out of repair; two
or three great stems of vines mounted to its roof,
and in summer no doubt made it very pretty. A
stone wall surmounted by a low paling separated
it from the road; three or four steps led up from
the road to the gate, which was also low, not more
than two feet high. The shrubs and flower-beds
were perhaps nicely kept in summer; they were
not much to look at now. A little path led to
the front door, but it was evidently unused. A
line of boards lay towards the kitchen door, indi-
cating that as the usual way of entrance.

The driver pulled open the stage door. Phœbe,
grasping the child in her arms, got out, giving
a hurried look towards the house. No one had

appeared at the call of the driver; everything seemed so deadly still. You could hear the breathing of the tired horses and the creaking of the old stage with their slight motion. She pushed open the low gate; it sagged and stuck at a certain point as she remembered it did when she was a little child. She hurried up to the kitchen door and opened it without allowing herself time to think again.

The room was all still and warm and in order. Coming down the little stairway that opened into it was her mother, who, dazed and frightened at the sudden apparition, gave a sort of cry and stopped. Phœbe ran to her, gave her a kiss, and then threw herself down upon the lowest step of the stairs, and hiding her face in the shawl wrapped round the baby began to sob. The mother, in terror, began to cry too, and moan and wring her hands and ask what was the matter.

" Oh, nothing ! " cried Phœbe, getting up and trying to master herself; " only I 've come home to you, mother. Oh, you must be good to me ! "

" But *what 's* the matter ? Why did you come? Where 's Barry ? Oh, my goodness, I always *knew* it would n't come to any good ! Oh, my poor child, why *would n't* you listen to me? This is more than I can stand. You must n't take on so unless you want to break my heart."

At this moment the driver, rather tired of waiting, knocked at the door, which stood half open.

ⵡ

Phœbe darted into the little bedroom that opened from the kitchen at one side, to conceal her agitation from the man. Her mother stood helpless and bewildered while he asked if there was anybody to help him in with the trunks. Mrs. Holden said she did not know; what trunks — where?

" Why, your girl's trunks; she as has just come home. Come out and look at 'em, if you don't believe me."

" I 'll go and ask Phœbe," said the mother.

" Oh, mother," cried Phœbe, who had thrown herself upon the bed beside the baby in a paroxysm of weeping, " pay the man and send him away! Don't let him in here; don't let him see you're feeling bad. Pay him and send him away, and let me be alone for a little while."

Thus entreated the mother went away, and collected herself enough to call the " hired man," Joe, to help about the trunks; but three times she had to break in upon Phœbe's passion of weeping, to decide where they should be put and to make change to pay the man the fare.

" I have n't got any change, — I have n't got a cent!" said Phœbe. " Why can't he come in another time? He passes here two or three times a week. Oh, don't, *don't* make me talk about it now!"

Mrs. Holden was so used to crying herself, a puling stream of tears that was never quite dried up, that she could not understand what the objection was to being asked about the spare room and the driver's change in the midst of weeping. Phœbe's tears and hers differed, — that was all that could be said: an April shower and a midwinter tempest; a perennial meadow brook and a suddenly swollen mountain torrent.

After the man had been paid, and had got into his seat and gathered up his reins and gee-upped to his horses, and gone his way much reflecting upon the widow's agitation and the unhappy looks of her returning daughter, the widow herself went into the little bedroom and unwrapped the now protesting baby from his shawl, and moaned over him and plied his mother with questions about him, and kissed him, and cried feebly.

" Do you feed him, Phœbe. He's hungry; the poor darling is hungry. I am *sure* he's hungry. Shall I give him a little milk? Or would some farina suit him better? I could boil it in a few minutes, if you could hold him till it's done. There, there, don't cry, petty, don't. Perhaps I might as well loosen his clothes; *something* hurts him — I am sure. Dear, dear, it's so long since I've had a baby to look after. Not since you. I almost forget how to hold one. Ah me! I little thought! — Phœbe, if you can quiet yourself a moment to listen to me; the child *must* be fed, or something done to pacify him. There's no good in crying so, Phœbe. If I'd cried like that I

should have killed myself years and years ago.
Goodness knows, I 've had enough to cry about,
but I try to control myself, and that saves everybody. Think about your baby, Phœbe, think
about me. You don't want to hurt us, and
you 'll kill us if you go on like that."

Poor Phœbe; she would not have minded, that
moment, if she had been told that she *had* killed
her mother and her baby. It was the blackest moment of her life; it was totally black, and nothing could have made it blacker while it lasted.
She was paying for the long strain and the unnatural silence of the past eight days. The discon-
tents and rebellions and complainings of ordinary
lives would make up quite as heavy an account as
she paid for all at once in that one awful hour of
despair. She was not generally discontented and
complaining, but of a full, sound nature and very
patient. It was not to be wondered at that her
mother was frightened, and gathered up the baby
and went out when she told her to. She hovered
about the door all the afternoon and listened, but
did not dare even to turn the knob or implore her
to drink the tea or eat the toast, relays of which
she had eased her maternal heart by preparing.
These slow-gathering, heavy-bursting storms have
this advantage, that they get themselves respected
and in a measure let alone. We stay in-doors and
keep out of the way of a tempest, but in frequent
paltry showers we arm ourselves and flit about defiantly.

Late in the afternoon Phœbe came out of her room, pale and spent. She took her baby in her arms and sat down silently beside the fire. Her mother fluttered about and made ready a fresh supply of tea and toast, prepared the table for the evening meal, and added whatever was possible from her not very abundant larder. She did not even try to "make talk;" she was awed into silence for once. When it was all ready, she humbly offered to take the baby and to keep him while Phœbe took her tea. But Phœbe held him on her arm, and came to the table with him. When they sat down at the board for the first time for so long, and in such painful circumstances, the widow's ready tears overflowed. But they did not touch the source of her daughter's grief nor call hers forth again. She soothed the baby, who fretted a little, and silently ate some of the food put before her. Her mother waited on her anxiously, getting up to bring this and that to her. She did not remonstrate or express gratitude, but took it all simply and did her best to eat. After the meal was over she got up and tried to help her mother put away the "tea things," but probably found it beyond her strength, and sat down silently by the fire again. The widow was busy for an hour or two in matters about the house. The "hired man" came in and helped her to bring down a cradle from the garret and make it ready for the baby.

" You 'll sleep with me to-night? " she asked of
Phœbe, hesitatingly. " It 'll be cold for the baby
up-stairs in your old room. Joe 'll make the fire,
though, if you want it."

" I don't care; it does n't make any difference
to me."

After she had prepared the baby for sleep, and
put him in the cradle, and seen him close his eyes
heavily and finally for the night, she came out and
sat down by the fire again. Her mother sat there
rocking herself backward and forward. Phœbe
knew she had to tell her mother something of the
reasons for her coming home. It was very hard
to speak now, in cold blood, but there was no
question but that she had to do it. If she could
have done it at the moment when she first threw
herself into her mother's arms, it would not have
cost so much.

" I hope you don't mind having me home again,
mother," she began, while they both sat looking
into the fire.

" Why, no, Phœbe: it 's been lonely enough
without you, gracious knows. Only " —

" Yes, I know what you mean. Well, we must
n't care what people say, and as long as I am doing
what I know is right I don't think you ought to
mind about it."

" But are you? — that 's the thing," and the
widow's voice faltered, as if she were struggling
with a fresh supply of tears.

"Yes, I believe I am. It's hard to talk against — Barry — and I hope you'll let this be once for all, and never say anything to me about it afterwards. I've found he did n't — feel the way he used to towards me. There was somebody that he was attached to from the time he was a boy."

"Powers o' mercy, then why did n't he stay at home and marry her, and leave us here in peace?" cried the mother, hotly.

"No matter. He did n't, and there's the end of it. But — and this is why I won't go back to him — he has — said things I can't stand; he must want to be rid of me, or he would n't have said them. Don't let us talk any more about it, mother. I've come back to you, and I'll try to be a help to you, and I hope you won't mind the baby. He's very good, if he's only well. I can earn enough at sewing to keep him and me in clothes — and — you won't mind giving us our board. You're getting old, and you'll be glad of a little less work. I've thought it all over, and I don't see that there's anything better can be done."

"But, Phœbe," cried her mother, now genuinely broken down, "my child, I don't like to hear you talk about it in that sort of way. Don't you know it's an awful thing to go away and leave your husband? Why, it's wicked. Oh, it might bring a judgment on you. Have you thought about it, have you prayed about it?"

"Yes," said Phœbe, setting her teeth together, "and it's done, and I don't want to talk about it any more."

"But you *must* talk about it," moaned the mother. "You haven't told me anything. You just come home, and say you won't live with your husband any more, and that there's the end of it. *What* did he say? What does he say's the matter? How can you expect me to know whether you've done right till you tell me all about it?"

"There isn't anything more to tell," said Phœbe, stolidly. "If you don't want me to stay, I'll pack my trunk to-morrow and go and earn my living somewhere else. There are plenty of places; I shouldn't have to starve."

The widow was frightened, and began to dread another tempest; she wept, and hurried to assure her daughter that she was more than welcome to her home, no matter how she came.

"But I can't help thinking, Phœbe"—

"Well, try to help speaking, if you can't help thinking, mother," said Phœbe, getting up and going towards the table. "Shall I take this lamp, or is there one outside?"

She had never seen Phœbe like this before: it was like having a child come back to you that did not belong to you. She dissolved in tears, and sat rocking herself by her lonely fire long after her daughter had gone silently to bed.

CHAPTER XXIII.

OUTSIDE THE KITCHEN DOOR.

THOUGH Phœbe had subdued her mother and got herself let alone that first night, it would have been too much to hope that she had made a permanent conquest. Weak natures are the hardest to conquer, and in dealing with them the stronger ones are generally fain to confess self-conquest is the only way to peace. Mrs. Holden had a feeble judgment and a vehement will. That this will vacillated, and was set now in this direction, now in that, made it none the easier to get along with her. The widow brooded over her child's troubles ; they were as her own, for she loved her passionately. She could no more have restrained herself from advising and trying to influence her than she could have made herself a strong, sensible woman *sur-le-champ*. After one night of weeping and wakefulness, she would tell her, under protest, that it was borne in upon her that she ought to go back immediately to Barry. Perhaps before evening she would have reached so different a conclusion that Phœbe could not stay in the room and hear her bitter reproaches of her son-in-law. She was wearing herself out, praying, crying, striving to see what they ought to do in this most dreadful situation.

"Why don't you stop thinking about it, mother? It's my doing; you are not to blame. Just leave it to me, and be as quiet as you can. People have got to live their own lives; even their mothers can't do it for them."

"But their mothers can't sit still and see them going to destruction. You'll find that when your baby gets a little older. Oh, Phœbe! you're positively unnatural and cruel to me. You seem to forget that it's only a few years ago that I was doing all for you that you're doing for that baby, and slaving for you day and night."

"Well, mother, I didn't ask you to, any more than the baby asks me to. And I hope I'll never throw it in his face that I took care of him after I brought him into the world, or that I'll think it gives me any rights over him after he's a man.

"You'll see; it'll look different to you then."

"May be, but things generally look one way to me."

Phœbe had been at home just three days, when a messenger came to tell Mrs. Holden of the serious illness of her sister, living on a farm about ten miles away. The summons was urgent; the poor woman was doubtless near her end. Mrs. Holden was dreadfully agitated by the news. She could scarcely make the necessary preparations for going. She thought Phœbe ought to go too and see her aunt before she died. But Phœbe did not in the least see it so. Her aunt was very little to her, being old and money-getting and narrow-minded. She was sorry for her sufferings, but she knew she could do nothing to alleviate them ; half a dozen women were probably standing around her bedside night and day. It would be intolerable to her to spend hours, perhaps days, in the turmoil of such a household, meeting all her relations for the first time since her trouble. She simply refused to go on the baby's account, and busied herself in forwarding her mother's preparations. Her mother could not accept the excuse. Malvina would bring her three children ; none of the others had ever stayed away on account of having babies ; it would look unnatural.

When the wagon drove away with only her mother in it beside the neighbor who had been sent to fetch her, Phœbe said to herself it *was* unnatural ; but she knew she felt a relief and breathed freer now that she was all alone. She was not glad that her aunt was ill ; it gave her a feeling of awe that one of her own blood had drawn so near the impenetrable boundary. But it did not touch her affections, and in the gloom of her own distress it did not seem a thing for desperate grief that any one should have reached the end of life. And for her mother, she felt that a change, another grief, would really be a benefit.

She had suffered so much in watching her mother's helpless perplexity about her troubles that it was a relief to think, for the time, they would fall into the background.

The day was comparatively a peaceful one. There was constant occupation for her in the household work and in caring for the baby. She laid out her work for the spring; she went up-stairs into the unused best room and threw open the windows, and planned for the house-cleaning and for some changes which her enlarged experiences of decent living now suggested. The day was beautiful; a sudden spring day after a long course of damp, raw weather. It was in the latter half of April, but up to that time there had been nothing to give one thoughts of spring and longings to be out-of-doors. The flood of warmth and sunshine seemed like the opening of heaven. One panted for the summer, and hated the barriers of winter.

After dinner Phœbe put the baby into a little wagon which Joe had brought in from a loft in the barn, and dragged him up and down the path before the house. She threw the windows of the kitchen wide open, and let the fire die out. She had to loosen the baby's wraps; April though it was, the heat was oppressive. The baby blinked and crowed; he liked the sunshine, but it was pretty strong for him. He looked a little pale; high tragedy is not good for nursing babies.

Phœbe decided for his sake to avoid the feelings
of high tragedy, no matter what facts were forced
upon her. She sat down beside him on the step
of the little unused porch. How delicious the
flood of sunshine, how sweet the still, warm air!
The grass was greening in the little plat between
the house and the gate; the earth was drying.
The crocuses were pushing up their heads in a
little patch under the parlor window. The long
spears of the daffodils were thrusting themselves
through the dead grass and fallen leaves and bare
shrubbery along the fence. One saw pink buds
swelling on the trees as the sun shone through the
naked branches. Phœbe thought almost with a
sensation of pleasure of the time when

> " All this leafless and uncolored scene
>   Should flush into variety again."

The tide of spring was bringing a little hope into
her heart.

" If I could be let alone," she thought, as she
drew a deep breath, "and have nothing but God
and the baby and out-doors, I could get along,
perhaps."

The sound of a wagon coming up the little
hill made her go quickly into the house. It was
only Farmer White and his man going to the
sugar-bush, with an empty barrel jolting in the
back of the wagon, but it broke in upon her
dream of peace. People would be the obstacles
to her " getting along," she had known from the

first. Man's inhumanity to man, intentional or accidental, seems to be at the bottom of more than half our mourning.

The lengthening April day drew to its end. The sun had set behind the far-off hills, but he seemed to have warmed the earth so fully with his all-day shining that no chill came on with the growing dusk. The baby was asleep in his cradle. Phœbe had eaten her solitary evening meal, and Joe had taken his in the little outer kitchen. The work of the day was over. Phœbe threw a cloak on her shoulders and pulled the hood up over her head, and went out into the still, warm twilight. She left the door open that she might hear the baby if he woke, and walked up and down the path, and then wandered off into the old orchard that adjoined the garden. Here had been the playground of her childhood. Her head nearly touched the tops of one or two low old trees which she had considered it a feat to climb then. The shade had seemed dense and mysterious to her; the rocky side of the hill that arose abruptly behind the orchard and the house had been the boundary to who can say what, in her childish fancy. And here her boy was to grow up; here drink in his first draught of conscious life. Well, it was healthy, it was simple; it might be an honest and honorable home.

As she wandered aimlessly on, the latch of the gate fell. She heard a step upon the board walk, and a sound as of some one knocking, low, at the kitchen door. If it were some neighbor come to feast his or her curiosity, he or she might go away again. She felt the same trouble at the thought of meeting any one; she wondered whether this feeling would ever go away, or whether she would grow "queer," as the country people called it, as she grew older, and, shunning her kind, be shunned of them and held in ridicule and aversion. She shrunk behind a tree and watched. The visitor did not go away. It was too dim to see whether any one was standing in the door; she had not left any light in the house. After a moment came a pang of fear for the child; the knock had been too low to be a neighbor's ordinary visit. She started towards the house; just as she reached the path she discerned the tall form of a man standing in the doorway. He took a step towards her, and husband and wife stood confronting each other.

"You!" said Phœbe, huskily, her breath coming quick. It was too dim to see his haggard, worn face; she only heard the almost harsh tone of his voice.

"Yes, why not? I suppose you knew that I was likely to come."

She did not speak, and he resumed, after a silence. "You know best what you went away for. This sort of thing is a disgrace to people who have any kind of place to keep in the world."

"When they have n't they don't mind," thought Phœbe, or something like it.

Now Barry had had a hard day of it, not to say a good many hard days. The heat, the worry, the bad fare, the humiliation, the vulgar people he had had to ask questions of, had set his teeth on edge. He had at last found his wife. It was a little like the Lost Heir : last night he would have thrown himself at her feet, perhaps ; to-night he felt more like throwing reproaches at her head. All his self-accusation vanished, and he felt himself injured by everything she had done and by everything she was doing, especially by the coldness and self-control that she was showing.

"I don't know what excuse you have to make for yourself," he said. She was silent. "But you never can make up to me for these last few days."

As she did not speak, he went on, harshly : "Do you know how the world looks upon people who quarrel and who can't get on together ? First it laughs, and then it sneers at them, and then it turns its back upon them. We have made ourselves a laughing-stock, and now we shall have to spend the rest of our lives trying to get people to forget our folly."

Poor Barry ! It seemed to Phœbe he was only thinking of what the world said about them, and not at all of any wounded love. In reality, he scarcely knew what he was saying, he was so sore and angry, so relieved and so ashamed of his past

fears and yearnings, and so fatally wrong-headed
in his treatment of her. They stood confronting
each other in the dusk, silent, for some minutes.

"I have come to take you back with me, at
once," he broke the silence by saying hoarsely.

"I am not going back," she returned slowly.

"Do you mean to say" — he began.

"I mean to say that I am going to stay here,
or somewhere else, if it seems best, and earn my
own living as I can. About the child, — I suppose
you came about him, — you know the law gives
him to me till he is seven years old. I don't think
you could get any court to let you have him. You
care so much about what people think, it does n't
seem to me it would be wise to try. I will do the
best I can for him while I have him. I can teach
him; the country is good for him. After that —
may be we shan't any of us be alive. There is
no use in looking ahead and worrying."

"You seem to have made your plans."

"Why, yes; I would have been very foolish
not to."

"Have you had any help about it?" he cried,
hotly.

"Take care," she said, in a restrained voice.

"Listen to me, Phœbe," he said, firmly. "I
have come to take you back. I am willing to over-
look everything, to forgive you, to treat this out-
rageous episode with eternal silence. I shall believe in you if you tell me I can trust you. All

the past shall be wiped out. I don't know another man would do it in my place. You have the choice before you, — respectability and peace, or disgrace and misery. Now choose, once for all."

"I *have* chosen. There is no use in talking."

"Do you tell me you refuse my forbearance, my forgiveness?"

"Your — forgiveness!" and Phœbe's smothered voice had deeper contempt in it than Barry knew how to bear.

"Yes, my forgiveness. Perhaps women don't know what it is to disgrace a man so before the world, to belittle his name and his child's by making them common talk."

"You are angry, Barry; it is best not to talk any more. I am not angry."

"No, by Heavens, I don't think you are. I think you are rather pleased than otherwise."

"I'm not as much troubled as you are about the opinion of other people."

"I think the standard of opinion of well-bred people is to be respected. It's dangerous setting up for one's self."

"A person's heart sets up for itself once in a while, whether one will or no," thought Phœbe vaguely, but she did not say it. Her silence seemed to irritate him more than anything that she had said.

"I don't make any threats," he said. "I don't propose to tear the child away from you and rip

open this scandal any further. But I give you
the chance of doing right by him and by me, and
repairing in a measure the wrong that you have
done us. If you come home, we have probably
both of us self-control enough to live peaceably
before the world, and get on as well as half the
married people do, whose dissatisfaction one does
not hear anything about. I place it definitely before you : Go back with me to-morrow morning
by the early train, and all will be right. I shall
make no reproaches. Refuse to do it, and I sail on
Saturday for Europe, and join the family there.
I shall live abroad ; my life in this country would
be unendurable to me with this social stigma on
it. You can understand what you will be responsible for. I shall not, likely, be a saint."

Phœbe did not say what a more fluent woman
would probably have said, — that she declined to
save him on these terms.

" I am sorry," she said, " if you are going to lead
a bad life, but I can't help it."

" I have told you that you can help it."

A silence. " Well ? "

" I don't know why you make me say things
twice that you don't like to hear. I am not going back. Why should we talk any more about
it ? "

" Why, indeed," he said, fiercely, as with a gesture of throwing something from him he turned
away and strode down the path.

"Don't you want to see the baby?" she said, faintly.

He did not answer, probably he did not hear. The little gate swung on its creaking hinges, and shut her back into the old life alone. The darkness swallowed up Barry's figure, and silence, such a silence, settled down upon the low, solitary house.

CHAPTER XXIV.

AFTER ALL !

A YEAR and a half had passed; the second summer of Phœbe's return to her home was over. The short autumn days had come, one by one growing shorter, growing chiller, warning of the dreary winter that would be upon them soon. Dwellers in isolated mountain homes do not look forward with zest to the five or six months of winter. The men make their preparations with very little enthusiasm for shoveling snow and building fires and housing cattle. It is even less hopeful for the women ; their housework is doubled and their liberty curtailed. To the two lonely women in the little house climbing against the hill, the coming winter brought gloomy anticipations. The widow was growing old, and the privation of fresh air and the long housing made each winter harder. Phœbe felt the imprisonment with this uncheerful companion to be almost insupportable. The summer days, spent in wandering about the silent woods with her baby, after the short morning's work was over, had been endurable, almost peaceful. But the winter brought interminable hours of sewing, irruptions of inquisitive neighbors from whose visits she could not escape, monotony of occupation and scene, and no solitude. The child, too, would fret at the confinement. The first winter had been bad enough, when he was just beginning to walk. What would this be, now that he was active and self-willed and "into everything," as his grandmother said. She was very fond of him, but she took the liberty of slapping his hands, and pulling him out of "everything" with a promptness that his more even-spirited mother disapproved. There were just two rooms in the little habitation which could be inhabited in winter with anything like comfort: the summer's sitting-room was the winter kitchen; the bedroom opening into it could be warmed with the same fire.

With a heavy heart Phœbe had that day moved the baby's crib down into this room, where she and her mother and he were to sleep during the cold weather. The low room up-stairs could not be made warm enough for the child. She had left her little refuge with a feeling that she had said good-by to herself in doing it. To be chained for six months to a fellow-prisoner seemed a fate many degrees blacker than solitary confinement.

A temporary respite had come, however. One of her many sisters had sent that morning and taken the widow away for a few days' visit. Before the walls of snow closed in around them it was well that these old women, with perhaps not many winters left, should see each other once again. She had gone with many regrets for Phœbe's loneliness, for it was well understood Phœbe would not darken any door in Malden if she lived to be a hundred in it. It was twilight; the little boy, tired with his day's play, had been put to sleep in the old cradle that he had almost outgrown. To have him near her as she sat by the fire, she had dragged the cradle from its corner; occasionally she touched it with her foot. She had her basket of work beside her, but she had not yet lighted the lamp upon the table. The fire was blazing on the hearth, and sent a cheerful glow through the room. She looked at it with affection; she almost felt as if she could have endured the winter with that to keep her company. But it was only an autumn pleasure; with the real setting in of winter would come the boarding up of the fire-place, the putting away the bright andirons, and the erecting of a black monster that would bake, boil, roast, and stew them and their "victuals," that would not "go out" all winter, and that would probably last many years longer than its victims. The windows of the kitchen would be stuffed with cotton; the doors would be "listed." Phœbe wondered what color the baby's cheeks would be by April.

She sat on a low chair by the fire, leaning forward on her elbows; looking now into the fire, now into the hooded cradle, now into vacancy. She wore a dark stuff dress; around her neck was tied a bright red silk handkerchief. She had grown rather thinner in the year and a half, and looked indefinably older. Her skin had a clear, healthy tinge, but the expression of her eyes was troubled, and her mouth had a firmer, more "set" look. Her rich, heavy hair was put back smoothly in a knot low in her neck. She had no look of carelessness in her dress; the room was in faultless order; whatever she did she did well and thriftily. There was not a cent wrong in the little account-book in her desk beside the window, nor a pan that did not shine in the buttery outside the door; the bread was sweet that she had baked that day; the butter that she was laying down for winter would bring the best price at the "store." Her "preserves" were better than her mother's had ever been; the linen, the clothes, were all kept in better order. The garden flourished under her care; the little farm was none the worse for her oversight of it. In a certain way she was interested in her work, and liked to feel she was doing it well. But there came times, and this was one of them, when she felt too weary to go on, — when, as people say sometimes, she did not feel as if she could put one foot before the other.

The fire-light made the room cheery, but her heart was heavy; the way was long, and to what end did it lead? The child might be taken from her; at best she could only keep him with her for a few years. She could not deny those who had a right in him, when they asked for him to give him a proper education. Her mother's health was failing; it was dreary with her, but blood is thicker than water, — it would be drearier without her. It was all pretty dark, whichever way she looked. She did not often allow herself to go over the past, but to-night she was alone, and sat long idle, thinking of all that had happened and that had failed to happen in the months since Barry had swung the little gate shut after him, on that warm April night, and gone away from her forever. Not a line had ever come from him. Why should he have written? She knew nothing but what she had gathered from one or two letters which *had* come.

The first, about two months after she had parted from Barry, had been from his mother, an earnest, loving appeal to her to give up her wrong decision and come back to him to save him. It was a letter which would have touched her very much, if she could have felt that he was to be saved from anything but his infatuation for his cousin. In that effort she declined assisting. She was a true woman, and unfortunately a jealous one, and nothing could move her that looked to condoning his infidelity of heart. The letter, she judged, was written after Barry's first meeting with his mother. It bore marks of agitation. She did not answer it at once. She never liked writing ; but this was so painful an effort that she put it off as long as possible. Her mother, who always insisted on knowing everything that befell her fellow-prisoner, and who could not withhold advice or abstain from trying to influence, had revived the recollection of the one interview she had had with Mrs. Crittenden, and rehearsed every cruel word. (All this Phœbe had been trying to forget.)

After she sent her cold and not very well expressed letter, she waited long months for an answer. She had looked for one earlier, she did not know why. When it came, it was from Lucy, and not from her mother. It was written in a frightened, uncertain way, just as Lucy would have talked if she had been compelled to confront this sister-in-law, who had got so far out of reach upon such a tempestuous sea that she could understand neither the elements nor her. Lucy did not know, evidently, how to address her, nor what to talk about after she had told her that dear mamma had received her letter just before her great illness ; that she was not yet well enough to sit up, but when she was better she would write to her. They were still abroad, waiting for mamma to be strong enough for the journey home. Papa had gone as soon as mamma was considered out of danger. It was very necessary for him to be in New York, and he had been very worried at being away so long. It was evident poor Lucy did not know whether she ought to mention Barry or not, and that she had finished her letter with the conviction that it would be better not to do it, and that Mrs. Crittenden was not well enough to be consulted. But before she sealed it she had had as strong a conviction in the other direction, and had opened it to add a P. S., which said that Barry was with them and was well, and as soon as mamma was strong enough they would go to the South of France with him, and he would bring them home in the spring, if the doctors thought it safe and wise.

Phœbe did not answer this letter at once; and since her reply there had been nothing. It was possible to imagine delays and miscarriages of letters, even to think that death had come to some of them, and that she was not considered near enough to them to have been written to about it. Her mother was not slow to tell her they were glad to have got rid of her; that the first thing she would hear would be that a divorce had been granted Barry for desertion, and that he was married to the woman whom he wanted. It seemed to give Mrs. Holden a great deal of satisfaction to talk in this way. She considered herself very forgiving and as possessed of an excellent Christian spirit. She often said she wished no ill to the Crittendens, and she felt that that showed a very exalted character. The edification of her example would have been greater to Phœbe if she had not rehearsed so unendingly the ill that she considered they had done to her.

Phœbe herself, deep in feeling, slow in utterance, was not unforgiving; a great way down in her heart there was the germ of a true faith, a holy life. How did it get there? "The wind bloweth where it listeth," and the rest. One must not limit the work to good counsel, of which Phœbe had not had very much. Nobody had held out a hand to draw her into the ark that seemed safety to her, but she had managed to get a pretty firm grasp of it, notwithstanding. Has not somebody said (if nobody has, somebody ought to, for it is true), Let me compile the books of devotion for a people, and who pleases may draw up their creeds? There was a little book that Lucy, on a birthday or something, had given with much hesitation to her silent sister. It had red edges and crosses on it; it would have frightened Mrs. Holden into a fit, and Phœbe kept it, very properly, very far back on a high shelf in her room. But more than once every day she took it down and locked her door and said her prayers out of it. This "Treasury of Devotion" and her Prayer Book were all the ecclesiastical spoils she had brought out of Egypt with her, but they seemed to have been all she needed for her sojourn in the wilderness.

To-night in the unusual silence and solitude she

sat idle long. At last with a deep sigh she got up, and going across the room lighted the lamp and put the shade on it, and brought her work and sat down by the table to sew. Once she thought she heard a step outside; she lifted her head a moment and listened, and then bent it down again and went on with her work, silent and steady.

By and by there *was* a sound outside, and then a knock. She started a little; not that she was nervous, but she never liked a knock after dark. The place was lonely; Joe was gone away to the village. If any one should come with evil purpose to her or to the child, what defense had she? Her hand trembled a little as she laid down her work and went to the door. She opened it quite wide, for she did not mean to show she had any fear, and raising her eyes looked directly into the face of — Barry.

He held out his hand; she did not know exactly what she did, but she put hers in it, and he stooped down and kissed her. He did not look defiant, but anxious, thinner, and older than he had before. He came in, and she shut the door and went and sat down where she had been sitting. It was possible she felt as if she could not stand up any longer without showing how she trembled. Barry, too, was not unmoved, though he came in slowly and went and stood beside the fire. When he first tried to speak his voice was not audible; after a

moment of silence he commanded it enough to
say, —

"You see, Phœbe, I have come back again,
though I believe I said I was n't ever coming."

Phœbe sat with a beating heart, wondering
whether, as her mother had been repeating to her,
he had come to tell her he had got a divorce from
her; she only said, trying to speak calmly, —

"I thought it likely you 'd want to see the baby
after a while."

"Well, I did. I 've wanted to see him all the
time."

"He 's asleep now," she said, looking at the
cradle. "Shall I wake him up? He 's been very
well all the time, and he 's grown to be — the
nicest little fellow."

"He always was that, was n't he?"

"Well, but he 's so different now. He knows
so much. And he 's so big, — a great deal bigger
than any of the children of his age around."

Phœbe's heart was heavy with the dread that
her mother had been for a year and a half instilling
into it: was Barry come to claim the child and
show her that she had no right to him? "I 've
taken the best care of him I could," she said.
"He 's all I have, and I should die without him."

And abruptly she put her face down on the table and began to sob. The sudden meeting had
been too much for her. Barry came over and
stooped down and tried to take her hand.

"I have n't come to take him away from you, Phœbe," he said, in a husky voice. "I 'm not a brute, though you seem to think I am. I 've come to ask you once again to come back to me. Is there any use in asking you?"

Phœbe shook her head, though she did not lift it, and he kept his hand upon hers.

"I can't get along without you, though I 've tried every way. My life is just spoiled. I 'd rather die than go on like this. And you are not any too happy here, perhaps. Why can't we make it up and begin again together? My mother, my father, all of us, entreat you to come back."

Phœbe's tears were drying up. She was wanted to help along the reform of the prodigal son. She did not feel the same confidence in the exaltedness of her Christian character that her mother felt in hers. She was afraid, when it came to that thought, that she was almost pagan. She could only hope that her salvation did not depend upon her being willing to reconcile Barry to living without his cousin Tartar. She lifted her head and passed her handkerchief across her eyes, and put it in her pocket.

"I can't see," she said, "how you can ask me, after what has passed."

"I can't see how I can myself. You see how I must be in earnest, when I can humble myself so much. For, Phœbe, I don't want to say anything that you won't like, but I can't see that you had

a just excuse for carrying it so far. I can see
I was to blame in a good many ways. I can understand you resented what I said that day; but
if you 'd loved me it would not have been impossible for you to forgive — just a fit of jealousy."

The color was coming and going in her face, and
she drew away her hand as he went on speaking.
He let it go, and turned to the mantelpiece again
and leaned against it.

"I don't want to justify myself, Phœbe," he
went on. "I 'm ready to be as humble as a man
can be. I am only here to plead with you to come
back, and to forgive me whatever I 've done wrong
or whatever you think I 've done wrong. I know
I went away to Europe selfishly ; it was not the
thing for me to go, leaving you so lonely. But
when I came back — and I 'd been counting the
days — you could not forgive me. You were as
cold as ice. You threw me back so. I was trying
to find some reason for it. I have seen that I
found the wrong one. I ask your forgiveness for
— being jealous of Peyton. It is not easy for me
to say a thing like that, Phœbe."

"I am sure, Barry, you know — There is no
use in talking. If it had been only that!"

"Well, what under heavens was it, if it was
not that? I don't know another thing Phœbe. I
swear to you I never have been able even to conjecture anything else that you could magnify into

a cause for quarrel with me. That was bad
enough. What I said that morning was unjustifiable, but I thought you might have put it down
to the right cause. I have felt bitter and resentful, Phœbe, and have only come back because I
can't keep away, — because I love you so much I
can't be happy without you. I have felt bitter
and resentful that you could be so unrelenting for
so small an injury. For a hasty word, it isn't
quite the thing to ruin a man's home and break
up everything. If I had done anything that you
could lay your hand upon and charge me with " —

" It seems to me," said Phœbe, getting up and
standing with her hand upon the table, leaning a
little towards it, and speaking slowly, — "it seems
to me a strange sort of — thing — to say this to
me, Barry, for you *must* know."

" Must know what? Phœbe, speak plainly.
Before Heaven, I tell you I know nothing more
than I have told you that would give you the
smallest reason to inflict on me what you have in-
flicted. I know nothing that any woman might
n't forgive after a half hour's fit of crying."

" See if a woman could forgive *this* after a half
hour's fit of crying," said Phœbe, with a dark flame
burning in her eyes, turning with a swift movement to the old desk beside the window, and bending down to unlock it. Her hand shook no longer.
A sort of still strength seemed to carry her forward, as it had carried her the day she walked

steadily out of her husband's house, leaving it in order. She took a paper from the desk, and pulling it out of the envelope handed it to him, with her eyes fixed on his face. He took it eagerly, read it perplexedly, re-read it; but there was no sign of agitation on his face.

"It's Tartar's writing," he said.

Phœbe, white to the very lips, looked at him silently. He stretched out his hand for the envelope, which she gave him; studied it for a moment; glanced again at the note, then at the date, then at Phœbe; caught the tragic look on her face, exclaimed, —

"You don't mean that you thought" — and then burst into laughter that rang through the little house. He threw himself into the chair beside the table, and laughed and almost sobbed. If he had been a woman you would have talked about hysterics. He buried his face on his crossed arms, and tried to hide the tears, perhaps, and to subdue the laughter. Phœbe, meanwhile, with whiter face and darker-burning eyes, drew back from him, and did not speak. "Those miserable theatricals!" he cried, lifting his head at last. "Phœbe, you poor girl, you most silly child, you don't tell me *this* was at the bottom of all your trouble! *This* — oh, it isn't possible that so much misery could come from anything so paltry! Don't you see — why, how could you ever have *helped* seeing — why, there's the date! You couldn't have thought Tartar was such an utter fool as that — and I. Well, upon my word, Phœbe, you'll have to be the one to ask forgiveness now."

And he got up and went to her to take her in his arms. ·But she held away from him, and said with coldness, but trembling from head to foot, —

" I don't understand ; I don't see what there is so much to laugh about."

" I beg your pardon," he said, earnestly, " I didn't mean to laugh. I believe it is the relief that makes me feel like laughing, as well as the awful absurdity of such a mistake making such trouble between people. Where did you find the paper ? Did I leave it at the house ? "

" It was in your desk," she answered, looking away.

" I used to empty my pockets every two or three days of all the letters in them. I suppose I stuffed this in among the rest. How well I remember now about Tartar's writing it ! It was the morning before we were to play. As I was going down the stairs, I recollected that I hadn't written out the note I was to read, and that, depending upon reading it, I hadn't committed it to memory. I was in a great hurry, and I called up to Honor to write it for me before night. Honor was in one of her pets, and said she had her hands full with learning her own part, and that I could write mine for myself. I answered

a little sharply, for I was late. Tartar called
down to me over the stairs not to mind; she'd
do it for me. And when I came home at night,
I found it on my dressing-table, waiting for me.
I remember I thought it was so good-natured of
Tartar, who is apt to have her caprices as well
as Honor. It's insupportable to think of such a
thing as that, such an accident of temper, doing
all this mischief, influencing all our lives. Talk
of a Providence!"

He strode up and down the room a few times,
till he had got himself a little under control, and
then came back to Phœbe, who stood as if turned
into stone.

"You blame me," she said, as he paused before
her.

"I don't blame you, exactly, but I think you
might have known me better."

"How could I know you?" she cried. "You
never used to talk to me. That summer you
grew all absorbed in business, and in winter all
in pleasure; and you stayed away, and I saw
from a great many things that they had wanted
you to marry Tartar — and — *you can't deny that
you were very fond of her.*"

"Fond of her! Yes, as a cousin. But I never
wanted to marry her, nor she to marry me. I am
willing to tell you the truth, Phœbe. I thought
always that she liked me, and that I could have had
her if I'd wanted her, and it flattered my vanity

to think so. I found out, that time she was at
my father's, just after we came home, that it was
all a mistake, and that she 'd never cared for anybody but — a very different man from me. The
discovery mortified me a little, but we 've always
kept good friends, and latterly it 's drawn us together very much, for she 's anything but happy.
You see, Phœbe, nothing *could* have been further
from the truth than your suspicions, — nothing."

" Not half so far as *yours*, if you will think
about it."

" There 's no use in going over *that*. I 've asked
your pardon, and it ought to end it. But if you 'll
let me say, Peyton's conduct to us all shows that
something has changed him very much; I can't
say it was entirely unreasonable for me to doubt
him. A man who could cut himself off from all
his friends, break up such a business as he had
worked up for himself, and go away, without an
explanation, to live the life of a rough frontiers-
man in a strange country, must have some flaw
somewhere in his character."

" Poor Peyton," said Phœbe, in a faltering
voice, — " has he done that ? "

" Yes," said Barry, coldly. " And you can't
much wonder at me. I 've never seen him, and
he won't even answer when I write to him. It 's
no harm, perhaps, telling *you*, but he 's treated
Tartar abominably. The poor girl has been so
ill. I doubt whether she 'll ever be quite well

again. She'd always been very sharp and pep-
pery with him, — it's her nature, and she can't
help it; but her feeling for him is the deepest
you can fancy. She went abroad with us from
a sort of pique, I think. They'd had some little
tiff or other. But when she got there she was
so deadly homesick nothing but her pride kept her
from starting directly back again. I knew something by that time of what was going on, and
she, trusting to some assurance I had made her
of what I thought his feelings were, sent back by
me a little gift for him, and a note that I suppose
said a good deal in a suppressed way. I don't
know how long it was before he answered her at
all. But when he did — well, it just killed her.
She'll never get over it. I've seen the letter,
and it was simply brutal. There's no use in talking, Phœbe. A man who could treat like that a
woman who had shown she cared for him could
do anything and everything. It's shaken my
faith in human nature. I had never had a friend
that was as much to me as Peyton Edwards. I
should as soon have thought" —

"Oh, Barry!" cried Phœbe, hiding her face in
her hands. "I — want to tell you — something."

"I'm not sure that I want to hear it," he said,
jealous suspicions very easily awaking into life
again.

"Oh, but you mustn't make it any harder for
me," she said, laying one hand upon his arm, and

with the other covering her face. "Promise —
promise me that you 'll forgive me" —

"I shan't promise anything," he said coldly,
stepping back, but she kept her hold upon his arm.

"I know you 'll be angry, Barry — and I am
more sorry than I can tell — but it all came about
without my knowing that I was going to do anything that would have so much influence upon
other people."

Barry by this time was as white as she was;
he would have shaken off her hand, but that she
kept a strong grasp upon his sleeve.

"I — I showed Peyton that note " —

"What note?"

"The paper — the one I 've just showed you."

"You did! I think you might have had better
business. Well?"

"And it was — just as bad to him as it was to
me. Barry — it is that that has done it all — I
never can be ashamed enough " —

"You don't mean to tell me, Peyton thought
Tartar had written *that* to *me?*"

"How could he help thinking so — any more
than I could? He never seemed to doubt; and,
Barry, if you 'll think a minute you 'll see it was
no wonder. Tartar and you were always intimate; you were forever staying in the city all
that winter, and seeing her every day; she left
everything, and went away to Europe with you
all at a minute's warning. How do you suppose

—people feel—that are left alone that way?
They have a good deal of time to think, and it
is n't strange if they don't always think right."

"Oh, Phœbe!" he cried, with a groan. "It's
a miserable business. Four people made so
wretched, a year and a half of such unhappiness,
the breaking of so many plans, the upsetting of
business interests, family comfort, the scandal,
the disgrace, —and all for what? Because that
little minx of an Honor would n't do as she was
asked—and because"—

"Because I could n't trust you, I suppose!"
and Phœbe began to cry, burying her face in her
hands. "Oh, I hope—the baby—'ll never
know—anything about it"—

"Well, we won't tell him, Phœbe," said Barry,
putting his arm around her. "We've been a
pair of fools,—I mean I have been a fool; I
don't pretend to say what anybody else has been,
—and all that we can do about it is to be wiser
for the future."

"And I suppose you think that will be easy,"
said Phœbe, lifting up her head and wiping away
her tears. "But for me—I am afraid it won't
be—very."

"Why, what's to stand in the way of it?" he
said, sitting down beside her and drawing her close
to him. He seemed not to be thinking very much
of what she said now, but to be devouring her
with his eyes, and feeling most of all that he had

got her in his arms again. She, however, had something to say, and she said it with her face against his shoulder and her hands before her eyes.

" I believe that, to-morrow — I should be unhappy — if I saw you pleased that other people — thought that you were handsome " —

" Well, you won't be troubled that way much," he said, laughing and kissing her hair, for he could not get at her face. "I don't believe you 've looked at me, Phœbe, or you 'd see I was n't very dangerous nowadays."

But Phœbe would not look ; it had cost her a good deal to make her small confession, and she preferred to have her hair kissed and to feel Barry's arms around her to looking in his face and seeing the ravages of time, and possibly a little lurking smile about her jealousy.

" You have n't seen," he said, " what a miserable-looking fellow I am, and you don't know, I suppose, how near I 've been to being no fellow at all. This time two months ago they thought it was all over with me. Feel how thin my cheeks are," and he took her hand and laid it on his face.

" You have been ill ? " she said, startled, lifting her head and looking at him. " Oh, Barry ! " she cried, throwing her arms around his neck and bursting into tears, "and you never sent for me ! "

" Considering that I should have been dead six

times over before you could have got to me, and
that I was beyond being consulted, and that you
probably would n't have come if you had been sent
for, I don't think you need reproach me very
much. Such as I am I'm here, and that ought
to be enough for you."

"What was the matter with you? How long
were you ill, and who took care of you?"

"If I said Tartar, you know you would n't like
it."

"No, I should n't," said Phœbe, growing crimson, and taking her arms away from his neck.
He made amends by getting his much firmer
round her, and by holding her so tight against him
that he could feel her every breath.

"You *are* — a jealous woman."

"You knew that before," she said, trying to
get away from him.

"No, by heavens, I did n't. I thought you were
too quiet to get jealous."

"Being quiet does n't help things," she said.

"No, it seems not. Well, about Tartar taking
care of me. If she had n't I probably should n't
have been here. For we 've had the most infer-
nal time of it. My mother and Honor last spring
came down with a fever, that they 'd picked up in
Naples probably, just as we were getting ready to
come home. Tartar was barely up after her own
illness of the winter, but my mother was so ill she
and Lucy had to forget themselves in looking

after her and Honor. They both pulled through ; but we were all pretty well used up, and before the invalids were fit to start for home I was taken with I suppose very much the same sort of a fever. It had been longer in developing, and it played the very deuce with me when it did develop. Lucy had by this time got so run down herself she was of hardly any use at all ; and if it had n't been for Tartar, as I said, Heaven knows what would have become of me. Come, Phœbe, I hope you 'll forgive her. Are n't you willing to accept me as a gift from her? It was n't any trifle, those two months of nursing, two thirds ill herself, poor girl."

" People in Europe generally send for a Sister of Mercy, when they 're ill in a story-book."

" Well, I was n't ill in a story-book, but in a cursed little Italian town, where you could n't have got a Sister of Mercy to save your soul (or nurse your body). Now, Phœbe, do the handsome thing. Tell me you forgive Tartar for having known your husband before you did, and that you thank her for saving his life, and that you 're prepared to love her like a sister."

He kissed her and kissed her, and did not seem to care what he said himself or what she answered him as long as he held her in his arms. But Phœbe, more earnest, could not consent to dry her tears. " You seem to think it 's all over. But I 've been too unhappy to believe that."

" You have n't been any more unhappy than I have," he said, a little more seriously. " But I 'm inclined to think we won't be any the worse for it. We began life wrong, Phœbe, God forgive us ! Have n't we wiped out the score a little, all these two or three years of misery? Come, there 's no use talking about it."

" Yes, there is use," said Phœbe, with tears. " Oh, Barry, it 's so hard — to look at just — sins."

" Well, it is n't the pleasantest kind of contemplation, I know," said Barry, with a sigh. " The fact is, Phœbe, I don't like to look back. I think I was about as well equipped to go to the devil as any young fellow I know. If I 'd turned wrong at a certain point in my life, Heaven knows where I should have brought up. I 'm not much to brag of now. But, zounds, if I had had my swing ! "

He released Phœbe, and walked two or three times across the room. " It makes one shudder," he said, " to look down the precipices one just has n't slipped over. I don't see, though, how my mother's son could have got so deuced near the edge."

" Phœbe, remember this," he said, stopping before her : " whatever remnant of happiness we have now we owe it to my mother. In our first desperation and misery I doubt if I should ever have had courage to do right but for the help that I know she made my father hold out to me. He alone would have cowed me. I was afraid of the world, and he was on the world's side. I knew by instinct what side she was on, though she was too pure-minded ever to have named to me the sin that I had fallen into. The thought of her always helped me. You must love her, Phœbe. She's better worth it than I am, and I know you love me." Then more lightly, " But I want to tell you one thing more : I believe I am discharged cured in the matter of caring what people think."

"I'm sure I'm glad of that," said Phœbe, simply.

"It's lucky," he went on, " for we'll probably never have money enough to make people respectful to us on that account, and I don't think we've behaved ourselves so as to make them respectful to us on any other. We'll just live for ourselves and the boy, and all that."

" All that" was probably meant to cover duty, the service of God, loftiness of aim, and unworldliness ; at least, so Phœbe understood it, and was satisfied.

CHAPTER XXV.

IN MY LADY'S CHAMBER.

IT was near midnight : the bell was ringing in the belfry of the not very distant church. Mrs. Crittenden, lying on the sofa in her little dressing-room, heard the door close and the sound of voices die away below the window as the last ones of the family went out to the midnight celebration. First Phœbe and Barry went, then Honor and her young English lover, then Tartar and Peyton Edwards, and lastly Lucy and her father.

They were all again at Marrowfat, and the blinds, dingy with the dust of two years, were again open, and lights shone from the windows. There had been a good deal for Lucy to do, but it was well for Lucy to be busy, particularly as no amount of business ever damaged her serene temper. There had been the house to open, new servants to get, the whole machinery to put in motion again. The Christmas party now assembled was not inconsiderable for a house just on its feet, and for such a young housekeeper. Barry and Phœbe, the boy and his nurse, Aunt David, Tartar and Peyton Edwards, had come from the city by the

21

six o'clock train; the young Englishman had arrived earlier, and was in a sense a permanent guest. Honor was looking very pretty; her hair had been cut short after her Italian fever, and was coming out in delightful little curls. Her eyes had a soft and shy expression, and she went about in a dream of bliss. Naturally she was not very useful to Lucy in the management of the house and the entertaining of the visitors; except, of course, the visitor with the blonde mustache and the many-jointed name.

It was a still night, very light, but with no moon or stars that one could see; there was a deep but well-trodden snow on the ground; the air was not sharp, though not mild or damp. You could hear sounds very far off; Mrs. Crittenden almost thought she heard the music swell after the bell stopped ringing.

She had had much experience in imagining how scenes and people looked that she was not permitted to see, and she was likely to have much more as the years went on, for it did not seem probable that she would ever again go far beyond the limits of her own room. She was told that there was great reason for surprise that she was still in the land of the living, and that she need never look again to be in the ranks of the working and enjoying. She had accepted the decree, and had settled herself into the life that lay before her with silent fortitude.

She knew when her active life got its death-blow : that night when she watched the stars out in this same room. The very springs of her being seemed to have been broken by that blow. She had never been a well or strong woman since ; she had just been going down, down, one illness after another, till she had come to the not uncommon lot of a " confirmed invalid." Too common ; like the Egyptian plague, there seems scarcely a house where there is not one dead, — dead to pleasure, to active duty, to natural, buoyant feelings. In our rushing, tumultuous modern life, perhaps it is necessary for some souls to be stretched on the rack for the world that will not pause to pray for itself; that the apostleship of suffering be laid on some elect ones. But it is sometimes impos-sible not to faint at their tribulations for us ; it requires faith to see that by their bonds we are to be partakers of their grace ; it is hard to accept for our dear martyrs what they have accepted for themselves. All that we now see of suffering we see through a glass darkly ; when the last word is spoken of that gospel, we shall change our esti-mates of its value, very likely. " There is only one power against sin, and that is, suffering. JESUS CHRIST has taught us that love alone is not sufficient."

To the eyes of those around her Mrs. Crittenden was a screne, even a cheerful sufferer ; when there were no eyes upon her, as to-night, the cheerfulness

went, though rarely the serenity. She could never
cease to love, almost to long for, God's gifts of
health and bright social life, and the power to en-
joy nature, what Phœbe, in her contracted vocabu-
lary, would have called "out-doors." She had an
eager mind and keen senses ; she was not the sort
of woman who easily sinks into helplessness ; she
was the last person to take kindly to a sofa and
bromide of potassium. Her steps downward she
had taken with a clear mind and a strong abhor-
rence of her fate. "If it be possible " —

But it was not possible ; and when she reached
the last step and was at the bottom and was shut
into her dim cell, where not a ray of earthly
hope could penetrate, there was a desperate revolt, an hour of darkness ; and then one of those
miracles of grace began which are the despair of
materialists and the edification of supernatural-
ists. Intense pain, alternated with languor inexpressible, and deprivation of all life's healthy
pleasures do not seem to the candid carnal mind
the elements out of which to form a strong faith,
a cheerful temper, and "a good understanding."
That this unlikely result was in evidence daily and
hourly in the Crittenden family no one could
deny.

Her life was lonely and high. The ill are always lonely: it is "a strange land" upon which
they have entered ; no one goes with them, and
they have to learn its speech and laws for them-

selves. Lucy stood closest, and went farthest with
her. But even she could not go far. She, with
healthy senses, could see the moonlight and the
sunlight, and smell the evening breeze as it blew
across from the hills. She could read with zest,
eat with enjoyment, sleep with profound forget-
fulness, move with the freedom of youth and
health. And yet her heart was full of love for
her mother; her life was consecrated to the care of
her. She had infinite tact and a good deal of imagination. But with all that, she could only stand
upon the borders of the land where her mother
lived, alone. In days of health

> "Not even the tenderest heart and next our own
> Knows half the reasons why we smile or sigh."

How much more exiled from human sympathy
must they be who always live in pain, " their lives'
sad undersong," who do not know a moment of
healthy vigor or an hour of unbroken sleep, upon
whom the thousand unhappy sensations of a dis-
eased body are continually pressing! That spirit
can rise above matter and through long years
keep its ascendency at such a disadvantage gives
one a respect for that which is not material.

Mrs. Crittenden lay listening to the music that
she seemed to hear, and picturing to herself what
the scene was in the church: the warmth, the glow,
the smell of the evergreens, the shining of the
laurel leaves, the soft depths of the fir branches,
the rich colors of the altar and its many lights.

She put out her hand upon the crib in which the
sleeping boy lay who had been left in her care,
while his mother should be away at church. She
whispered, leaning over him, —

> " Soon will a thousand bells ring out,
> A thousand roofs the choral shout
> Prolong, where Kings with Shepherds meet,
> His manger with their gifts to greet.
> What shall we do, mine infant dear,
> Who may not those glad anthems hear ?
> How shall we serve Him, thou and I,
> Far from that glorious company ? "

Poor little boy ! he had had an illness, and the
hand that lay in hers was thin and frail. She
wondered wistfully if his life would be better or
worse than that of his father, of whose future she
had spent so many years in dreaming here in this
very room, here on this very pillow. Ah, Barry,
Barry ! you have wrung our hearts; you have
killed our hopes; you have failed to make a name
and place for yourself among your fellows. Who
could be less of a success than you ?

And yet there was deep peace in her heart that
night. Barry's son might have a worse fate than
to be like his father. The courage of her convictions had come back to her. Yes, she had
done right. If she had helped him to lose the
world, she may be had helped him to save his
soul. And to people bound to beds of pain the
saving of one's soul looks so much larger than
even a great measure of temporal success. Yes,

she was glad that Barry had undone himself in the
eyes of the world. Without the sin, she would ask
nothing better for this pretty baby, whose small
hand she held, than what his father was starting
with now, — a true love and a low fortune, the
fear of God and small countenance from men.

At last voices sounded again below the window,
and steps crossed the piazza, and the hall door
opened. They were coming back, one after another; it was nearly two o'clock. Their voices
were subdued and quiet, as became those who
were coming back from such a service. One after
another they came softly to the door of the dressing-room. First, it was Phœbe, who entered with
a wistful look towards the little crib.

"He has n't wakened?" she said, in a whisper,
leaning down towards her mother-in-law.

"No," she answered, with a smile. "There
has n't been anything to do, though I promised
you I would take care of him for you."

"You said that once before to me," said Phœbe,
with sudden emotion in her voice and face. "I
wish — I had" —

"I don't understand," said Mrs. Crittenden.
"When did I say it?"

"That day — when Barry went away with
you" — .

"Oh, I remember," whispered the mother, drawing her down to her, and putting her arm about
her neck. "Dear child, we did a cruel thing.

I always reproached myself that you were left. I knew it was wrong. But you have forgiven us."

"Forgiven you — oh!" — said Phœbe, with a sort of shudder.

"What do you mean? You can't? Or that you think it is the other way? Oh, let me tell you this to-night: I thank God for you; you are one of the blessings of my life. I could n't ask anything better for Barry. Love me and trust me, Phœbe, and forgive me for anything painful in the past in which I have ever had any part."

If Phœbe's life had hung upon it she could not have said what she felt. It was fortunate that her mother-in-law understood her and interpreted correctly her kiss and clasp of the hand.

"What is this?" said Barry, coming in. "My mother still awake? A merry Christmas to you, mother, and a robuster grandson to keep you company next year."

He stooped down and kissed her. The little movement around him made the child wake up; he put out his arms to his father, who took him up and said, —

"Tell us all merry Christmas."

He laid his sleepy head down on his father's shoulder, with his eyes wide open, and did not show the least intention to speak.

"It's pleasant for a parent to be obeyed," observed Barry, "but it's a pleasure I don't often taste."

"Here are some flowers for you, mamma," said Honor, at the door. "May Reginald bring them to you?"

"It seems to be in order to say good-night here," said Tartar, following.

"Yes, but it isn't in order to say anything else," cried Lucy. "Mamma won't have a moment's sleep if you all don't go away."

"Oh, it won't hurt me to give Tartar a kiss. And isn't Peyton in the hall?"

Peyton answered for himself, and gaunt and tall stooped down to kiss her hand.

"This is quite worth staying awake all night for," she said, still holding his hand, and looking up with shining eyes upon the group that stood around her sofa. "Last year half of us on one side of the ocean and half on the other."

"Yes," cried Barry, with a laugh. "I think we'll all agree this Christmas is worth two of last. Come, Tartar, tell us if it isn't!"

"Answer for yourself," said Tartar, turning away, her dark skin suddenly darkened by a blush. "What was the matter with last Christmas? I for one enjoyed it thoroughly. It had been the dream of my life to be at Rome on Christmas."

"Oh, nothing. Only it didn't seem to me you were in the very highest spirits, if I remember right."

"Well, you don't remember right, since you had the fever. You rarely do. Lucy, did n't you tell us we ought to say good-night?"

She stooped and kissed Mrs. Crittenden lightly, and went out into the hall, picking up her bonnet and muff, and hurrying to the stairs that led up to her room. But Peyton was as quick, and as she put her hand upon the newel-post he put his over it.

"You must take that back," he said.

"Take what back?" she asked, looking up at him defiantly."

"*Was n't* there anything the matter with last Christmas? Come, you 've got to tell me that there was."

"There was n't anything the matter with it; the sun shone in a perfect glory."

"Oh, I was n't talking about the day. I was talking about you."

"Well, then, you did n't express yourself with accuracy."

"I 'll be accurate now. You said that you enjoyed it thoroughly."

"Why not? I remember I had a little headache towards the afternoon, but the morning had been heavenly."

"Had you been crying, that you 'd got a headache, Tartar?"

"Crying? What had I to cry about? Peyton, you'll please remember I haven't given you the right to say such things as that to me."

"Oh, yes, you have. You can't take *that* back, you know."

"We'll see !" she cried, tearing off a ring with a great diamond in it, and dropping it upon the floor of the hall. While Peyton stooped to pick it up, he had to take his hand off hers. She profited by the release to fly swiftly up the stairs.

But he followed her in three bounds, and caught her at the landing-place, where there was no light except from the hall below.

"You'll make me hate you," she cried, panting.

"I'm not afraid," he said, holding her hands. "You did it to make me kiss you, and I don't mean to disappoint you, ever."

Her slender hands had not as much power of resistance as her tigerish heart. He got the ring on again, and he got his kiss, but he didn't get her to recant about last Christmas.

"It was a perfect day, and I enjoyed it thoroughly ; more, a great deal more, than I shall this. Of that I'm very certain."

The others were coming up by this time, and he had to let her go. His eyes followed her. Why should she say such things? That, perhaps, will always be a problem to him, but nothing will ever disaffect him.

Tartar will go on saying what she does not

mean, and Phœbe failing to say what she does, to
the end of their mortal pilgrimage ; and Peyton
and Barry will go on loving them and cherishing
them, admiring them if not understanding them,
thanks to that law of love, affinity, election, sympathy, whatever it is that brings Jack to Gill and
keeps him constant to her.

www.ingramcontent.com/pod-product-compliance
Lightning Source LLC
Chambersburg PA
CBHW020937030726
47496CB00005B/1230